Mystery of the Mountain Lake

A Novel
By

William Etheredge

This book is a work of fiction. Any references to historical events, real places, or real people are used fictitiously. Other names, characters, places, and events are products of the author's imagination, and any resemblance to actual events, or places or persons, is entirely coincidental.

All mistakes and inaccuracies are the fault of the author

Copyright © 2022 by William Etheredge
All photographs, including the cover and design by the author

This book is dedicated to my wife, who has supported me in all things like no one else, and to all those who have had to pay dearly for their mistakes and have persevered.

All rights are reserved, and belong to the author. For rights to reproduce this book or portions thereof in any form whatsoever, including information about bulk purchases, author inquiries, film rights, or comments, please message 404-438-7272, or email tiwanawiki@gmail.com

Details in this book are not meant to be accurate, and the author makes no apologies to anyone whose feelings get hurt because of any inaccurate representations of anything. The purpose of this book is simply to entertain, and I sincerely hope you enjoy it as that.

To Ruth,
I hope you
have a great life!

1

❋ ❋ ❋ ❋ ❋

The evening began clear and warm on the day of the storm at the Tiwanawiki RV Park, named for the mighty creek that feeds the lake. It is my favorite part of the day, just before sunset. The breeze off the Wakitani Taniki, known to the locals as Lake Homer, begins to cool. The faint algae smell of the lake mingling with that of wood smoke and burning grease from Eddie's grill infuse me with that peaceful, easy feeling that I have come to depend upon as the end of another semi-productive day in the Appalachians approaches. I hear the sound of a lawn mower in the distance; Hector, never one for ceremony, clearing some grass that is beginning to go to seed on the south side of the camp. And, another perfect sunset, the spectacle that never ceases to amaze and delight as the sun slips past the far end of the lake.

The park wraps around the eastern end of the roughly arrowhead shaped Lake Homer, a 500 acre natural wonder in the Western Carolina mountains, the eastern part of the Smoky Mountains. The western end of the lake being the top part of the arrowhead, with the sloping Durban Hills beyond, leaving a fairly unimpeded sight line of the aforementioned 'picture postcard' daily views from the park. The daily tradition of park residents lining their chairs along the eastern shore of the lake in the evenings began immediately after the opening of the park sometime in the early 60's. Several of the current residents continue the tradition of 'herbal refreshment' that the original hippies enjoyed back in the day.

Yours truly included.

"Don't bogart that dogleg, Shorty." Sitting in my fancy lawn chair on the ridge by the water's edge I felt a tap on the left temple of my RayBans. Janie Shain had a six foot long telescopic antenna broken off the old Lincoln that was abandoned decades ago in the woods near the south end of the lake. After she scavenged it she had Hector solder a small alligator clip to one end. She never left home without it.

I took one more big toke and fastened the doobie to the clip. She shortened the rod and muttered "'Preciate it," as she inhaled a nice lungful of the locally sourced 'wiki weed' as we like to call it. Janie was our resident 'free-spirit flower child.' A twice-retired RN, with careers in the high burn out fields of Trauma and Hospice nursing, she hung up her stethoscope after putting two kids through college, bought herself an RV, and said so long to the fast lane. Now in her sixth summer at the Tiwanawiki, she seems happy as a clam to sit back in the evenings, sip an ice cold Budweiser and inhale a few puffs of wiki weed as the sky explodes in the myriad of colors that accompany the Smoky Mountain sunsets. Life is good, as the old saying goes. I think that saying includes that it is better than the alternative, but you get the idea.

In my other life I was a roofing contractor, inheriting my father's business after a stroke disabled him at the ripe old age of 49. Three years later my mom and I buried him after aspiration pneumonia took him the rest of the way out. I had been working for him since high school, gradually learning the business, so I was ready to take the reins full time when the stroke hit. I was 27, and by the time I made it to 35 my wife had left me, my Mom moved to Boca Raton with Fred, their next-door neighbor for the past 30 years whose wife had passed away the same year as Dad, and the business had begun to decline. Cheap, 'undocumented' immigrant labor, and cut-throat corporate insurance scam artists had drastically lowered the profit margins for honest, family-owned businesses, to the point that I was having trouble seeing my future continuing along this road, and I had begun to contemplate a career change. Into what, I had no clue, but I felt like drastic change was imminent.

The confirmation for this line of thinking came out of the blue. I had driven down to Jacksonville to enter into the bidding wars for roofing contractors after Hurricane Omar had destroyed about twenty square miles of businesses and residences. I stopped at one of those large gas station/food marts to gas up the truck and grab a couple of taquitos and a sugar free Red Bull when I did something I had never done before or since. It was a total impulse buy, but when my numbers came up in that night's Florida Lotto drawing, I let out a scream that threatened to blow out the windows of the little room in the La Quinta Inn where I was staying.

After splitting the jackpot four ways and paying the taxes, I walked away with a check for about $13 million. Not enough to live on forever, I thought, but certainly more than enough to exit the Rat Race, sell my company, and open my mind to what the rest of my life might look like. No wife and no children meant the future was wide open.

That life began with the purchase of an 1800cc Italian cruiser motorcycle, and spending the next few years touring the Americas, especially the coastal regions. Exploring the Smokies one fine spring day about two years into my sojourn, I happened upon the Tiwanawiki RV Park, in a horrible state of disrepair and disuse, but a large *For Sale by Owner* sign. Kismet, you say? Perhaps.

After parking and walking through the brush to the fallen-in office building and standing on the ridge behind it, looking out over the lake, I felt a pull that I had never felt before. Looking around, I looked at the property with a more critical eye. Yes, it would take a lot of work, but the lake was incredibly beautiful. I made up my mind then and there, whipped out my mobile and called the number on the sign.

That was 10 years ago. The $13 million dropped under $10 million as I piddled around for the next few years, working the park in between annual rides up and down the Eastern Seaboard. I loved that bike, man... still do as a matter of fact. I still have it, it's on its second engine after the first one gave up after about 200,000 miles. I have had good luck with investments and I am back up to about $12 million in my accounts along with twelve of the best RV spots on the planet, complete with water, electricity, sewer, satellite TV, free Wi-Fi and the most magnificent views imaginable. I pretty much live free, the park pays for itself, and I have a couple of full time residents that help me out with the maintenance and stuff. Also, there is more than enough spice in my life with the characters I see everyday along with some of the regular annual and seasonal folks that keep coming back every year.

I think I mentioned earlier that life is good.

"Looks awfully dark up to the north," came a voice to my left. Eddie and Mary Beth Avery, two of my regulars who seemed to have made the park their home base, were out for their evening stroll around the lake. Owners of a large orange and yellow

Fleetwood, I remember the day they pulled up about 5 years ago. I half expected Walter White and Jesse Pinkman to pop out in yellow haz-mat suits and doomsday-looking respirators. An exclamation of "Yo, we're cooking now, BE-OTCH" would not have surprised me. What did surprise me, however, was the dressed to kill, obviously very devoted, neat little middle aged couple that walked out. Eddie, seeing the sign in front of the office that said 'Please honk your horn to let me know you are here,' had stopped, raised a finger at me, patted his wife on the shoulder, and bounded back into his rolling motor home. "AhhOOOGAH" had resonated from under the hood.

"Yep, we may get a little shower this night" I replied. That would prove to be the understatement of the century.

Janie

It was a hot, humid, mosquito filled night when Jolie Daisy DuBrow went into labor. Daisy lived in Tourbeaux, a little bayou community about sixty miles due south of the Louisiana state capital of Baton Rouge, but considerably farther away in culture. Jolie Daisy worked in the only business in the town, *Crawdaddy's*, known in those days as a 'speakeasy' which the locals called simply *Daddy's*. *Daddy's* was home to live jazz and blues. Sometimes a group would come through and stay for a week, others were one-nighters or maybe three or four nights. The hooch was cheap, and so were the dancing girls, of which Jolie Daisy was one. Therefore, after Janie was born after a miserable night of labor, Jolie Daisy left the line blank where the father's name would have been on Janie's birth certificate. After all, it would have been impossible to know which of the dozens of musicians and crew members it could have been.

Jolie Daisy had an idea though. There were only a handful of white musicians, or paying customers, for that matter, that had come through Tourbeaux. Jolie Daisy was maybe a shade lighter than milk chocolate; Janie popped out as pink and peachy as could be.

Jolie Daisy couldn't let a baby slow her down, or interrupt the life she loved, however, so by the time Janie was in her terrible twos, the Louisiana Department of Family and Children's services had received word about a toddler living in a flop house in the swamp. They swooped in and 'rescued' young Janie and put her into the system. Her mother put up very little fuss; in fact she was secretly happy to be shed of the responsibility and happy that the baby would be cared for.

The two never saw each other again.

Janie proved to be a very bright and agreeable little girl, in spite of her inauspicious beginning. She had taught herself to read before she got to kindergarten, and she was adopted by Jimmy and Freida Shain when she was five years old.

Jimmy and Freida were members of a fringe fundamentalist religion, and began taking young Janie to prayer meetings several times a week. Jimmy was intolerant of anything he deemed to be a sin, except, of course, when it was him doing the sinning. He began to creep into Janie's room at night after Freida had gone to sleep.

Janie, however, being very bright and perceptive way beyond her years, figured out real quick that this was not normal behavior. So it happened that one night, Jimmy had gotten a little carried away and put something in Janie's mouth, upon which she clamped her teeth down and began to gnaw, eliciting a bloodcurdling scream from Jimmy that brought Freida running out of her benzo haze. She flung open Janie's door and flipped on the light just in time to see Jimmy slap Janie and pull away, turning towards Freida, who saw the bloody mess a split second before Jimmy clutched himself with both hands and fell against the wall, sliding to the floor whimpering "Jesus God Jesus God help me help me…"

Freida scooped up the smug faced Janie and wiped the blood off her cheeks and chin with her pajama sleeve. She snatched the keys off the hook in the kitchen, went out the door and into the family Buick and drove the two of them down to the church, where Pastor LaSalle and his wife TaShanna lived in a little house out back. TaShanna came to the door and ushered the two inside. After taking Janie into the bath to clean her up, the three went into the storage shed behind the church to get them some clothes out of the donation boxes. Freida explained what had happened and they ended up staying with the LaSalles for a few days. Jimmy Shain got twenty five years at Angola State Prison, but he only had to serve about a year of that sentence. He was granted parole about twenty four years early by a shank in the chow hall one morning. The shanker was never identified.

Freida moved into a small rental house owned by her aunt who lived just outside of Memphis, Tennessee. While never losing her faith, she gave up the strict tenets of the fundamentalists. She was determined to provide Janie with everything the girl would ever need, including the knowledge and the self confidence to make up her own mind about things.

Freida got Janie enrolled in school, and began taking classes herself. She earned her GED rather quickly and then became a Certified Nursing Assistant.

Janie proved to be a gifted, but distracted, student. She could easily make straight A's in all her classes without ever opening a book. She took to sneaking out of her classrooms and wandering the school, eventually discovering an out-of-the-way closet full of discarded musical instruments, leftovers from a music program the school had been stripped of a decade earlier due to budget issues.

Janie had music in her DNA, and, sneaking out of her classroom several times a day, quickly taught herself to play the various stringed instruments she found in the closet, tuning each string to a note that sounded right to her, far from standard tuning but very much in tune. She was intrigued by the different sounds that similar notes would make on the guitar, banjo, and mandolin.

One of her teachers soon became suspicious and surreptitiously followed the youngster one day. She was shocked to hear the beautiful melodies coming from the closet as she stood around the corner. She went back to the classroom without saying a word to Janie.

That evening Freida received a telephone call from the teacher.

"Has someone been teaching music to Janie?" she asked.

Freida replied that to her knowledge Janie had never seen a musical instrument. Instruments had not been allowed in the Shain household or in the church. The Louisiana DFACS Foster program were very poor historians when it came to Janie's parentage as well. The teacher explained what had been going on at the school and that she felt Janie had a rare talent that should be explored. The teacher said she had spoken to the Principal of the school and he agreed that the school could loan them the instruments for Janie to learn on at home. Freida agreed to let the teacher bring them to their house; she brought along an old electric piano that she had inherited that was collecting dust in her house. She gave Freida the name of a respected music teacher as well, who agreed to tutor Janie at a reduced rate.

When Janie was eleven years old she entered and won the Tennessee Bright Junior Pianist competition in Knoxville, at the University of Tennessee. She was the youngest competitor there, and won with her own arrangement: a mash-up of a Rachmaninoff concerto and Elton John's *Funeral for a Friend*. She played for twelve minutes without the benefit of sheet music.

The standing ovation she received lasted more than fifteen minutes. It was no contest.

Freida, meanwhile, had gotten a job at the Veteran's Hospital, first as a CNA then quickly obtaining a Licensed Practical Nursing certification, taking night classes. Sometimes Janie would come to work with her and bring along her mandolin and sing for the patients, who absolutely adored her. It was those days in the hospital where she developed the overwhelming desire to become a nurse rather than pursue a career in music.

Freida had fallen for one of the doctors who did rounds in the hospital, he finally took notice of her and they began to date, much to the happiness of the now teen-aged Janie. Janie would grow up and follow in her mother's footsteps, marrying a trauma surgeon four years after graduating from Saint Mary's School for Nurses and going to work at the Level Four Trauma Center at Bigelow Hospital in Jackson. She and Dr. Tomlinson shared their first kiss one night while doing a code blue on a dead meth head, and their last one ten years later when Janie discovered the good doctor had adopted the hospital's practice of going after younger nurses.

She obtained a lucrative settlement for herself and their two daughters, and decided that fifteen years was enough of trauma nursing. She became a home health nurse for a time, and eventually gravitated into Hospice nursing. She found that she loved to be the one to be there at the end for her patients, often bringing her mandolin to their bedside and 'singing them to heaven.'

Of course, everything has its price. By the time Janie hit 45, and seeing so much death and disease, she decided she had had enough. She couldn't help getting close to some of her patients, and it became increasingly difficult to separate herself. The final blow came when she admitted a forty seven year old patient with End Stage Liver Disease.

Jeremiah was a singer/songwriter, guitarist and harmonica player. Janie found herself making unscheduled visits, bringing along her mandolin. They would spend hours playing and singing, often making up new songs as they went along. Without meaning to, Janie had fallen head over heels in love with Jeremiah, who also introduced Janie to the magical, wonderful herb he was able to procure legally now, with his cancer diagnosis. He also introduced her to a friend who was able to obtain better strains by other than legal means.

Her heart was broken when Jeremiah passed away. After his funeral, she went home and examined her finances, and her life. Both of her children had graduated college and were settled into their own lives. She had hefty sums in two different retirement accounts, well into the seven figure range with the two combined. She was fully vested in the Bigelow account and could begin accessing those funds whenever she wanted. Her savings account at her bank was well into the six figure territory, so she took a long drink of an ice cold long necked Budweiser, took a long toke from a small pipe, and said, out loud to her empty house, "I'm Done!"

She spent $70,000 on a GMC with an over the cab camper in the bed and headed for the open road, spending the next several months seeing the coastlines of the North American continent. She grew her hair long, began wearing flowers and multi-colored ribbons in her hair, wearing tie dyed shirts and bell bottomed jeans. She had her tubes tied, burned incense and played music wherever she stopped.

It was at one of these lengthy stops, in a little South Florida Beach town named Lauderdale-by-the-Sea that she finally made the acquaintance of a Mike Stevens, (whom she affectionately called 'Shorty,' since he was about a foot taller than she), and followed him that summer up to the Smoky Mountains.

The late blooming free spirit had found a home, finally, at least for the summers.

William Etheredge

Eddie

Eddie Avery had been driving the East Bay bus line for the Bay Area Rapid Transit since he had graduated from Benicia High School. He loved the bus and most of the passengers were regulars; people going to and from work at the Kaiser Hospital at the south end of his route; staff and students at the Solano County Community College at the north leg; others getting on and off at various other stops and businesses along the way; and many who got off at the train station to head into the city. One loop generally took him about forty-five minutes

Eddie's shift was Monday-Thursday normally, from 5:15am until 3:30 in the afternoon. However, normal had come to mean, more often than not, six days a week and sixteen hours a day. He always took Sundays off, no matter what. He didn't mind the extra shifts, as he had nothing better to do anyway but watch science fiction shows and movies.

After about thirteen years of driving, Eddie noticed a new fare that had begun to ride to the college in the morning and back to her home stop in the evenings. He had surely noticed pretty girls before, lots of them, but something about this girl was different. She had a noticeable limp, but never needed any help even when the bag she carried was obviously heavy, bulging with textbooks. But there was something else.

The bag! That was what had caught his eye. He had noticed the MGM logo on one side for a while, then one day he noticed the other side of her bag had a picture of the Stargate, Eddie's favorite Sci-fi movie, ever! His interest was definitely piqued after seeing that.

Eddie was typically extremely shy; it was all he could do to greet his passengers as they boarded and mutter "Have a nice day" as they left his coach. But after about three weeks of watching his new passenger get off at the college in the mornings and back home in the evenings, he finally got his courage up and broke the ice one evening. She happened to be the next to the last passenger on the bus that day, the only other one snoring on the back seat.

"So do you think Michael Shanks is a better Daniel Jackson than James Spader?" he blurted out just as she was stepping off the bus.

She stopped on the first step, whirled around and looked him dead in the eye for a few seconds. Finally, with a stern look on her face, she spoke tersely, "That is quite an interesting question. I shall have to consider how I can respond to it."

At that she whirled back around and marched off the bus, her ponytail swishing back and forth as she headed down the street toward her home. Eddie had been dumbfounded as he had looked into the eyes of the future Mrs. Avery. He realized she was the most beautiful creature he had ever laid eyes on. He couldn't understand how he hadn't noticed it before. Mary Beth had a sort of sneaky beauty. At first glance, you think, "Well, she's kinda cute." Then one day she looks at you and you forget your name, where you are. You forget how to breathe, and you wonder how in the world you could ever have thought she was anything other than absolutely stunning.

The next morning Mary Beth got on the bus, handed Eddie an envelope which felt fairly thick, and took her seat on the bus. Eddie, stunned, stuck the envelope behind his overhead mirror and drove on. She had not said a word, and, as Eddie kept glancing into the mirror, she never looked up. When he finally stopped at the college, he said "Have a nice day" as she walked down the steps. When she got to the sidewalk she finally turned and looked up at him.

"You too. See you this afternoon, Edward." Then she was gone.

Eddie thought "How does she know my name? I don't know hers." Then he caught a glimpse of himself in the mirror and saw 'Eddie' written backwards on his shirt. "Duh!" he exclaimed, smacking himself in the forehead.

"We gonna sit here all day, Driver Dude?" came a voice from behind him. Eddie snapped out of his reverie, glancing up at the mirror at the young fellow with the blond dreadlocks three seats back. He closed the bus door and took off, hardly breathing until he reached the end of his route back at the train station. Snatching the envelope, he headed for the driver's lounge, where he was allowed a ten minute break after each run and a thirty minute lunch break.

He looked at the front of the envelope, where, in purple ink, was written 'For Edward.' He could barely open it, but finally got the papers out. Neatly folded were two sheets of long yellow legal paper. One paper had the heading 'Daniel Jackson,' the other 'Colonel O'Neill.' The left column under each heading was labeled 'Attributes,' and the right side contained two columns with the actors names who portrayed these characters; Spader and Shanks, for Daniel Jackson, and Russell and Anderson for Colonel O'Neill.

It bears mentioning here that in Eddie's opinion, he is the world's number one fan of the Stargate franchise, which, in his estimation, is light years ahead of any other film or series with the word 'Star' in its title. Trekkies and Jedi beware!

As he looked over the lists, he suddenly remembered where he was, looking at his watch, he realized over twenty minutes had elapsed since he had sat down. "Shitballs!" he exclaimed as he jumped up, shoving the hastily folded papers into his back pocket and scurrying out the door.

He approached the 41 bus to find a small army amassed at the door. "Sorry, sorry" he muttered as he went around to the driver entry and hopped in, opening the bus door to the throng of disgruntled commuters.

His heart was thumping out of his chest as he continued on his route, occasionally looking at his letter from his as yet unnamed passenger during the lengthier stops. Finally he reached the end of the route and, as he rolled to a stop at the station, pulled out the letter and finished reading the lists. He read her summary on the back of page two, expounding on the pros and cons of each actor, ultimately giving the nod to the two television series actors, noting "... longevity and superb writing..." and ending with "Submitted for your approval. Miss Mary Elizabeth Crown."

Eddie thought her writing and her ideas were incredible. He had always considered the movie to be superior to the series, but she had swayed him with her arguments. He could barely contain his excitement as he anxiously awaited the evening so he could see her again.

He rolled up to the college around 4:15 and there she was. Eddie was as nervous as a trapped squirrel as she boarded the bus. "I think I love you Mary Beth!" he blurted out as she dropped her token into the slot. She stopped and glared at him.

"It's Mary Elizabeth, and you don't even know me!" she exclaimed, and, pigtail bouncing, marched to the very back of the bus and sat down.

"What is wrong with me?!?!" Eddie shouted to himself as he pressed the accelerator. "I am such a friggin' idiot" he thought as his face burned with shame. He began to sweat and felt his bowels begin to loosen. Eddie rarely used profanity, but kept muttering "Fuck, fuck fuck" under his breath. He was about a minute from her stop before he finally mustered the courage to glance up into the mirror at her. She was staring right at him, and, when their eyes met she gave him a crooked little smile that melted Eddie's heart. He brought the bus to a stop and she made her way to the front, but didn't get off.

She sat in the seat by the door and said, "I trust you won't mind if I ride the route with you, since you are obviously in love with me. School's out for the semester and I'm not sure when I will be back on this bus. The jury is still out on whether I wish to continue my education at that school."

Eddie, who could not have been more stunned if he had seen a Goa'uld worm crawling out of the AC vent, closed the door and the bus lurched forward. They discussed everything Stargate on that round trip, as well as pros and cons of college. When they finally came back around to her stop, she stood to get off and said "I had a nice ride. I am glad you agree with me on the Stargate stuff, that the SG-1 series is far superior to the movie. Perhaps next time we can talk about Doctor Who." With that she was down the steps and gone. Just before she turned down her street and disappeared from sight, she turned. Eddie, entranced, watched as she blew him a kiss and waved. "See you later, Eddie!" she yelled, and limped out of sight.

Eddie was surprised the next morning when she got on the bus. Sitting on the seat next to Eddie's, she rode the route with him several times. Eddie discovered she was three years younger than him, at twenty nine. Her father had been killed in Vietnam when she was just four, and she lived with her mother, who had never recovered from losing her husband. She was studying English Literature in college and wanted to be a writer. The next semester started in two weeks, and she and her mom were having some financial problems.

She got off the bus finally, shortly after noon, and told Eddie she was getting a bit tired after sitting so long but she would see him again soon.

Eddie had moved out of his parent's house many years earlier and currently lived in a rooming house. He had moved out on his own mainly because his father had dominated the television, only watching the news. So Eddie basically moved out so he could watch what he wanted. His life was fairly simple, and he had never really thought about things he may have been missing. Meeting Mary Beth had awakened something inside him. They were getting along so well after about a week of her riding his route with him in the mornings he could hardly believe it was real. Finally, at the end of the week, Mary Beth looked at him as they came to a stop near her house.

"So, now that you know me a little bit, do you still love me?" she asked him, a sly smile on her face. Eddie put the bus in park, put on the flashers, and slid over into the seat next to her. He wrapped his arms around her and began kissing her face, ears, forehead, cheeks, and, finally, before they locked lips, he declared "I never want to ever live another day without you!" She wrapped her arms around his neck and said "Do you want to be a bus driver your whole life?"

Eddie pulled back and said "It's what I love to do."

She pulled him close and whispered in his ear "I'm glad that you love it. So many people have no clue what they want to do. And you may call me Mary Beth if you want to."

And so it was that, at the age of 32, Eddie Lee Avery finally kissed a girl. And he liked it.

Mary Beth went back to school. She and Eddie were married three months later. Eddie moved out of the boarding house and into the house with Mary Beth and her mother. Mary had been unable to have children due to a childhood accident and when Mary's mother passed away a few years later the two of them lived happy, blissful lives for next two decades or so, spending their vacation time in cosplay at Comic Cons and such, until that fateful night, about three years ago.

It was pouring rain that December evening, the time of year when twilight begins around 4:30 pm, and it is pitch dark by 6. The fog from the Bay seems to be alive and creeps into the surrounding areas like a plague. Eddie had cut back on the overtime, but this particular night his relief driver had called out sick, so he was pulling a double. About 6:15 he was pulling away from a stop, and just as the door was closing a fairly large woman in a white frock ran out in front of the bus, waving her arms and obviously in a great deal of distress. Eddie stopped and opened the door. She ran in, dripping wet, mascara running down her face from bloodshot eyes. He saw that she was not, in fact, a large woman at all, but a pregnant one. VERY pregnant. Her belly looked as if it were about to explode as she held it tightly with both arms.

"Kaiser," she panted, almost completely out of breath. She made her way about three seats behind Eddie and plopped down, holding her belly and starting to wail. Eddie closed the door and floored the accelerator.

He had gone about fifteen feet when suddenly there was a pounding on the door. He looked over and could barely see a shaggy looking guy jogging beside the bus, pounding on the door and shouting "STOP! STOP THIS MOTHERFUCKING BUS NOW GODDAMMIT!!!"

The pregnant woman screamed "NO! He's trying to kill me and my baby! Don't stop PUHLEEZE!! AAAAIIIIEEEEE!!!" Eddie gunned the accelerator for all he was worth. He risked a glance up into the mirror and saw the woman begin to slide into the floor. Thankfully there was only one other passenger; an apparently stoned young man on the back row with ear buds in his ears, seemingly oblivious to his surroundings.

Eddie drove steadily on, not making any of the stops. He was becoming a bit frantic himself, knowing he should be driving faster but being aware of the unsafe conditions as he slowed around curves and keeping safe distances from cars in front of him. The woman had lain in the floor between the two rows of seats and suddenly let out a scream that made the hair on the back of Eddie's neck stand up. "OH my GAWD he's coming OUT!!! EEEEEEEEE!!!" He radioed his dispatcher to tell them what was going on and call 911 to put the Kaiser Emergency Department on alert.

About a half mile from the hospital the woman's screams stopped. Eddie spared a quick look back. She was flat on her back, her knees up and splayed out, and she was unconscious. Eddie could see the entirety of the baby's head sticking out, bloody and blue. He looked ahead, and could see the hospital staff waiting, about a hundred yards up the road. He stopped the bus, flashed his lights, put on the emergency flashers, and opened the doors to allow the emergency personnel access, who were already headed towards the bus with a stretcher and other medical equipment. He jumped back to help the woman, who was beginning to groan as she roused. He could see the baby's shoulders, and he gently lifted them. "Can you push?" he asked the exhausted woman. He risked a glance back and could see the hospital staff hurrying down the sidewalk in the driving rain toward the bus. The woman screamed as she bore down with everything she had. The rest of the baby popped out into Eddie's waiting hands. He lifted it gently and cradled it in his arms. It was warm but still.

Eddie looked into the woman's face as she huffed and puffed and rubbed her stomach. He had read enough books and watched enough hospital shows to know that the placenta had to come out next. Eddie was considering giving the umbilical cord a light tug as the woman pushed when all of a sudden, coming through the door like a shot, was the crazed shaggy fellow who had been beating on the door a few miles back. Apparently he had known a short cut or maybe grabbed something on the back of the bus and held on. He leapt over Eddie, landing with both feet hard onto the woman's abdomen. The placenta gushed out, along with a huge rush of blood. The crazed maniac then stomped the woman's face twice, turned and punched a shocked Eddie hard on the bridge of his nose, snatched up the baby, and ran back out the door.

The hospital staff were about thirty feet from the bus. The fellow slipped, dropping the baby. He jumped up, grabbed the umbilical cord about a foot or so from where it attached to the baby, and began swinging the baby in a circle until the baby finally tore loose and, trailing blood, flew up into the air, landing with a thud on top of the bus. The lunatic let out a whoop and took off down the street.

One of the orderlies managed to climb up onto the top of the bus to attend to the baby, who was gray and cold. The nurses ran into the bus. One of them stopped at Eddie, who was knocked unconscious and covered in blood from both his busted nose and the woman's ruptured uterus. The woman herself was very pale and cold, having lost almost all of her blood. Her eyes were open, fixed and dilated. All her breath was gone.

Police arrived from the 911 call the dispatcher had made. They were able to quickly locate the shaggy villain, who hadn't made it very far into the darkness before collapsing himself. Roused by the flashlight and the sounds of the police officers telling him not to move, he jumped up, pulled out a large knife and charged the cops, who emptied their service weapons into his chest.

Mary Beth

Mary Elizabeth Crown had grown up in the shadow of a man she never knew. She was barely a year old when young Joey Crown was drafted into the Army. After boot camp and basic infantry training he was sent to the Southeast Asia jungles to hunt down Charlie. When he was a week shy of finishing his tour and coming home he went on one last patrol with his unit. A tree viper fell onto his shoulder. Before he knew what was happening he had been bitten three times in the neck. He never made it back to camp.

Mary's mother Catherine was devastated to the point of paralysis. Catherine's mother and aunt were both old, and little help with the now toddling Mary. With no other family of her own to speak of and out of contact with Joey's family; in fact she had only met her mother-in-law once, at their wedding, where she would give Catherine the malicious sneer of disdainful disapproval every time their eyes met. It was quite unfashionable in the early 1960's for a bride to be six months pregnant on her wedding day, and the haughty Mrs. Crown possessed nothing even mildly resembling understanding, compassion, or forgiveness in her emotional toolbox. That was their only meeting. Catherine had called Mrs. Crown after getting the news about Joey's unfortunate demise so close to his return home, and was promptly greeted with a dial tone. Mrs. Crown had hung up on her without uttering a word.

The next few years of Mary's life were spent with her hearing, at least four times a day, "If your father were here he would _____." The blank was filled with phrases such as 'beat your ass,' 'be so ashamed,' 'be so mad at you,' etc. Growing up with such negativity it is a wonder Mary developed any ambition at all.

But she did.

Growing up watching such television shows as Star Trek, Lost in Space, and The Twilight Zone, as well as reading books by Mark Twain, Isaac Asimov, and Ray Bradbury, she developed a strong urge to write. She was impressed by the imaginations of the television writers, how they could keep coming up with so many new ideas. She loved that she could get lost in a good book, and be transported to worlds beyond her stifled life.

Mary wrote a short story in the 6th grade entitled *The Bewilderment of Sally*, about a girl who could put herself into a trance and see things from the past exactly as they occurred. She used her unique skill to help her Detective Uncle Frank solve crimes. She submitted the story to the Ellery Queen Young Mystery Writers contest and was shocked when a few months later she received a check in the mail for $500 and a gold plaque proclaiming her first place credentials.

Catherine told her, "Your father would be so proud."

By the time Mary was fifteen she had had three more stories published, one in the prestigious Omni Magazine. On her sixteenth birthday she and her mom went to the Motor Vehicles Department to get her driver's license. She passed the test with flying colors. Driving home her mother's LTD was T-boned on her side by a large Ford F-250 whose driver was trying to shoo a bee out the window and didn't see the red light...

Her mother, sitting beside her in the passenger seat, sustained a small cut on her chin from a piece of glass flying from the broken window. Three days later Mary awakened finally, on a ventilator and in a body cast. Her mother was sitting next to her bed, holding her hand and looking pitifully at Mary's bandaged face.

"I wish your father were here."

Mary had a shattered hip and several broken ribs, one of which punctured her left lung. She also sustained a broken shoulder and several leg fractures as well as a cracked skull. Thankfully she avoided a major head injury, but it would be years before she could walk without assistance and a lot longer before she had the urge to write anything. She had lost her muse in the accident.

Her recovery was slow. She battled numerous infections, and it was eighteen months before she could put any weight on her left leg as her pelvis, hip joint, knee and ankle were shattered in the crash. She also had several fractures to the long bones as well. On more than one occasion the doctors strongly considered taking the leg off, the damage was so severe. Nineteen surgeries were performed before they finally said "That's all we can do. The bones are all in place, it is up to her now."

She spent over a year in traction, developing sores on her back. She wished on more than one occasion that she had died in the

Mystery of the Mountain Lake

wreck. She questioned everything about herself, wondering why she had had to be in such a godawful hurry to get a stinking driver's license. She had nowhere to go, anyways.

Finally Mary was fitted with a walking cast and began the arduous task of physical rehabilitation. She was only allowed to touch her toe to the floor, but she could not tolerate even that. She howled in pain and would have hit the floor had she not had a therapist on either side of her. Two years after the crash she was transferred to an inpatient rehab unit, which was also a nursing home, where she would spend the next five years, until finally she was able to ambulate fifty feet down the hall and back with the help of a rolling walker. She went home, her driver's license already expired. She would never get it renewed.

Therapists began coming to her house. Her mother, never the most stable individual even before losing her husband to a Vietnamese snake bite, was little help for Mary, either physically or emotionally. After about a year of three-times-a-week visits she was finally able to graduate from the rolling walker to a regular one. One of her therapists would bring magazines and would leave them for her to read. The main one she brought was a regional magazine called *NorCal Living*. Mary read them from cover to cover. She had also developed an increased appetite for science fiction, books and television shows. She loved the space travel ones like Star Trek and discovered Doctor Who as well, late Saturday nights on Public Television. She started seeing advertisements for a new movie called Stargate and began to beg her therapist to take her to the theater in a wheelchair to see it. She had only ventured out of the house a handful of times since she came home, never farther than the mailbox. Her therapist, sensing a change in Mary's spirit, seized the moment.

"The movie hits theaters in about four months," she said. "I will take you, pay for everything. The biggest, buttery greased tub of popcorn they sell. Whoppers, M&Ms, Large Coca-Cola, everything you could possibly want. You name it. BUT..." She looked Mary straight in her big eyes. "You ain't going in no dad-blasted wheelchair! You gonna walk in that theater using nothing but a walking stick!"

That did it. From that moment on, Mary pushed through the pain and started getting up and moving. She read *NorCal Living* and begged her mother to go to the store and get her the ingredients she needed to try out the amazing recipes contained in the magazine. She even wrote a long letter to the editor of the magazine, telling her how much she loved the publication, about her accident and how cooking the recipes was helping her recover, getting her up on her feet and moving around in the kitchen.

By the time Stargate opened at the San Pablo 12 theater, she had not only gotten rid of the walker but also the four point cane and was using an old oak walking stick she had purchased at a yard sale. She refused to allow Tanita the therapist to let her out at the curb, or even to park in a handicapped space. She walked halfway across the parking lot, sometimes picking up the stick and carrying it several steps. She sat in the theater, mesmerized, and convinced Tanita it would be okay if they kept their seats through the intermission and they saw the movie a second time.

Although neither one of them would remember it until years later, and although it was still a few years before they met for real, holding the door for them going out was gangly bus driver Eddie Avery, who had taken the afternoon off to catch the second show.

Mary slept like a rock that night. She awakened the next morning with a totally new outlook on life. She had not graduated from high school and began to look into it. She realized she needed a computer. She had put the $500 in the bank she had won from the Ellery Queen contest, and along with the other moneys she had received from her other published stories she found she had about $1500 in her bank account. Her mother was pretty much out of the picture by this point, so she talked with her therapist about getting a computer. She showed her her bank statement, but the therapist knew something Mary didn't.

While she was in traction and on a ventilator the first few weeks after the accident, a lawyer had visited her mom in the hospital. Catherine retained the ambulance chaser's services, and was told the truck driver's insurance company was offering $75,000 for a settlement. The attorney told Catherine that was an insult, and they could get a great deal more than that, but he was simply doing his duty by reporting the offer to her. Catherine took the offer despite vehement protests from the lawyer, but Mary never knew anything about it.

When she confronted her mom about it, she discovered Catherine had been consuming about a half gallon of vodka every day and there was only about $5,000 left.

"I want that money. I am ready to finish high school and go to college so I can become a real writer," Mary pleaded with her mother. Catherine finally acquiesced and gave her half of it.

"That was my car you wrecked," she slurred.

Mary eventually got her computer, got connected to the internet, and began researching what she needed for her diploma.

The very next day a letter arrived from the editor of *NorCal Living*. Mary had completely forgotten about the letter she had written, as it had been several months and much had been going on in the Crown household since then. The editor apologized for taking so long to write back, but she said she was very moved by Mary's letter. Not just her story of despair and renewal, but she really liked her writing style. She said she had looked for her published work and read the Omni story as well as the others. She wondered if Mary would have any interest in writing a monthly column for the magazine, telling readers the story of her ordeal over the course of several issues, as a special to the magazine. She said she could have two thousand words per issue, however, since they were a non profit, she could not offer a salary. She could, however, give a $25 stipend per issue to cover expenses.

The editor went on to say how much it meant to her that Mary enjoyed the recipes that were printed each month. She said the magazine received dozens of new recipes every month from readers but could only print two or three of them. Would Mary be interested, also, in helping her with an idea she had been kicking around for compiling an annual cookbook to offer as an adjunct to the magazine. She could send Mary all the recipes along with the pictures and stories some readers included. She could edit, arrange, and organize the ones she felt worthy enough to include into a nice cookbook. She could organize them into Appetizers, Sides, Main Dishes, Desserts, Soups, etc. Mary would receive $500 upon publication, and $1.00 for each copy sold. Mary's name would appear on the front cover, along with a picture and a short bio on the back inside cover.

Included with the return address was an e-mail address. She immediately drafted and e-mailed out her acceptance. Since she had just set up her e-mail account, this was her first e-mail. She thought it would have been pointless to try to write a letter anyway, as the flood of tears gushing from her eyes would have caused considerable blurring.

2

✴   ✴   ✴   ✴   ✴

I folded up my chair and walked down the ridge to my home. I had built one of those tiny houses behind the old office building. Later I built a large deck connecting the two buildings. Later still I enclosed the deck with a lot of screen and glass. That deck area I now use as a movie and recreation room, with a pool table and pinball machine. My tiny home became my bedroom with a kitchen. I had also built another building that we call 'the shop,' or sometimes the shed, off from the tiny home which housed an elliptical machine, treadmill, and a weight lifting station. I kept a couple of kayaks, an aluminum john boat and some fishing gear, life jackets and other stuff along those lines in there. Hector kept a little bait tank in there as well, which he rarely used any more since he had put two large tanks out by his trailer. I carried mine and Janie's folding chairs into this shop building.

Hector Mendoza, my first permanent resident and jack of all trades handyman and maintenance man, was in there, looking through some of the fishing supplies.

"I am needing to restock some twenty pound lines and these big hooks," he said, the last part coming out as 'beeg hukes.'

"Have you been hooking some big fellas?" I asked him. Hector fished the lake with short pieces of fishing line with baited hooks, tied to jugs which he floated around on the lake. He had a nice little side business going, catching bass out of the lake and making tamales with them. He had a deal going with a local Mexican/Honduran restaurant called *Payaso's Locos,* which meant roughly 'Crazy Clowns.' Hector supplies them with a steady supply of pork, beef, and chicken tamales; he has a big smoker at his place, as well as a giant steamer. He can do about two hundred tamales at a time. His bass tamales are considered to be a delicacy, as he can only do them about once every month or two. He is very particular about the fish he keeps to make them with, they must meet his stringent size and color requirements. *Payaso's* has a big neon fish sign in the front window; when it is flashing the public knows they have the fish tamales. They sell out quickly.

"We shall see." He jotted a few things down in his little notepad, stuck it into his back pocket, and headed for the door. He stopped in the doorway and looked back at me. "Nasty weather coming. Tell your buddies tonight. You are going to be in the ring, right?" I said I didn't know but I probably would, since I had nothing else planned. I hardly ever had anything planned, and that was just the way I liked it.

Hector was one of the first people I met when I first came to this area. I actually met him at *Payaso's*, I was drawn in by the blinking fish sign that day. He became my first full time resident right after I bought the place.

Hector

Hector's father had been a fisherman. One day while out in the gulf of Mexico the crew reeled in a large grouper, and as they were preparing to fillet the monster it gave a huge flap and jumped right off the edge of the boat. Unfortunately for Hector's dad, he was standing in the mooring rope, upon which the grouper hung his dorsal fin, yanking the rope against the foot of Hector's dad and pulling him overboard. He hit his head so hard on the rail as he went over the side it was doubtful that he was alive when he hit the water. Young Hector was six years old.

Hector vowed then to never get on a fishing boat.

His mother loved him very much, and taught young Hector how to clean and cook fish; how to make the tastiest tamales in the town. He would take his cane fishing pole to the bridge that crossed the small intracoastal waterway that separated his little village of Jajenda and the island of Mejoriña. He would catch a small fish occasionally and throw it back; maybe 2-3 times a week he would catch something big enough to take home. This routine went on for some time, as Hector became devoted to his mother, helping her in her garden as well as cooking.

One day when Hector was around nine years old, a tall, dark-skinned older man approached him on the bridge. "You are Mañuel's son?" the stranger asked. Hector looked up at the man. His hair was long, sticking up in knots all over his head. He had a long, bushy beard with large gray spots in it. His eyes were red-rimmed and watery.

"I was on that fishing boat when he was killed by the big fish. I wish we could have saved him but it happened so fast. God takes us when he wants us and there is nothing we can do about it."

Hector looked at the man and snuffed back a tear. Or tried to. The tiny drop rolled down his cheek. Hector made no attempt to wipe it away. "I miss my Papi every single day." he said, wincing from the heartache.

"I am Eduardo Santillo." the black man said. "My heart is broken for you. I, too, lost my father at a young age. Raiders in our village in Dominica killed him. He was protecting our family from them." Eduardo looked at young Hector. "If you will be here at this time tomorrow I have something to give you and something to tell you. It is up to you whether or not you listen to what I have to say and take heed." With that Eduardo Santillo tipped his head, turned around and walked on.

That evening Hector told his mother about the strange encounter with Eduardo. She didn't know what to say; she had never heard Mañuel speak of anyone with that name. She got Hector busy chopping some onions and peppers in preparation for making the tamales she sold down at the fishing wharf.

Hector lay awake that night, listening to the sounds of the night, thinking about what the old man had said. He wondered what sort of thing he had to give him, what kind of secret he had to share.

The next day Hector stood on the bridge. He put the little bait fish onto his hook and dropped the line into the water. Standing there holding his cane pole, thinking about Eduardo, the fish nearly yanked the pole from his hands. He tightened his grip and thought "Oh boy, this is a big one!" He twisted the pole and ran back and forth on the bridge, waiting for the fish to tire itself out so he could get him in. Suddenly Eduardo was there, his big hands in leather gloves, pulling the line and wrapping it around his hand. Finally the fish broke the surface of the water. It was a lunker, alright. Its head looked as big as a soccer ball! Together the two of them walked to the end of the bridge, Hector carrying his little stringer and his net, and they hauled in the ten pounder.

"We gonna eat some good tonight!" Hector shouted. He could barely contain his excitement. This was by far the biggest fish he had ever hooked.

"Bring it back up on the bridge, *mijo*. I want to talk to you for a few minutes then I guess you'll be wanting to get this monster home so your mama can cook it!"

"I will cook this fish myself. I can do it all." Hector stated proudly. "I can clean it, fillet it, light the fire, and cook it with the lemon and the herbs."

"I have no doubt it will taste magnificent." Eduardo smiled. Hector noticed that when the big man smiled it seemed to light up the sky. "Now sit down right there and listen to what I tell you." Hector watched as Eduardo removed a small black pack from his shoulders and sat it between them, Hector sitting on the ledge on the edge of the bridge. Eduardo squatted on his haunches in front of him, his gloves off and his hands on the bag.

Eduardo started. "There is not much future in this little village for a bright young man such as yourself. See, Hector, your Papi talked about you all the time when we were out on the gulf. He bragged so much about how smart you are we all grew tired of hearing it." Eduardo grinned. "I think really we were all jealous." His face grew serious.

"I believe God has a higher purpose for you."

Hector noted that was the second time the old man had mentioned God. He stared at him, barely blinking.

"There is a small city about five hundred miles from here, perhaps you have heard of it. It is Cancun." Hector nodded. He had heard of the place but knew very little of it.

"Off the coast of Cancun there is a small island called Cozumel. Not many people live there, but long ago many battles were fought there. Many ruins and forts from some of those battles remain. They have become of great interest to people who have lots of money and like to look at old things. Most of the island, and indeed, much of Cancun itself is controlled by companies that cater to these rich people, and they bring them in by the ship load, huge ships a thousand times larger than our little fishing boats. On Cozumel alone those big ships pull in there three times a week and hundreds of people get off of them to spend the day off the ship. Some just want to walk the beaches and pick up sea shells and tan their skin. Others want to go out and see the ruins of those old battles and the other sights to be found on the island. Others want to go up to the town area about three miles from the dock and shop in the shops that some people have there, selling jewelry, clothes, fake Aztec and Mayan baubles and trinkets, and food and drinks."

Eduardo paused to let all this sink in. He knew Hector was wondering what all this had to do with him. He continued, "They get to these places on buses. And they need guides to tell them the history of these places, show them where to go to buy the souvenirs they crave. The best of these guides will make more money in a single day from the tips from these rich *touristas* than we fisherman make in a month."

Hector thought for a minute. "Why aren't you down there, then, making all that money?" he asked the old man.

"Two reasons." Eduardo eyed the boy intently. "One, I am old and ugly. These young privileged travelers wouldn't want to look at my ugly face on a long bus ride." He opened the pack finally and reached inside.

"The second, and most important reason of all," he started as he pulled a book from the pack. "These rich *touristas* cannot speak any Spanish at all. Oh, they can say quesadillas and enchiladas. But to be a guide, a very successful guide, you must be good looking, charming, funny, entertaining, and..." He handed Hector the book. "You have to speak English. You must be able to answer their questions, compliment the men and the women, make the children laugh. To do these things you must know how to speak very good English."

Hector looked at the book. On the cover was a picture of two small boys wearing straw hats and carrying fishing poles and buckets. There were symbols and letters at the top but Hector had no idea what they said. He knew his ABCs but couldn't read. He had never seen the inside of a school.

"What do I do with this?" he asked Eduardo, mystified.

"You are going to teach yourself to read and write and speak in English and Spanish." He reached into the bag again, and pulled out a small portable tape recorder.

"You take this pack with you. Inside are many tapes, more books, writing tablets, pencils, everything you need to get started." He pulled out two grade school writing tablets and alphabet books, one each in Spanish and English. "I feel like I owe my life to your Papi. It should have been me getting yanked off the boat that day, not him. You take this pack home and talk to your mama about what I told you." He stuffed the tape recorder and the books back into the pack, closed the flap, and handed it to young Hector as he rose to leave.

"I know your Papi left you much too young, and without much of a purpose. Like I said before, there is no real future here. This is as good as it is going to get. The next hurricane will likely wipe the rest of this place off the earth anyway."

With that, old Eduardo pulled a hat out of his back pocket, pulled it onto his head, turned and headed down the bridge toward the island. Hector watched until he was out of sight. He solemnly draped the pack over his shoulder, grabbed up his big fish and his gear and headed home. It was still early in the day, he realized, but he had no more desire for fishing today.

When Hector arrived home, he noticed things were not quite right. His mama, who was usually outside tending their little garden, was not outside anywhere. Sitting in front of their house, which was really just a four room hut, was a large truck. Hector recognized it as belonging to Pancho, the man who was his father's friend who owned the bake shop on the other side of their village.

Pancho was sitting on the stool in the main room when Hector entered the small clay and straw abode. His shoes were off and he was wearing an undershirt; his shirt was draped over the back of the dining table chair.

Hector, frozen in the doorway, looked to the left as his mama came out of the back room, looking down as she buttoned the top buttons on her dress, her hair down out of its customary bun. She looked up, startled at the sight of her son standing in the doorway.

"Hectorito! I did not expect you home so soon!" She noticed what he was carrying and rushed over to him, trying to inconspicuously pin up her hair. Hector noticed she was barefooted as well. "Look at this fish!" she exclaimed, a bit overly dramatic.

Pancho had slipped on his shoes and grabbed his shirt off the kitchen chair. As he headed for the door he tousled Hector's hair and smiled his big baker's smile at him as their eyes met. He touched Mama's arm and nodded toward her. "I'll be back in an hour or so. That will give you two time to talk and clean this big ole fish. What a wonderful meal this young man has provided for you this day!"

Gabriela ushered young Hector into the house as Pancho cranked up his big noisy truck and drove away. "I have to tell you something Mama!" Hector held up the small black pack as he put the big fish on the kitchen counter.

His Mama put her hands on his shoulders as she turned him to face her. "I must talk to you first, *mijo*, and then afterwards we can talk some more. Come, sit on the sofa.

"Your Papi has been gone more than three years now. I know how much you loved him, how much you miss him. I loved him even more. I will always love him. He was my heart and my life.

"But he is gone on to heaven, leaving you and me here to live on, and we have done our best. Life was difficult while Papi was here, and you see how difficult it is now."

She looked away, a tear starting to form in her eye. When she looked back at him, she was smiling, her face beaming. "You know that Pancho and your Papi were good friends. They grew up with each other, they both fished off the same bridge you do when they were *niños*." She looked down and began to fret with her hands as the tears began to roll down her cheeks. Hector noticed for the first time how thin she had become.

She suddenly stopped wringing her hands and placed them on her knees. She shook the stray hairs out of her face and raised her head. Her red, wet eyes pierced Hector's wide eyes. She reached out and took his hands.

"Pancho wants to marry me and adopt you as his son." She did not look away, and realized she was holding her son's hands very tightly. She loosened her grip a bit but held on as she continued to look into his young eyes. Neither of them had blinked.

Finally Hector dropped his mother's hands and stood. She watched him as he took a few steps away from her. He stood with his back to her for a minute that seemed to Mama like an hour. Finally he turned to face her, tears streaming down his young cheeks as he ran back to her and threw his arms around her neck, his tears dampening her shoulder.

"I know my Papi loved me and he thought I was very smart. Eduardo told me. I know you loved Papi, too, and that he loved you. I know you have been so sad since Papi has been gone."

Hector pulled his face off his mother's shoulder and stood up. He looked over at the black pack and back to his Mama. "Papi always said Pancho was a good man."

He suddenly stepped away from her as he picked up his pack.

"Mama?"

"Yes *mijo,* what is it?"

"Do you think Pancho can help me learn to read and write?"

Eddie and Mary Beth

When Eddie came to he was strapped to a stretcher being rolled out the door of the bus. He wasn't sure what was going on with all the flashing red and blue lights as well as the flurry of activity around him. He squeezed his eyes shut and tried to think. The memory of the last thirty minutes or so came back to him so strong it was like a hammer to the head. He tried to raise his head and realized it was strapped to the stretcher by a cervical immobilizer. "The baby," he croaked as rain began to hit him in the face.

"He's awake," one of the emergency responders called out. They had the stretcher on the sidewalk now, rolling him towards the hospital. The paramedic leaned over him and shined a penlight into his eyes. "PERRLA" he barked to the orderly, who scribbled something onto a notepad. "Do you know your name, sir?" he asked the wide-eyed Eddie

"Yes I know my friggin' name! Where is the baby? That maniac snatched him out of my hands just before he cold-cocked me!"

"What is your name sir? Can you tell me where you are?"

Eddie drew in a deep breath and closed his eyes, calming himself and gathering his scrambled thoughts. After a few seconds he opened his eyes and looked at the tech.

"My name is Eddie Avery. That is my bus. I just helped a woman lying on the floor of it deliver a baby when a crazy person jumped on top of her, snatched the baby out of my hands and socked me in the nose. That's the last thing I remember."

"A&O times three" the tech yelled out. He looked back at Eddie. "How are you feeling? Can you move your hands and feet?"

"I am fine," Eddie said. "I think my nose is broken and my friggin head hurts, but I can feel everything. Now will someone please tell me what the FUCK is going on? I need to call my dispatcher and tell them what happened and why the route is delayed. I need to call Mary Beth." He was bordering on hysteria. "UNTIE MY GORRAM HANDS AND GET ME OFF THIS THING" he screamed.

He felt a hand on his shoulder. "Calm down sir. We will get you situated in a minute as soon as we get inside out of this rain."

Eddie heard the swoosh of the automatic door and felt a bump as the stretcher entered into the brightly lit Emergency Room hallway.

"Take him to six. Someone give me report," the nurse ordered as they came around the desk. They wheeled him into a room with curtained walls. The nurse followed, writing on her clipboard as the medic gave her a brief rundown of Eddie's condition. Eddie was doing his very best to stay silent and patient and let the medical personnel do their job. But his patience was nearing an end, which was evidently obvious to the nurse as she looked into his wide eyes while she applied a blood pressure cuff.

"You gonna be a problem for me if I take you out of these restraints?

Eddie looked up at her, tears beginning to stream from his eyes and into his ears. "Of course not," he said hoarsely through quivering lips. "I just want someone to talk TO me instead of AT me." The nurse looked over at the cop, who was waiting patiently in the curtained doorway.

"Give me five minutes and he's all yours," she told him.

The nurse, Amanda, checked Eddie's vital signs and did a quick neurological assessment, deciding Eddie was okay to be unstrapped. "I will go get you some washcloths so you can clean yourself up a little." Eddie sat up and for the first time saw all the blood caked on his waist and thighs, as well as his hands and arms, and began to shake. The cop replaced the nurse by his side and helped him twist to the edge of the stretcher

"Can you stand, d'ya think? You need to go over to the sink and take a look in the mirror."

Eddie slid forward until his feet touched the floor. The cop supported him under his arm as he slowly got to his feet. After a few seconds he raised his hands from the stretcher and nodded at the cop. As he slowly made it over to the sink, he gasped when he saw his reflection. Both his eyes were bloodshot and already turning purple around them. His nose was flattened and deep red, and his mustache and goatee were matted and crusty with dried blood, as was the front of his uniform shirt. He realized he had been breathing through his mouth; now it was obvious why.

"Jeez. The bastard really knocked the crap out of me." He turned away. "My head hurts real bad right now." The cop assisted Eddie over to the chair that was next to the stretcher and stepped out of the little room, quickly returning with another chair. He sat and looked Eddie in the eyes.

"I just need to ask you a few quick questions then I will leave you be."

"Can I call my dispatcher first? There are people waiting for the bus..." Eddie looked at the ceiling. "This is a nightmare," he mumbled.

"All that's handled," the cop told him. "That bus is now evidence in a double homicide. BART has already dispatched another one to finish your routes. Don't give that another thought. Now, what can you tell me about what happened?"

Eddie looked dazed. "Double homicide...what the..." Eddie trailed off and, cupping his head in his hands, began to rack and sob.

"We will get to that." The young cop immediately regretted giving Eddie that information too soon. He knew this was going to be a learning experience for him. The nurse walked back in to get another set of vital signs and set down a stack of towels and washcloths.

"Are you allergic to any medications, sweetheart?" she asked him in her syrupy sweet nurse voice. Eddie looked up at her and shook his head. "I need you to say it for me, hon."

"No. I do not have any allergies." Eddie replied.

Eddie looked over at the cop, who had his notepad out. He nodded and started talking, the cop stopping him from time to time to ask a question. Eddie would answer him. "No, I had never seen her before," and other responses along those lines. As the cop finished with him, Eddie suddenly remembered the placenta popping out and bouncing off his thighs. He shuddered as he related that to the cop. He looked at his crusty pants and began to cry again.

The cop stepped out and motioned to the nurse. "I'm finished with him. I think he needs something." The nurse held up an IV kit and some syringes filled with clear liquid.

"Way ahead of you, chief," she smiled. When she went back into Eddie's room he had dug his phone out of his pocket and was relating to Mary Beth the events of the evening. The nurse assisted Eddie back onto the stretcher and sat down to do the IV as Eddie wrapped up his conversation and turned off his phone.

As the nurse pushed the plunger home on the second syringe, Eddie closed his eyes and his mouth breathing became a little deeper.

Mary Beth had already sprung into action while she was still on the phone with Eddie. A veteran of experiencing and living through traumatic experiences, she knew exactly what to do. She packed up some clean underwear and casual clothes for Eddie, along with some bottled water and a few snacks. Pushed out of her mind was the big news she had planned to share with Eddie when he got home that evening...

When Mary Beth had graduated from college, *NorCal Living* had offered her the full-time salaried position of Associate Editor and Head Writer. The past five years she had held the position of Editor-in-Chief, and had tripled the subscription rate during her tenure, helped by adapting the magazine to the blossoming field of electronic publishing. She had also maintained her deal with the cookbook, *NorCal Cooking,* which was now receiving orders from Canada as well as many places east of the Mississippi. New England had become a major area of growth for it. In fact, the royalties from the cookbook was more than her annual salary.

The past few days, without Eddie's knowledge, she had begun to examine their investments and their retirement savings and had been pleasantly surprised at the seven figure nest egg they had amassed. She had already written up her letter of resignation, along with her recommendation for the person to take her position. She did wish to continue with the cookbook, however, as she had always thought of that cookbook as the child she could never have, as well as the savior and the giver-backer of her life. Apart from Eddie, that is. She had waited to talk it over with Eddie before turning in the letter, so it was still undated.

She knew Eddie had been driving that bus for his entire adult life, and hemorrhoids and backaches had caused him to begin contemplating life after BART.

But that talk would now have to wait, she thought, as she loaded her bag into the waiting taxicab and headed for Kaiser hospital.

When Eddie awakened he was no longer on a stretcher, but on a bed. He glanced to his right and saw a sink and an open door, through which he could see a toilet. He noticed his arm had a plastic IV catheter taped to it with a clear plastic tube attached. His eyes followed the tube up to a bag with clear liquid dripping into a little chamber at the end of the tubing. He realized he was no longer wearing his clothes but a blue hospital gown, and he was clean. He felt the sheets touching his bare legs. A look of panic crossed his face as he threw back the covers and raised up his gown. His underwear was still on!

"Don't worry honey bunny. I helped the nurse get you cleaned up. You have a male nurse, but he didn't see your jewels." Mary Beth smiled. Eddie followed her voice until he saw her sitting in a recliner by the window to his left, up by the head of the bed.

He saw through the window that daylight had broken. "How long have I been out?" he asked. He touched his nose gingerly. It was still sore but he was breathing a lot better.

"The ER doc popped your nose back out. They said we can go home after you pee."

At the mention of the word pee he suddenly felt a feeling of urgency he realized had been there since he woke up, and was now forcing its way to the front of his mind. "Come around here and let this rail down before I pee all over this bed then!" he exclaimed.

They went home with prescriptions for antibiotics and pain pills, along with instructions to follow up with his regular doctor the next day. As they settled on the couch, Mary Beth asked Eddie if he wanted to talk about it. He had been told everything that was known so far. The woman was the ex-wife of the maniac who had committed suicide-by-cop. They had split up when it was learned that she was pregnant by another man. He had not taken the news very well, and she had gotten a restraining order against him. Just as she and the baby's father were getting ready to go to the hospital, the ex showed up, in a very bad temper. He stabbed the boyfriend as he was putting their bag into the car and was turning on her as she spotted the bus going by. She slammed the car door on his arm and made a run for it. Eddie knew the rest of the story after that.

"I don't really feel like talking right now." Eddie looked up as the first rays of dawn began peeking through the curtains. "I need to call Ray, as I don't think I'll be driving the bus tomorrow, well, I guess today. I suppose he's probably already figured that out, since I was supposed to go on duty two hours ago.."

"Call him if it will make you feel better. I am going to whip us up some breakfast and some coffee. You're going to notice how hungry you are in a few minutes." At that his stomach grumbled a little. "She knows me so well," Eddie thought, smiling to himself.

Mary Beth laid a folder on the coffee table as she got up and went into the kitchen. Eddie called his boss and updated him on his condition. Ray informed him that he had several years worth of vacation time built up that he had never taken, so he didn't need to worry about a thing. He could take as much time as he needed. Eddie hung up the phone and accepted a cuppa from his lovely wife. He picked up the folder. "What's this?" he asked.

Eddie really didn't take much convincing after Mary Beth laid out the numbers for him. She then put the cherry on top.

"We don't have any children, our parents are gone, it's just you and me baby!" He looked at the figures she had written down. He looked at her figure as she settled beside him on the sofa and laid her head on his shoulder.

"Well, according to Ray I have about five years worth of vacation I can take before I officially retire. With over thirty five years of service I can retire with full benefits for the rest of my life," he mused. He leaned back and took a bite of his egg and cheese croissant. "But what shall we do, *Mon Cherie?*"

Mary Beth climbed over onto his lap, her knees on either side of him. "I have been thinking about that. You love to drive, and we love getting dressed up in different cosplay outfits and driving down the PCH to San Diego every year for Comic Con…"

"Yes we certainly do. And?"

"You know there are Comic Cons and Dragon Cons and Paleyfest and Renaissance Fairs and stuff all over the country, all year round. You like driving large vehicles." She pulled out the brochure for the Fleetwood Bounder.

Eddie got the full picture then. He wrapped her in his arms as the rest of his sandwich fell on the table. As he carried her into the bedroom and laid her on the bed, he gushed "That is the best idea I have ever heard in my whole damn life!"

"Don't turn off the light" she whispered into his ear.

3

✱ ✱ ✱ ✱ ✱

The ring was an area to the south of my place, between mine and Janie's spot. It had a fire pit in the center surrounded by several wooden benches that were made from logs Hector and I cut and placed the first year I owned the place, using the trees we had cleared out to open up the views a bit and expand the park. It had become a very popular spot for the residents, especially in the evenings after sundown. Hector was constantly making alterations to the ring, and had recently created some small stools that fit neatly under the benches and could easily be brought out and fitted into little metal-lined holes in front of the seats. These stools were very sturdy and quite handy. Folks used them as a table for food, a prop for their feet, and even a chair to use to get a little closer to the fire on a cool night. I would often awaken to find Howard or Janie, or sometimes both of them, sitting out at the ring strumming their guitars early in the morning, their coffees steaming on the stool.

As I exited the shed and headed back around to my little house, Eddie yelled, "Hey, bossman! We gots burgers! Come on over to the ring." No surprises here. Eddie had become the resident grill master. His burgers were always incredible, as were his chicken and pork chops. He was always cooking, when he and Mary Beth weren't rocking their Fleetwood, and watched as each person partaking of his culinary creations took their first bites, grinning like a possum at the satisfied faces.

The fire was crackling when I took my seat at the ring. Indie was in her customary spot already, her laptop open on the stool in front of her. Eddie brought over a metal camping plate with a fat, juicy burger and some browned potato strips, which he also cooked on his big pellet grill. I looked up at him to say thanks.

"Just the way you like it *jefe*. Mustard, pickles, onions, and two slices of cheese! You gotta get your own drink, though."

As if on cue, Janie came flouncing out of her door, the ribbons in her hair and her thin scarves lifting on the slight breeze, which had begun to pick up a little. Her multicolor-tipped fingers were wrapped around two frosty, dripping long necked Budweisers, fresh from her cooler. I briefly thought to myself that putting in the ice machine had been one of Hector's best ideas.

Janie plopped down beside me, her warm, soft hip and thigh pressed against mine. Handing me a cold brew, she elbowed me in the ribs and said, "Give me a bite of that burger, Cowboy." I started to tell her to get her own, but she called me Cowboy, and by the way she looked at me I knew I was going to be one lucky cowboy in a little while.

Yes, life is indeed good.

Howard stepped into the ring then, carrying his acoustic bass guitar case. I possess zero musical talent myself, but I can appreciate real talent when I hear it. Howard can chord that bass like a guitar and has a really nice singing voice to boot. There are times when he and Janie get their groove on and it is a real treat to behold. He still loved to play, but seemed to have no desire to ever be on a stage again.

Howard declined Eddie's offer of a burger, saying he had "noshed on some nuggs" a little earlier. Instead, he opened his case and brought out his bass. He began to strum a little to loosen up his fingers and checked the tuning. He worked a few scales up and down the neck, then stopped. He looked over at Indie, in her usual mind, oblivious to everything around her as she sat hunched on her perch and typed away.

Howard cleared his throat, struck a chord on the bass, and in his best emcee voice, announced: "And now, Ladies and Gentlemen! For your dining and dancing pleasure, it is a stunning and persuasive pleasure to present to you...the world premiere of..." He simulated a drum roll by tapping his thumb and little finger back and forth quickly on the body of the guitar. "NESSIE!"

Indie's head snapped up immediately as Howard began playing and singing.

> "Nessie, oh Nessie. Your eyes are so bright.
> When next you come back in the night.
> Will you bring us some eggs
> Since you don't have no legs."

He played a little run and kept time tapping his thumb hard against the body of the bass, next to the sound hole where the finish had been rubbed off a bit, then started again.

> "Nessie, oh Nessie. Your skin is so dark.
> We can hatch them and have
> our own Jurassic Park!"

He finished with a flourish, running scales up and down the neck and stood quickly, brandishing his bass in one hand as he bowed to the sounds of applause and whistles from everyone, with the notable exception of Indie, who glared at him like he had just confessed to being the zodiac killer. She whizzed a pine cone at him, which skimmed the top of his head.

"You, sir, are not a nice person." Indie pouted. Howard laid down his axe and went over to her, enveloping her in his arms and kissing the top of her head.

"You know I love you! Just don't forget me when you go on your book-signing tour. Me and Janie can accompany you and sing *Nessie* at every stop!"

She began slapping at him then. "Get your filthy hands off me, you fucking cretin!" she cried, standing and stomping at Howard's feet as the big man mussed her hair. "OOOOOOOOO! Get away from me!" She threw her head back and looked up at him then, her eyes blazing, cheeks red and hair sticking out everywhere. She was breathing hard, and grabbing Howard's collar, pulled his head down to hers and laid a big wet kiss on him that had his fingers twitching. Then she put her hands on his chest and gave him a hard push, snapped her laptop shut, and went marching off towards her RV. She took several steps and whirled around, looking back at Howard, who stood with his mouth open and hands on his hips.

"You gonna stand there looking like an imbecile all night, or are you coming?" she barked at him.

Howard sprang into action then, snapping his guitar case shut and grabbing the handle. "See y'all tomorrow." he said over his shoulder without taking his eyes off the big bouncing buttocks of the aspiring novelist and scurried away.

Howard had been coming to the park off and on for about four years.

Howard

"You be careful now, and dontchu drap one o' them melons, boy." Howard glared at his step-father with blazing contempt, but quickly looked away fearing the wrath that would surely come later. The short, skinny twelve year old towhead had been forced to make these long hard trips to central Florida four or five times a year with Otis Stantsil for the past eight years since his mother had married the hateful fellow. Otis had made the acquaintance of a farmer there who grew about two acres of the sweetest watermelons every year. He let Otis have them for a quarter apiece, the catch being he had to go gather them out of the fields himself.

So every month or so during the summer Otis and Howard would put the heavy oak sideboards on the old International pickup truck and drive the twelve hundred or so miles from the trailer they shared with Howard's mom Stella in Coburn, a small town in rural southern Indiana. Otis would park the truck in a little turn-around on state road 16 and sell them for three bucks each, then drive back down and get some more, until the season was done. Then, in the fall, they would make a trip about two hundred miles farther down, into south Florida to the Indian River citrus farms and load the truck with naval oranges, grapefruits, tangelos, and tangerines just in time for the holiday season.

The rest of the time Otis would sit around and drink cheap whiskey, scolding Howard and Stella relentlessly. Most of the time he scolded them with words; occasionally with the back of his hand or his belt.

Howard learned very quickly to stay clear of his step-father, especially when he was in his cups. He hated the trips to Florida in the loud old truck; no A/C, no heat in the winter, no radio. It was the last part he hated the worst, as he had to put up with Otis singing crappy old country songs about drinking and cheating hearts.

At home Howard mostly kept to himself, writing poetry and reading the encyclopedias and the dictionary; he would even read the telephone book. The year of his fourteenth birthday, he received for Christmas a small transistor radio with a little ear plug he could use to listen privately. This opened up a new world for young Howard, as the only music he had been privy to up to that point had been the depressing country music that Otis sang and occasionally on the *Grand Ole Opry* TV shows. Howard detested that sound, probably because Otis liked it.

    With his new radio, Howard discovered new types of music. The radio picked up much better when he was outside, so most of that winter he sat outside listening to the station from nearby Harton, playing the top 40 bubble gum hits of the day, which sounded beautiful to him. He longed to fly up, up, and away with the 5th Dimension in their beautiful balloon; he wanted to go roller skating with Melanie, who had a brand new key. He had no idea what that meant, but she sure sounded pretty singing about it. The station signed off at dusk, so he would come back into the house then. By that time it would be too cold to stay out anyway.

    Every now and then Howard would notice a TV ad for records such as *K-Tel's Rock Hits of the 60's*; when it would show The Grass Roots singing *Midnight Confessions* he would hear Otis mutter "Goddamned long haired faggots."

    As spring approached, two things occurred that changed things for young Howard: his Uncle Tommy came wheeling up one day in a new Ford Bronco, fresh from an eight year hitch in the Air Force. Howard had met his mother's brother only a handful of times, but now he was out of the military and became a fixture in Howard's life, riding him around in his Bronco with the top off and Tommy James and the Shondells, Uriah Heep, Grand Funk Railroad, and Creedence Clearwater Revival blasting from the 8-track player.

    The other thing that happened was discovering the superstation WLS out of Chicago, which would come in crystal clear after sundown when Howard held the radio in a certain spot. Howard had normally just turned the radio off after the Harton station had signed off, but one warm night he stayed out and fiddled with the radio, seeing what else he could find. What he found was the sultry voice of Yvonne Daniels introducing the world to "The best new band in Chicago, Styx, with their hit song *Lady*." When that song was followed by the screaming distorted guitar of Jimi Hendrix telling the *Foxey Lady* he was "coming to getcha," Howard knew what he wanted to do with his life. He wanted to play guitar and make music that sounded like that.

    From that day on, he couldn't wait for the sun to go down so he could listen to the Chicago station. He had had no idea the music he heard from there could exist. Deep Purple. Cream. Led Zeppelin. Jethro Tull. Black Sabbath.

He began to pester Otis and Stella to get him a guitar so he could learn to play. For that long summer and through the next winter he longed to play the music he loved. He endured Otis's abuse, continued to discover new music and write his feelings down in poetic form.

Uncle Tommy had gotten a place over in Harton and had begun working at the Ford dealership there, selling cars. Howard didn't see him nearly as much; he still came around sometimes on Sundays, and it was one of those Sundays the following summer while they were out riding in the Bronco that Howard told his uncle of his love of rock music and his strong desire to learn the guitar so he could make his own music.

Tommy stopped the truck and looked at him. "Man, you got to get after it if you want it." He got out of the Bronco and walked over to the passenger side. "Get the hell out. You're fifteen, I need to see how well you can drive." Howard jumped out and got behind the wheel. He had been watching and was a quick study, getting the hang of the clutch and accelerator, only choking the car out a couple of times and giving them whiplash once.

"Not bad for a beginner, but you have a lot to learn. By the time you're sixteen you'll be perfect. Now, about this other stuff." He put his hand on his nephew's shoulder. "Nobody's gonna give you anything in this world. If you want something badly enough, you'll find a way to make it happen." The next several Sundays, and occasional week days when Tommy wasn't working, Howard learned to drive that four speed Bronco like a natural. They even went off-road a few times, Tommy showing him how to lock the hubs and engage the four-wheel-drive, fording creeks and going up and down embankments.

When Otis came up to Howard one June morning and told Howard to get in the truck, they were going to Florida, Howard begged him to let him start working for him and making some money so he could buy himself a guitar. As they drove down the road, through Kentucky, Tennessee, and Georgia, Otis sat quietly listening to the boy's pleas. Finally, having heard enough, he backhanded the still runty Howard hard in the mouth, yelling "Shut the fuck up about that shit. I ain't a-havin' no 'flower child' pot-smoking faggot hippie living in my house."

Howard sat back, stunned, tasting the coppery taste of blood in his mouth from his bleeding lips. He spoke no more to Otis the rest of the trip. He loaded the watermelons and rode home in silence. He resolved to never look the hateful Otis in the eyes again, and to never even speak to him. He realized then that he hated his mother for marrying the sorry son of a bitch. That realization shook something in him, and when they got home Howard went straight to his room, got out his notebook and began writing down his frustrations. As the days went by, Tommy sensed a change in Howard, and, after Howard had been to Florida and back a couple more times and Tommy kept after him, Howard told Tommy what had happened the first trip that summer. That evening, after Tommy took Howard home, he took his sister outside and talked to her, after Howard had gone into his room.

The next day Tommy came to the house early, collected Howard, and told him "You are coming to spend the day with me at my house in Harton."

Howard had never been to Tommy's house before, and was shocked to learn that Tommy had a very lovely, very lively, thick-hipped roommate, named Susie. Tommy took Howard into the kitchen to get a drink, and leaned over near his mesmerized nephew, who had not taken his eyes off the buxom Susie. "She's also my bed-mate." Howard whirled around and grinned up at Tommy, who gave him a big wink, clapped him on the shoulder, and said "Come on, Romeo."

Tommy took Howard into the spare bedroom, where lo and behold, there, on a stand, shining and gleaming in the light of the sun coming through the window, was the most beautiful thing Howard had ever seen. Thoughts of Susie disappeared as he walked over and ran his hands over the contoured body and the strings and fretboard of the brand new Epiphone acoustic guitar. "I didn't know you could play!" Howard exclaimed.

"I can't, really. A guy I was in the service with had one and showed me a few chords. I figured we could learn together." Tommy opened the dresser drawer and pulled out a magazine sized paperback book: *Beginning Guitar, Learn to Play the Alfred Way*. Howard grabbed the book and started looking through it.

"It shows you proper technique, how to tune it, how to make the chords and play the notes!" Howard was excited, looking at his uncle and back at the guitar

"Go ahead, pick it up and sit on that stool over there and have some fun. Susie and me are gonna run to town and pick up some groceries and stuff. See you in a little while."

The rest of that summer and into the next Howard spent as much time as he could over at Tommy's house. He quickly graduated from the Alfred book and Tommy had located an advanced set of lessons called *Music Theory for Guitar*. The instrument came easily to him; Howard proved to be a natural at it. Soon he could hear a song on the radio and would be able to play it on the guitar and sing it in no time.

Otis had no idea what was going on...

Something else happened that winter and spring while he was learning his way around the fretboard. Puny little Howard hit a growth spurt, gaining about a foot in height and seventy five pounds in bulk. He noticed it was a lot easier to move the watermelons around that first trip down south.

One evening Otis came out on the porch where Howard was sitting listening to the radio. He had his clippers in his hand. "School's fixing to start. Come on out back and let's cut that mop off."

"I ain't getting my hair cut no more." Howard said, without looking up. Otis looked at him and grabbed his arm.

"I ain't got time fer this shit. Come on now, dammit." Howard yanked his arm out of the mean Otis's hand and stood, now able to look the tyrant in the eye.

"I said you ain't cutting my hair no more. Now go on and leave me alone."

Otis reached across his chest and swung, intending to backhand Howard in the mouth. Howard caught his wrist in mid-swing, feeling all the years of living in fear and hate come rushing to the surface.

"Oh, so you's a big man now, huh." Otis swung his left fist at Howard's jaw. Howard, who still had a death grip on Otis's right wrist, yanked his head back so Otis's punch barely grazed his chin. As Howard took a step back, Otis lurched forward and as his head came down Howard connected with a right uppercut, connecting flush with the evil man's chin and snapping his head backwards. Howard released the grip on his step-father's wrist and Otis' eyes rolled back into his head as he crumpled to the porch floor, out cold.

Howard knew that nothing good could possibly come from this encounter. He went in, grabbed his book of poems and threw his clothes in a bag. He walked past his mother, oblivious as always to what was going on. "I'm going to Uncle Tommy's," Howard told her as he walked out the door, grabbing his radio off the chair and stepping over the unconscious Otis, down the steps and down the driveway.

His bewildered mother looked down at the sleeping form of her husband on the porch, breathing deeply but not moving, and ran into the kitchen and called her brother. She stood at the window watching her son as he disappeared from view, reaching the end of the driveway and turning to walk down the street.

He had walked a couple of miles when Tommy came pulling up alongside of him. "What's going on, Zoom?" (Tommy had started calling Howard *Zoom* in honor of the speed in which he had taught himself the guitar).

"I've had it with that piece of shit, and I ain't going back. Can I stay with you and Susie for a while?"

"Get in, man. We'll figure it out."

Things got better for Howard after that. Already sixteen, he quit school and took the GED test, passing with flying colors. Tommy helped him get a job at the dealership, washing cars and assisting the mechanics in the shop. Soon he was changing tires, doing oil changes and tune-ups. He got a sweet deal on an old F-100 that came in on a trade. It had a camper shell on it, and a kicking stereo system! He saved his money, paid off the truck, and played Tommy's guitar every night. Finally, after about a year and a half, he told Tommy "I'm going to Chicago." He had saved up around $2,500, and he had his mind set on a Fender Stratocaster and a Marshall Amp, just like Jimi played.

Tommy looked at him. "What are you saying, dude? You wanting to move up there? Do you know anyone who lives there?"

"No, I just want to see it. I want to go to a big guitar store and buy me a Stratocaster with a whammy bar and a Marshall stack. Then I'm gonna find a couple of guys who want to rock as hard as I do, start a band and write songs and get laid and play concerts."

Tommy looked at his now strapping young nephew, with his long blond curls touching his shoulders, and smiled at him, shaking his head.

"Can you wait a couple days? Let me get some things squared away at work, and me and Susie will come with you!"

In Chicago, the first stop was a Howard Johnson's, the one with a restaurant. Tommy got them two rooms for a week. They found the biggest guitar store they could find, and Tommy and Susie ended up leaving Howard there for a few hours, as he put the store clerk through his paces, trying out every guitar, effects pedal, and amplifier in the store, until he found the sound he wanted. He noticed a bulletin board up by the door, and after he made his purchases, spending almost all his money on a guitar, amp, some pedals and a pedal board, and lots of cables and electrical adapters and such, he stood looking at all the notices people had posted, trying to sell their gear and looking for specific things. One notice caught his eye, and he snatched it off the board.

After having the meal of their lives at Lou Malnoti's deep dish pizza palace, Tommy and Susie returned to find Howard sitting on the curb outside with several boxes and bags stacked up, and a piece of paper in his hand. Tommy took the paper and looked at it as Howard loaded his stuff in the back of the truck.

"Singer/Bassist looking for hot guitarist and drummer to play original hard rock music. I have the PA and the voice, I need the songs to sing and other players to play them."

There was a number at the bottom, and a name: Storm Geiger.

"I called him. We need to go to 510 Watsonville Avenue. I'm supposed to be there at five o'clock."

They went back to the hotel, where they were able to get a city map at the desk. Howard disappeared into the restaurant as Tommy studied the map. "It's gonna take us about thirty minutes to get there, so we better get going pretty soon," Tommy told Howard as he came out with a large cheeseburger in one hand and a large drink in the other.

Susie asked if it was okay if she stayed behind in the room, "I'm tired and my belly is so full," she complained with a shy smile. Tommy kissed her and the two men piled in the truck and took off, Howard driving and Tommy navigating.

On the way to Watsonville Avenue, Howard tuned his FM radio until he found a station. The next thing he heard changed his life again. He cranked up the stereo in his old F100 as he and the rest of the world got their first taste of a Dutch boy named Edward Van Halen, as the sounds of *Eruption* filled the cab of the truck.

It would be twelve years before Howard ever made it back to the state of Indiana, by then playing in front of three thousand people at the Indianapolis Convention Center. He wowed Storm Geiger, who began to get a little impatient with Howard during that initial meeting, as Howard took his time getting his gear unpacked and setting everything up while a fascinated Tommy looked on, helping when he could. But finally he got everything situated and strapped on his blue burst Strat and began to warm up, playing *All Along the Watchtower*. Storm turned on his PA and stood a second mic in front of Howard who discovered he could harmonize in perfect pitch, and as they wrapped up *Lorelei* by Styx, Howard looked over at Tommy, who was beaming. Howard showed his notebook to Storm, who began to quiver. "These songs are amazing! Have you written the music yet?"

Tommy and Susie caught a bus back home; one of Tommy's co-workers picking them up at the bus depot. Howard moved in with Storm, who had one rule: no drugs or excessive partying. He was serious about the band, and knew he had found gold with Howard's writing and guitar playing. Soon Wild Dog Donnie Dew moved in with his drum kit, and the band Buster Hymen and the Penetrators was born.

They jelled quickly as a unit, as the chemistry between the three of them was amazing. They put together about thirty cover songs so they could get gigs in some of the smaller bars around town, and worked on their original tunes in the meantime. They began working in a few of the originals during their shows, and were getting good feedback from their audiences, which had begun to grow as they played larger clubs. They eventually shortened their name to The Penetrators, and played their hearts out every chance they could.

Finally, they secured a gig at a festival sponsored by a local radio station that had several bands appearing, including Cheap Trick and The Police. They took the opportunity by the horns, and played a forty five minute set of only their original songs. They were unaware of their audience, however, and after their set was up and they were packing up their gear, they got a surprise visit from two members of The Police. Stewart Copeland and Andy Summers had been watching from the wings. The two rock stars approached them with their hands out and big smiles on their faces. Andy grabbed Howard's hand and blurted out, "What in the hell are you guys doing here? That stuff you are playing is what those pussies out in LA are wishing they could play. You would blow everyone off the Sunset Strip! You need to go to Hollywood, fellows."

The Penetrators took their advice, moving out to LA and made a demo tape, got some gigs at some of the clubs in the valley and eventually getting in the *Whisky-a-Gogo*, the *Troubador*, the *Rainbow,* and the other clubs along the strip. In their minds they were indeed blowing away almost every other band they shared a bill with, and as months and years clicked by they watched these other bands get signed to big deals and going off on big tours while they continued to play the clubs.

"Man, we're a hundred times better than these lame-ass poser bands. Why can't we get a deal?" Howard lamented one night after another rousing set at the *Whisky*. "People love us. Listen to them out there screaming for an encore."

As those words left his lips, the devil walked through the door of the little dressing room.

"I hear what you're saying, Kemo Sabe," said the devil, wearing the disguise of a Mr. Steve Willard, with huge diamond rings and a shiny suit. "Allow me to introduce myself." He handed Storm his card, who looked at it and passed it over to Howard.

Steve Willard, Glam Entertainment, the card glittered.

"You boys do have a great sound, no doubt," the devil began. "But you look more like a bunch of grease monkeys that you do rock stars. Haven't you noticed what these other bands have that you don't?" The devil paused for effect, as he looked at each one of them. "Record companies don't give two shits anymore about how good you play or how good your songs are. I mean, look at Poison. Their songs have as much substance as a fart on a roller coaster. They only care about how slutty of a chick you can make yourself look."

The devil had their attention, and he let his words sink in as he turned his back to them. After a moment, he spun back around. "You have to tease up your hair and spray a can of Aquanet on there, use some red lipstick and eye shadow and lots of mascara. You gotta make the girls jealous and make the guys question their own sexuality when their dicks get hard looking at you."

"We have a manager already," Storm said, handing the devil his card back.

"Keep it, and think about what I told you. When you get serious about getting a deal and getting on MTV and becoming famous and going on big tours call me." Then the devil went out the door.

Six months later The Penetrators made the call to the devil. One year later they had a deal with Mercury records. It was 1988 when *Ride the Bull* hit number 22 on the Billboard hot 100, where it spent twelve weeks on the chart. The video, which featured several very buxom 'woo girls' bursting out of ripped Penetrators tee shirts and bandanna shirts, swaying back and forth riding a large smoke snorting black bull with a gleam in his eyes and a large nose ring, was one of the most requested videos on MTV's Headbanger's Ball show for several months.

Back home in southern Indiana, Stella made an emaciated and now nearly dead Otis Stantsil watch the video one night.

"I guess he may not be a fucking faggot after all," the mean old grouch grumbled as he watched the girls wooing ecstatically as they swayed on the bull.

But fame was fleeting for the Penetrators. Shortly after they made it to Indiana at the Indianaroo festival at the Convention Center, a group called Nirvana from Seattle hit number one on the charts. The era of glam rock was over; the era of 'depressed flannel shirt wearer' rock had begun.

Shortly after the Indiana show, the Penetrators were doing a show at the Fox Theater in Atlanta when a drunken fan somehow got up onto the stage and fell against Howard, knocking him off the stage, all the way down into the orchestra pit, about a thirty five foot drop straight to the concrete floor. Howard suffered a broken wrist, dislocated elbow, fractured hip, and three fractured vertebrae. But the worst fracture was to his psyche. Arm in a sling for six months and unable to walk for six more, the spotlight went out for Zoom Strider; better known to his friends as Howard Martin.

Things only got worse from there. Howard became addicted to oxycodone and morphine. The Penetrators, dropped by Mercury after the grunge scene took over, found themselves in debt due to the terms of their contract with the devil, to the tune of $375,000 to Mercury and $200,000 to Glam Entertainment. The money they had generated with record sales and touring didn't come close to paying studio time fees, video production fees, promotion fees, management fees, hotel fees, etc. etc. etc. Unfortunately for Howard, who was listed in the contract as the principal songwriter and 'leader' of the band, the bulk of the debt fell on him personally. He felt that he would have been much better off if he had landed on his head in the fall and just died.

Howard filed for bankruptcy and moved into a trailer park in Riverside, California, and began the slow process of healing his mind. It was there that one late night, at the depth of his depression, he saw an ad on television.

"Have you been injured because of someone else's negligence? Get the settlement you deserve. One call gets it all!"

The light bulb went off. Howard made the call, sued the Fox Theater and came away with a seven figure settlement. He paid off his bankruptcy and opened a rock and roll club in Oceanside called, of course, The Bull.

The Bull was a large rectangular shaped building with a live music stage complete with a bar, tables, and dance floor in each end. The two rooms were pretty much mirror images of each other, one side featuring rock bands playing cover tunes and the other side reserved for bands who played their own music. Howard liked giving good, original music, hard rock bands a place to play.

The center area had rest rooms, of course, but the feature attraction was The Bull. It was identical to the one in the video, complete with the nose ring, the leering eyes, and smoke coming from the nostrils.

All was well for the next few years. Howard had lost touch with the other Penetrators: Storm, Wild Dog and Lucky Longfellow, the guitarist they added when they began to tour, had all scattered. Howard found it easier to play bass after his injuries, and would sometimes jam with some of the bands that came through the club, during their sound checks, and occasionally doing a song or two with them at night. Things were good.

Then, one night he got a piece of advice from one of his managers that would eventually prove devastating.

"We need to modify the saddle on *El Toro* (as the staff referred to the bull). We can cut a groove into his back, and stick a vibrator in there. Then cover it back with the saddle which we thin out a little bit in the center. We put the control for it next to the bull control so we can speed it up and slow it down. The girls already like riding that bull, they will really love it then, and so will their boyfriends, after they come off that thing with their cootchies wet and tingling. I can adjust the intensity as the bull heats up. Believe me, it will be a huge hit!"

And a hit it was. Word spread about the magic bull at The Bull. And life was good and all was well. Until it wasn't.

Jenny Seaver had recently caught her husband of two years cheating on her. Her best friend finally convinced her to go out one Saturday night.

"You've been moping around here for a month, bitch. Come on, let's go get some get back. I can't deal with you like this any more."

So off to the Bull they went. Jenny got herself liquored up and did some dirty dancing, getting her grope on to an excellent cover of Dokken's *Just Got Lucky*. She made her way off the dance floor and headed to the restroom, mumbling to herself. "He doesn't know how freakin' lucky he was to have me. That son of a bitch is gonna know, though." She had made up her mind to go find her grope buddy, take him somewhere, and screw him silly. But she never got the chance; she never made it back to the band room.

Coming out of the restroom, she noticed a couple of girls lined up at *El Toro*, and looked at the girl riding it. She looked like she was having a ball. She got in the short line and waited her turn. She was very flirtatious with the guy working the controls.

"I got something special for you," he chuckled to himself.

Jenny like the bull. She liked it a lot. She felt a little flushed when her turn was up, and she got back in line. She tipped the controller a fifty and told him "This time don't stop until I tell you to." He pocketed the fifty and slapped Jenny hard on the butt as she headed to *El Toro*.

"You sure you're ready for another ride?" he yelled at the grinning Jenny, as she rubbed her behind where he had smacked her.

She mounted the bull and screamed "Let 'er rip, tater chip! Wooooo!"

He started slowly and gradually increased the intensity until the vibrator was maxed and the bull was bucking about 50%. Jenny was shaking her head and grinding on the saddle, slapping the bull with her free hand and about to break the pommel off the saddle with the other. The controller sped up *El Toro* a little just as Jenny let out a shriek, her legs tensed and stuck straight out as she threw both hands up to her hair. *El Toro* jerked backward just as Jenny threw her head back at the moment of ecstasy, and she went flying off backwards, landing awkwardly on her neck and back and damaging her spinal cord. She would never walk again.

The ensuing lawsuit and media frenzy was more than Howard could take. Six months later, his girlfriend got worried when she hadn't heard from him and went to his house. She found him in bed, his mouth and cheek crusty with white, foamy gunk, his lips blue, and the empty bottle of oxy on the nightstand. She called 911, the paramedics came and were able to revive him, and Howard lived, in spite of himself. His insurance took care of the lawsuit. He sold the club, bought a Winnebago, and started driving.

4

* * * * *

Eddie and Mary Beth had slid down to the hard packed ground in front of their bench, they were laughing so hard. "So which one is going to be rocking tonight, 8 or 9?" Mary Beth laughed at Janie, referring to the lot numbers where Indie's and Howard's motor homes sat.

"Probably Howard's. I hear he's got some kind of old bull saddle in there!" I had just taken a big pull off my beer, which spewed out everywhere, including Janie's arm as we all howled with laughter after that one.

"Gross!" she said, elbowing me, which caused my foot to kick at my stool, sending my now empty plate spinning towards the fire. About that time Hector walked up, snatched the plate and stood there, a semi serious look on his face. We were all on the ground, and looked up at Hector, silent now but still with big idiot grins on our faces.

"What'd I miss?" he asked, which started us all howling again, Eddie pounding his palm on the ground.

"Oh! I think I peed myself!" Janie had tears streaming down her face. I pulled myself up to my feet and grabbed her hand. I was about to ask Hector to make sure the fire was out, as I had to take Janie inside to see if she had peed herself, when a huge bolt of lightning hit the lake with an accompanying peal of thunder that was deafening. Large raindrops began to hit us as Eddie and Mary Beth gathered up their utensils and food and headed for their spot at number 7. Hector grabbed up the shovel that we kept nearby and began shoveling dirt on the fire.

"I got this, chief. Take care of your tenant." Hector knew Janie and I had become something more than friends, but he always referred to her as my 'tenant.'

Janie and I went through the glass door into my recreation room, and I lowered the glass to cover the screen. When I turned around, she had already disrobed and was perched on the edge of the pool table, her panties dangling from her raised right hand. I kicked off my deck shoes as I walked over to her. She jammed her panties into my face as her other hand went for my belt buckle. "You smell any pee on there?" she whispered into my ear as she nuzzled my neck and I proceeded to lose my mind.

Some time later, I don't know how much, we were sitting on the screened porch I had recently added to my tiny house watching the lightning hit the lake and listening to the big rain drops hit the roof. My mind began to wander back to the first time I met this little minx who currently was rubbing my chest with her feet.

Mike and Janie

After Denise had thrown our marriage away for her kick boxing instructor, a ruggedly handsome Puerto Rican ex-fighter named Mateo with scars on his face, I was lost. Winning the lottery certainly helped. I believe it was David Lee Roth who said "They say money can't buy you happiness. But it can buy you a big enough yacht that you can pull right alongside it." Or something like that.

Well, I didn't buy a big boat, but I did get myself a big bike, the biggest Italian cruiser I could find. The Moto Guzzi 1800 Continental. I had to go to New York to get it, and when I left the dealership I turned right instead of left and went past Maine on up into New Brunswick and Nova Scotia, then across Canada on up to Alaska. Then I turned around and headed south, ending up in Cabo San Lucas. I met Sammy Hagar, the aforementioned Roth's replacement in some band from Pasadena, and drank some of his signature Tequila.

I cruised through Zihuatenejo and Acapulco and on down into Central America, scooting across the coffee mountains of Honduras and up the Gulf of Mexico coastline, all the way around to the Everglades. I took in all the sights along the way, and as a fairly young, single guy with plenty of disposable income, the sights were plentiful, especially in the coastal resort towns. But my butt was getting a little sore from being on the road for the better part of two years, and when I made it across Alligator Alley and took a left on A1A, I pulled in for a lunch stop in a place called Montego's in the town of Lauderdale-by-the-Sea, a very small beach town just north of the Miami-Fort Lauderdale megalopolis.

Montego's was fairly busy for a Wednesday afternoon. The restaurant featured a walk-up bar on the beach side, valet parking out front, and an open air dining area inside and out, complete with bamboo ceiling fans and a live reggae band. I thought it was the perfect place for a lunch stop, and parked my scoot next to the building, took off my riding boots and dug my slides out of my saddle bags, as well as a pair of shorts. I went in, purchased a Montego's souvenir shirt from the clerk at the hostess station, and headed to the bathroom to change.

I decided this was a nice place to spend a few days and planned to seek lodging after eating. I was doing what I had been doing the past two years-going with the flow, playing it by ear, whatever euphemism you choose. I passed the indoor bar on the way back from changing and ordered a cold draught and some chicken nachos. I told the bartender I would be right back as I went to pack my clothes back into my saddlebags. I came back to the bar to find my frosty glass and appetizer waiting for me.

I sat with my back to the bar and took in the view of the restaurant and of the beach beyond. The nachos were excellent, the beer was cold, the band sounded great. I was sure I would be having another, so I asked the bartender if my bike was going to be alright for a few hours where I had parked it. She looked out past the three piece band out to where the big bike was, and said sure, adding that she went off duty in four hours if I wanted someone to show me around. I told her I appreciated the kindness and that my schedule was wide open.

She wasn't really my type but I could tell there was a cute girl hiding behind the multiple piercings, the red-eyed raven's head tattoo on her neck along with a blue-eyed black panther sleeved on her left arm, to contrast with her green eyes and reddish brown curly hair. Like I said, not really my type, but who knows? She may be a good local guide, and I knew we could have some fun.

I finished my nachos and drained my second beer, laid a twenty and a ten on the bar and walked through the restaurant and out to the beach, through a passageway to the left of the outdoor-facing bar. It was a beautiful afternoon, and I had been on the bike for four hours straight, so it felt good to walk and stretch my legs. I went to the shoreline and let the waves splash against my knees, considered going deeper, but turned left instead and headed north.

The beach was perfect. There were few people out, and I abruptly changed my mind. Stripping off my shirt, hat, and RayBans, putting my keys and wallet in my slides and covering them securely, I went out about thirty feet into the sea. It was so refreshing, and I stepped off a coral ridge and went neck deep, I treaded water, watching all the little pompanos darting about as my feet disturbed the sandy bottom.

After about fifteen minutes I came out, gathered my stuff, and walked on. I passed a set of apartments that looked to have once been a motor hotel, then nothing but dunes and vegetation for the next mile or so. On I walked, occasionally slipping back into the water for a dip to cool off; it was a warm May afternoon.

I'm not sure how long I walked, but when I looked back the way I had come I could not see Montego's. I walked across the beach towards the dunes, spotting a walkway which I surmised must surely lead to A1A. I felt confident that there must be a store or a soda machine near, beyond the dunes and over the ridge.

As I neared the path, I heard the sound of a mandolin being played extremely well, and a husky, bluesy female voice singing *Boat on a River*, by Styx. I knew the song, and followed the voice on up the path. As I cleared the dunes, I saw I had stumbled upon a small RV park of sorts. There, sitting on a stool under the awning of a Winnebago, sat what looked to be a traveler from the 1960's, Haight Ashbury era flower child. Long, wavy, dirty blond hair littered with multi-colored ribbons and flowers; big, round, sunglasses and guitar earrings; tie-dyed shirt with a psychedelic *LOVE* logo and cut-off jeans. Flip flops with flowers attached to them completed the look, and she was playing the dickens out of that mandolin and singing that old Styx song beautifully. She smiled as I stopped to listen. She finished the song and took a long drink out of a long neck Budweiser that sat beside her on the table.

"You look thirsty, Cowboy," she said. "Get you one out of that cooler inside the door." She gestured to the door of the RV and began playing *39*, the old Queen song about space travel and time-dilation theory. I did help myself to an ice-cold long neck and took a seat on the steps. She finished the wonderful song with a series of hums and whistles and put the mandolin into its case.

"So, what brings ya to these parts, tall, handsome, stranger?" She held her bottle towards me. I tapped it with my own and explained I had been having lunch down at Montego's and decided to go for a walk. She asked what I had for lunch, and chuckled when I told her. "Gotta be a damn tourist." She shook her head. "They have a really good shark sandwich that is only available for lunch. It is wonderful. This evening they have a special that is as out of this world as that last song I sang. Dolphin Creole. Best thing you ever put in your mouth."

I didn't know what to say. Dolphin?

"Wipe that look off your mug," she laughed. "Not Flipper. This dolphin is a fish, not the porpoise."

I laughed at that. "I suppose I have led a sheltered life. I had no idea."

I finished my beer, and she said, "I have an endless supply. Have another." I told her I had better not, as I planned to be driving later. She said, "What, you leave the wife and kids back at the condo?"

I felt my tongue beginning to loosen as I launched into a long spiel about my life the past few years.

"So you're telling me that you have absolutely no place to go and all the time in the world to get there?"

I studied her face as she no doubt studied mine. I could feel tension starting to build as I realized she was older than I first thought, but in really good shape. I wondered what HER story was. "Well, now you know all there is to know about Mike Stevens, but I don't even know your name."

She stood up, laid her mandolin inside her motor home and closed the door. She stuck her hand out to me. "Janie Shain. Its about five so we better hoof it on down to Montego's, that dolphin special usually runs out around seven-ish, and it's a good hour's walk from here." She picked up a small wallet and stuck it down the collar of her shirt, I assume into her bra, or bikini top. She told me her story as we walked back down the beach.

She couldn't have been more right about the Dolphin Creole. It had just the right amount of kick to it and melted in my mouth. The taste was heavenly. After we ate, we went outside, where I locked my wallet in my saddle bag. Janie ran her hand over the seats and said, "Got an extra helmet?" I opened the other bag and pulled out my helmet and my spare, a plain black one. No self-respecting bachelor who rides should NEVER, under any circumstances, be without an extra helmet, right? That's my motto, anyway.

Janie snatched the helmet and climbed on the back of the big Moto. "Well, come on. We have about an hour and a half. You have to see this. I know a short cut to keep us out of drive time traffic on the interstate." I must have had some kind of look on my face, as I stood there dumbfounded. "Are you gonna stand there all day looking stupid and catching flies, or are you gonna fire this monstrosity up?"

I donned my helmet, climbed aboard and started up the big Italian superbike. I assessed my sobriety state and determined it had been more than long enough since I had imbibed. I was getting high from the vibes coming from the back seat of my bike, but I was good to go chemically.

"Where are we going" I asked.

"You just drive. I'll tell you where to turn."

She navigated me down a series of side streets, which took us south weaving in and out between the Everglades, the Turnpike, and I-95, until we finally hit Alligator Alley and headed west.

About 8:15 we pulled into the parking lot of a condo called Lighthouse Lagoon Beach and Tennis Resort in Naples. I had passed this very place earlier today. I parked close to the entrance and Janie jumped off, grabbing my hand and pulling me inside the building. I was barely able to get my helmet off and hang it on my handlebars. "What's the rush?" I protested.

"Just come on."

There was a very cool fountain in the lobby; she told me to wait right beside it as she disappeared down a hallway next to the check-in desk. Two minutes later she reappeared and yelled, "Come on, Shorty. Follow me!" We went through the lobby, out and around the pool, and past a large stand of sea oats bushes until we reached a little secluded bench set back between a couple of bushes on top of a sand dune. "We made it!" Janie squealed. She looked out over the gulf as we sat down, and after about thirty seconds, she jumped back up. "Something's missing. Wait right here, I'll be right back."

She was off like a shot, returning in about two minutes carrying a little brown bag. Out of the bag she pulled two long neck Buds, ice cold. She handed one to me, and reached into her shirt collar and came out with a small, thin, metal case. She opened the case and took out a hand rolled cigarette and a book of matches. She lit the cigarette and took a long pull. It smelled more like burning cabbage than a Marlboro, though. She passed it over to me and I took a toke.

"Sensimilla." I said.

"Look!" Janie said excitedly, pointing out over the water. The sun was beginning its final descent toward the horizon, and the sky was ablaze with orange, brown, purple, and yellow streaks which reflected off the placid gulf waters in a trillion little twinkles. She tapped the side of my RayBans. "Don't bogart that joint, Cowboy!" she chuckled, the first of what would be about a half a million times she would utter that line to me.

I thought then that she must be crazy, going through all this just to see a sunset. It was spectacular, though, I had to admit. We sat in silence the next several minutes, watching the sea swallow the last of the day's sunlight. We were secluded in that spot; in that moment no one else existed. The faint sound of sea gulls and the gentle lap of the surf were all we could hear. I thought to myself

"This may be the start of a beautiful friendship." I didn't know how right I was.

We sat there on that bench until it was nearly dark. I don't remember when our hands had entwined, but I realized we had been holding them for quite some time. I looked over at her to find her looking at me, the first time we had looked at each other without our sunglasses on.

"That was the most amazing thing I have ever experienced." I told her, my gaze unwavering as I looked into her eyes as the light faded from the day.

"Yeah, well I'm kind of a spur-of-the-moment kinda gal. You gonna kiss me now, or am I gonna have to keep waiting on you?"

"Now is as good a time as any, I suppose." I wrapped my arms around her then, and pulled her close. It was a good kiss. It was a great kiss. And it kept getting better.

"Where did you disappear to when we got here?" I asked as we started back around the sea oats.

"I know the evening manager here. She gave me our sunset doobage." She smiled, squeezing my hand as we walked back into the lobby.

"You might get cold in those shorts on that long ride back in the night." I told her.

"Nah, I'm not going back until tomorrow sometime. I told you, I know the manager here." She pulled a card out of her back pocket. "You can go back if you want to, but I'm going up to 327 and order some pasta." I realized then that she had led me to the elevators, which dinged as one of the doors opened. She got in and looked up at me with gray-blue eyes which I was really seeing for the first time in the light. "Well? Whatcha gonna do, Cowboy?" The elevator door started closing as she stood back in the car.

I stuck my hand in and stopped the doors from closing. "I'm not ready to tell you goodbye yet." I said as I stepped into the elevator car.

"Push 3 then, and kiss me again, dammit. You seem to know what you are doing."

I ended up staying in South Florida about three months. I didn't spent all of it with Janie; in fact we only spent the night together a handful of times. But we really hit it off. We talked a lot, and it was amazing that we had had such similar experiences and shared the same outlook on life, although I would later find out that her back story was a heck of a lot more eventful than mine. We bared our souls to each other, generally when our bodies were also bare. I've never been a believer in 'love at first sight' but this was most definitely a strong 'like' from that first moment I walked up on her playing that mandolin.

I had rented a condo up the road in Pompano Beach for three months, and when that time was up I had to move out, and I knew it was time to move on. There were no tears, no long sad goodbye, just a sharing of info with the promise to keep in touch.

And we did stay in touch. I e-mailed her pictures from the rest of my jaunt up the coast, and we talked on the phone often. I was in Ottawa in November, where it was 5° while she was still in south Florida: 88°. She laughed at the pictures of me wearing a parka while she showed off her new bikini.

I made it back down to the Carolinas after spending most of the winter snow skiing with the oddball but fun-loving Quebecans, and decided to take a little trip over to the Smokies, as I had heard there were some nice rides there.

It was during this little hop that I happened to pass by *Payaso's Locos,* had my first taste of fish tamales, and made the acquaintance of a fellow named Hector Mendoza.

William Etheredge

5

✱   ✱   ✱   ✱   ✱

As we sat there listening to the rain and watching the lightning, I was struck with a thought. I was definitely going to have to get that pool table surface professionally cleaned. I was drifting down into a sleepy peace when Janie suddenly snapped me out of it with a foot tap to my chest.

"Did you see that?" she asked with an edge to her voice that I found slightly alarming. I was wide awake.

"Look over the lake the next time the lightning strikes." I became aware of a roar that seemed to emanate from beyond the Durbans. Lightning flashed and I saw a huge funnel shape above the lake.

"Tornado!" I screamed. "Shit shit SHIT!" The rain had picked up considerably and the roar was getting louder. "Come on!" I grabbed her hand as we made for the office, and held each other close as we huddled in the doorway leading into the bathroom, which I figured was probably the safest spot. We could hear the wind then, and loud thumps hitting the roof.

Janie shivered. "I'm scared," she whispered into my ear, her breath warm. I enveloped her in my arms and legs as we sat there in the doorway.

"It's okay, sweetie. I'm here. Everything's going to be alright."

She looked up at me then, as we heard more thumps hitting the metal roof covering the deck. It sounded like the wind was trying to tear it off. I was glad, then, that I knew the roofer who put it on and knew he was not one to cut corners.

"You realize, of course, that we are NAKED!" she blurted out. "If the tornado hits us, this is how we will be found!"

I laughed at that. I hadn't thought about it, but yes, we were naked as hell. "I've always said you play slide guitar and sing as well as Bonnie Raitt. I guess we'll give them something to talk about."

We sat there, cuddled together, and rode out the storm, waiting for the worst that never came. The roar ended, the thumps stopped, the rain continued, and Janie and I finally unfolded ourselves from the doorway and slowly made our way back to the pool table and felt around for our clothes. We went into the tiny house and crawled into bed. I suppose it could have been the near death experience, or just the feel of Janie's trembling body in my arms and against my skin, but I was ready as she rubbed her hand on my belly, then ventured a little further south and gripped the firmness she found there.

"Mmmm, what do we have here, Cowboy?" She purred into my ear as she kissed down my neck and chest, her head disappearing under the sheet.

Have I mentioned that life is good?

The sun was streaming through the windows when I opened my eyes. I sat up and looked over at the hippie/nurse/love goddess lying next to me, the sheet pushed down to her waist, flowers and ribbons still stuck in her mussed up hair. I eased off the bed to go put on a pot of coffee when she stirred. "Is it still raining? What time is it? Die we die last night and go to heaven?" She still hadn't opened her eyes.

"One question at a time, hot tramp." She grinned at the Bowie reference and sat up and started singing.

She sang so sweetly. I joined in, very off key, as I couldn't carry a tune in a bucket.

I was singing so loudly that I didn't realize that Janie had stopped singing. I had sung the last line of the chorus alone. She had propped on her side, on one elbow, and was looking straight into my eyes. Straight into my soul, it seemed. At that moment I thought she really did look like a goddess, with the sunlight forming a halo around her rat's nest of hair.

"So you 'love me so' now, do you?"

Uh oh, I thought. Shit just got serious. I finished putting the coffee on and walked over and sat on the edge of the bed. At some point I had pulled on my boxers, and I was suddenly glad of that. I felt naked. I noticed Janie had still not pulled the sheet up past her waist. She stared at me.

"I love being with you." I started. "I love the way you look right now, with your hair all messed up and your breasteses looking at me."

I get very suave when I'm nervous.

She made no move to cover herself. She put a hand on my thigh. "Uh huh." She said. "Keep going."

"I love listening to you play your guitars and sing, especially when you think you're by yourself."

She tapped her fingers on my thigh. "Uh huh."

"I love the way you laugh at my stupid jokes, even when it's not the first time I've told them to you. I love the way you're so patient when the folks around the park ask you to check their mosquito bites and their scrapes and pains." I fell silent as the coffee pot began to gurgle. "I think the coffee is finished." I said, starting to rise.

With the agility of a lynx Janie leapt up suddenly, somehow getting around me and into my lap, straddling me, pushing me back onto the bed.

"You stubborn son of a bitch!" she screamed as she held me to the bed, hands gripping my shoulders and shaking me. I watched her breasts bobbing up and down. "Why won't you fucking say it? Just tell me already you damned mule headed fucker!" Her eyes were blazing. It was a little out of character for her to cuss like this.

I flipped her over on her back and pinned her squirming self down by her shoulders. I screamed in her face "OKAY! OKAY! I FREAKIN' LOVE THE SHIT OUT OF YOU! I NEVER WANT TO EVER BE WITHOUT YOU ANYMORE AS LONG AS I HAVE BREATH IN MY BODY!"

I relaxed my grip on her shoulders as she reached up to wipe my spittle off her face. I straightened and happened to glance out the window to see the tops of Johnny's and Hector's heads as they were stopped, staring at the house. Luckily they couldn't see inside, and I was smiling when I looked back down at Janie, who had tears going into both ears as she reached for me and pulled me down to her face. "I love you too, you stubborn bastard," she gasped into my ear as her hand slid into the front of my shorts.

I forgot all about the coffee.

William Etheredge

Lucille

"See those two big stars right there, that look like they are in a row with those three other smaller stars over here?" Artie Sherwood pointed into the clear night sky as his wide-eyed daughter tried to follow his finger. "If you line those up with the bright star directly beneath them, then follow a straight line from the one on the left through that star, you get to that one there." Artie traced an imaginary line the little first grader was trying desperately to follow, but couldn't.

Artie, oblivious to his daughter's mounting frustration, continued. "Then, if you do the same thing on the other side, you get to this bright one over here. That is the hem of the dress, the two at the top are her shoulders, and the middle one that all the lines go through is her belly button. She is the goddess of all the sweet music you hear."

Lucille thought to herself "He's just making this crap up."

"I know you think I'm just making this up." Artie said lightly.

Lucille was slightly taken aback. How in the world did he know what I was thinking??

Artie stood up and took her by the hand. "Let us go inside and see what Eliza is up to." The Sherwoods had decided before Lucille was born that they would not be called Mom or Dad. Their child would be considered an equal from the time she was born, and she would be taught there is only one mother, mother Earth.

"There's my two favorite humans!" Eliza chirped as her 'terramates' came back into the house. "Just think," she squatted so she could look young Lucille in the eye. "Tomorrow we will celebrate your seventh sun revolution! What shall we do on your special revo day? I know we will have some cinnamon cocoa and some fairy sprinkle cupcakes!"

Lucille smiled at her mother. She loved the fact that her parents were different from the other kids' parents she had seen at the school. She knew she was special, so why shouldn't her parents be special, too?

"That sounds delightful." She squealed as her father snuck up behind her and snatched her up, slinging her over his shoulder. The dark-haired little munchkin continued to squeal as Artie ran around the house, bouncing her belly-first on first one shoulder then the other. Her squeals were punctuated by 'oofs' as air was squeezed out with each bounce.

'Tha...at's...en...nough...uff...uff!"

Artie flipped her off his shoulder and went into the space they referred to as the 'common room.' Artie's cousin Fauna and her 'Earth-mate' Mick were in there, stretching and twisting the homespun wool yarn they weave into the ropes they use to make chair hammocks. They sell the hammocks in their booth at the annual Renaissance Festival, which lasts about ten weeks each fall in a huge field about forty miles east of Portland, Oregon. The little farm they shared with several other families was about an hour to the north, in a little unincorporated area in Washington known as Shaballa.

Fauna, who was six months pregnant, looked at Lucille, who had coaxed a grape popsicle out of her mother and had walked into the room with a little purple line forming on her chin. "I got YOU something special for your revolution day! Wow, it is hard to believe you have already been with us for seven full sun cycles!" She continued to twist the yarn until they had that strand completed, tied off the end, and said, "Don't you go anywhere! I cannot wait until the morrow. You must have your gifts now!" She bounded off into the sleeping quarters she shared with Mick.

"She's really excited. I wonder what it could be?" Artie smiled.

Fauna skipped back into the common room carrying a big box. She sat it down on the center table and waved Lucille over. "You are going to have to finish that popsicle and clean your hands and face before you can touch this, as it is all quite special." Fauna knelt and placed her hands on the box and gazed lovingly at her little cousin. Lucille had gnawed the frozen sugar ice down to the stick; she stuck the rest into her mouth, pulled it off the stick, and raced back into the kitchen, her mouth obviously full as a second purple line appeared, sliding out of the corner of her mouth.

Eliza dampened a cloth rag and wiped the youngster's upturned hands, then after Lucille had gulped down the last of the cold delight, wiped off her chin and shooed her back into the common room.

Lucille bounded back into her spot, next to her older cousin in front of the box. "Show me your hands," Fauna told her. "Okay, you pass. Now, open the box!" Lucille opened the box and looked inside, looked back at Fauna, then up to Artie, who just smiled, cocked his head, raised his eyebrows, and held his hands up by his shoulders, palms facing up as if to say "Well?"

Lucille pulled out a plastic box that looked like a fishing tackle box. She sat it on the table and opened it. Like a tackle box, it had a couple of shelves that rose up as the lid opened, with several small compartments containing many different types of little objects, some with holes through them. There were polished stones, beads, crystals and several odd shaped squarish rocks with objects painted on them. Lucille picked up one of these and turned it in her fingers.

"Those are runes." Artie said, smiling at his cousin.

"In the bottom are special enchanted strings. They are to fashion bracelets, anklets, and necklaces. Look inside the box again."

Lucille brought out a large square wooden box and opened it. Inside were more charms and strings.

Fauna said, "You can make them however you want; there is no specific way the artifacts are to be placed on the strings. Only you can decide how they should look, and which colors and shapes to combine. Then, when you have created a goodly amount, you can give them away as gifts, keep them for yourself, or," Fauna paused as she looked into Lucille's wide eyes. "Or, you can come to our booth at the Festival and offer them to the souls that pass by and enter; for a special fee, of course." She gave a little giggle and pointed to the box. "You have not finished, yet."

Lucille looked into the box one more time. She pulled out a small box with strange drawings and oddly shaped letters and characters printed on it. As she studied the letters, she finally made out the words *Madame Tureau's Beginning Book of Tarot*. Lucille opened the little box and pulled out a small deck of Tarot cards and a thick book of instructions.

"Oh, thank you, Fauna!" She jumped up and threw her arms around the older woman's neck. "Now I can tell people their futures, just like you do!"

So by the time Lucille had finished the twelfth grade of her "Human School" she had reached the eighth ring of her "Earth Warding," and it was time for her to begin her five year journey to find her place and her 'sparkle' on Mother Earth. It was during her 'Sparkle Jaunt' that she decided that the whole 'The Earth and

Moon are alive and we feed them with our souls' belief was a bunch of hogwash, but her life's training did teach her one important fact about it. There was a shitpot full of money to be made from it!

Her new buddy that she had met at a big spring bazaar in Kearney, Nebraska had been instrumental in shaping Lucille's new outlook on life. Shiloh Dorsey had set up a booth right next to Lucille, selling fancy scarves and leather goods, as well as biker gear and memorabilia. They had watched each other for a little while, examining each other's goods and chatting superficially until they were packing up their tents for the night. Shiloh finally asked Lucille if she was a local.

"Nope. I am a leaf on the wind." Lucille pointed to her customized Chevy Van. "I took the back seats out of my van and made it into sleeping quarters."

"Ha. Sleeping quarters, huh? I like that." She took a joint out of her purse, lit it up, and passed it over to Lucille. "That all you do in there, sleep?"

Lucille and Shiloh quickly became close friends, getting high and talking about life. Shiloh was fascinated by Lucille's upbringing in the commune of quasi-Druids; and she regaled Lucille with stories of her own childhood, growing up with a long-haired, tattooed white hard-rocking hippie daddy and black soul food restaurant owner mother.

"They didn't give two fucks what people thought or said about them. I never had any doubt that they were totally in love with each other; I never heard them say a cross word to each other."

Lucille was no virgin, having been with a few boys, but finding them to only be interested in seeing what she had under the flowing robes and scarves she wore when she was working her booth; and showing little interest in what was going on between her ears. And, although she and Shiloh began to travel together to various state fairs and festivals, sleeping together most nights in the van, their relationship never became sexual. They talked about it, sure, and occasionally shared a lucky fellow they would meet at a festival, but ultimately they decided their friendship was too important to bring that aspect into the mix.

One night after a long hot day at the Summer Fun Fest in Little Rock, Arkansas, they were unwinding in their lawn chairs in the shade of some trees where they had the van parked, listening to Billy Thorpe's *Children of the Sun,* drinking some cold beer and passing a *Maui Wowie* joint. Lucille asked Shiloh what she thought about the song.

"*Children of the Sun*, huh? That's right up your alley, isn't it? Don't look at me, I hear you talking that 'Earth Mother' bullshit to your customers when you are doing their 'readings.' I just always thought it was a gimmick to separate the rubes from their money."

They smoked some more and got into a very deep discussion about life and death, Jesus and the Saints, food for the Earth, food for the Moon, and all the other things they had been putting off picking each other's brains about for the couple of years they had been traveling around with each other.

By the time they finished talking, the Billy Thorpe tape had long finished, the stars were out, and a fine layer of dew had began to form on the metal rails of their chairs. Lucille looked at her friend, her eyes shadowed by the soft interior light of the open van. She stared into her eyes for a full minute, then cracked a huge smile and said "Wanna go get some pizza?"

They both laughed so hard they had tears streaming down their cheeks and snot dribbling from their nose.

Now well into their thirties, Lucille and Shiloh still are great friends, these days on Facebook rather than face to face. Shiloh married a man who owns a burrito truck called *It's a Wrap!* and they travel to events and sell to the revelers.

Lucille still loves to travel but has began to settle down a bit. She still sleeps in the same van, which is on it's third engine and second million miles. She was packing up her Christmas booth in Gatlinburg, Tennessee one January day when she heard someone talking about the famous fish tamales at some place called *Payaso's* over the mountain in North Carolina, and decided to go investigate.

At *Payaso's* she made the acquaintance of a very handsome delivery man named Hector Mendoza, who took one look at her and the van she crawled out of. "You sleep in that thing, don't you?" When she nodded, he told her about the Tiwanawiki park. "You should come and stay some time. You will love it!"

Hector

Pancho proved to be very patient and fatherly with young Hector. He himself had gone to school in the city until the age of sixteen. He could read and write Spanish, although not very well. He remembered some of the pronunciation for English letters and numbers as well. As they examined the contents of the bag Eduardo had given Hector, they found he had included the English and Spanish versions of the book *Tom Sawyer,* as well as both versions on cassette tapes. "This is wonderful!" Pancho had exclaimed.

Hector was a slow but very deliberate and determined learner. He did not get frustrated when faced with something he found difficult, but persevered. For the next eight years his life consisted of getting up before dawn and helping Pancho in the bakery; fishing until mid afternoon to try and catch their dinner; helping his Mama in her garden and the other household chores, then work on his studies in the evenings. Sundays he did nothing but go to Mass in the morning and play soccer with the other kids in his village.

Hector grew strong and handsome, and learned to speak English very well. One of the fishermen he met at the pier was from Belize, where English is spoken. He assisted Hector with his grammar and pronunciation.

On his eighteenth birthday Hector got home from the fishing pier to a surprise. Mama and Pancho were in the living room, with a box that had *Happy Birthday Hector!* written on it in big letters.

First out of the box was a new suit of clothes and shoes. They were the finest clothes Hector had ever seen. He looked into the box and saw two more suits. He didn't know what to say.

"Take all the clothes out of the box." Pancho instructed. "There is more to be seen."

Hector took out the clothes, and underneath them there was a leather wallet. He picked it up and looked inside. It was packed full of money!

"You have to be kidding me! I have never seen this much money before in my life! This cannot be for me!" He was fanning the bills in his hands. "Where did this come from? This is a fortune!"

Pancho patted the seat next to him. "Come. Sit beside me." Hector looked at his Mama, who was beaming at him, tears streaming down her cheeks.

"Mama!" Hector cried. "What is it?" He reached for her, but Mama just shook her head, wiped her eyes, and pointed to the seat next to Pancho.

"Do what he says," she told him, getting up and moving to the other side of Hector as he sat next to Pancho.

"Now listen to what I'm telling you, *mijo*." Hector looked over at Pancho with wide eyes. Pancho rarely called him anything but Hector. Hector studied Pancho's face as he wiped away a tear of his own.

"For nine years you have worked hard for me, and for this family. Your have never asked for a single centavo for yourself. I have never in my life known a man so determined and self assured as you. You didn't know it, but I have been paying you the same salary I would have had to pay someone else who worked for me, from the very first day you began to help me. I have been waiting for you to ask me about money, but you never ask. Plus you save us a lot of money by catching the fish and cooking us such excellent dinners all the time." Pancho studied Hector's face for a moment, making sure his words were being received. Satisfied that he had Hector's full attention, he continued.

"You have become an excellent driver of my old bread truck. It is time for us to go get your official driver's license. I know you have studied the booklet."

Hector was still as a stone, soaking up Pancho's words. He was still in a state of shock as Pancho reached into his shirt pocket.

"What is in the wallet is only part of your salary." He pulled a key out of his pocket and handed it to Hector. "Go to the back yard."

Hector stood, in a daze, and walked toward the back door. Sunlight reflecting off glass made him squint as he opened the back door to find a glittering green Toyota Corolla. Pancho put a hand on his shoulder. "It's far from new, but it has been very well maintained and should last you a long time if you continue to keep up the good care." He handed Hector an official looking piece of paper. The title to the car, with Hector's name written as the owner!

"And it is paid for!" Pancho declared.

Hector stood frozen on the stoop. Pancho clapped him on the shoulder. "Come on, you drive. Let's go get your license."

Hector stayed home about six more months before he finally, taking the advice of his mother, decided to leave their small village to pursue his dream. His Mama told him, "I am going to be fine. You see what a good man Pancho is, how well he looks after us. I know he is not your father, but he loves you as if he were. And he loves me deeply. I have no idea why, but he does." She smiled at him.

"I know he does Mama. I guess I am ready. I am nervous, though. I know I am going to a whole new world."

"You will do great, I know it." Pancho had come out onto the porch where Hector and Mama were talking. He handed Hector a set of index cards.

"These are some people I know in Quintana Roo. Call Javier as soon as you get there, he is expecting your call. He will help you get situated. The others are waiting to hear from you too. They will all help show you around and get you settled in and make you feel at home." Pancho looked at Hector with warmth and love in his features.

"I love you with as much love as I have in my heart. I will miss you at the bakery and here in our home, but it is time for you to find your place in this world. Don't forget to write and come back and visit."

With that Hector loaded up his suitcase and drove off, looking in the mirror at his Mama and Pancho waving at him until he turned a corner and drove out of sight. He pulled a map down from the visor and opened it beside him, his course already plotted out.

Hector did quite well in Cancun and Cozumel. He worked several jobs in various hotels and tour lines. His English was very good; he only had a little difficulty with some of the thick British accents, as well as the Southern U.S. dialects, but he was a quick study.

He also became a quick study of the plethora of *mamacitas* that began to show him close attention. He eventually met a lady named Connie, who was instantly intrigued by him. He had found it endearing to his customers to share bits and pieces of his life's story; it seemed to fill them with a desire to give bigger tips when they heard of his very humble beginnings and his drive to better himself. Connie was mesmerized by his stories, and spent as much time as she could away from her family to be near Hector. After her vacation was over she wrote to Hector, and when he didn't respond, she wrote him again telling him he was the most amazing man she had ever met, and she had met several, as her family owned one of the largest and most successful horse farms in middle Tennessee. This time he did respond, telling her that he liked her very much as well, but they were thousands of miles apart.

She immediately wrote him back, giving him a set of dates that he was to take off from work. She was going to fly down to Cancun and wanted to spend all her time with him. She did exactly what she said, and they spent a week together, falling desperately in love. They spoke to each other by telephone every night after she went home. Finally she convinced Hector to move to the United States, telling him that if they married, he would become a United States citizen.

The wedding was a fairly small affair attended by their families. Pancho and Gabriela received first class round trip airline tickets complete with a chauffeur to and from the airport.

"What happened to Connie?" Lucille asked him after he told her his story that night after they met at *Payaso's*. Lying next to the raven haired beauty in the back of her Chevy van, listening to the crickets chirp and the sound of their hearts beating, Hector sighed. "She died of the cancer, about two months before I met Mike."

6

* * * * *

Some time later, how much later I have no idea, I left Janie in the shower (we had started out there together-have I mentioned yet that life is good?), put on my clothes and ventured outside to assess the storm damage. There wasn't a cloud in the bright, deep, blue sky, and it was already warm. I spied Lucille up by the lake looking at something. I started up that way and stepped on something squishy that popped as my foot slid forward. I was suddenly filled with nausea as I looked down and saw what I had stepped on. It was a large bullfrog. "Yuck!" I exclaimed, and as I looked around I noticed several of the large amphibians lying about. Remembering the thuds we heard on the roof last night, I said out loud, to myself, "Surely not."

I grabbed the ladder off the side of the shop building, extended it, and leaned it against the roof of the deck and climbed up to have a look. There must have been twenty five of the critters that I could see, already baking in the sun.

"Those are going to be smelling ripe in a little while." Johnny said as he walked up.

"Will you grab my gloves and one of those buckets out of the shed and pitch them up to me please?" I asked him as I stepped over onto the metal roof. Once again I felt thankful that I knew the builder of the structure and was confident that it would hold my weight. Humility is also one of my strong points.

Johnny had tied a length of rope to the bucket's handle and threw the other end up to me. "Good thinking. How bad is it over your way?" I yelled at the old history professor. I say old. Johnny was sixty, and, although his hair was mostly gray, it was still quite thick and he looked as if he could get into fighting shape fairly quickly. He always looked dapper, and had just a slight bit of paunch beginning. I had noticed he and Lucille had become quite chatty with each other and I wondered if...None of my business!

81

Everyone at the park were well into adulthood and could do whatever, or whomever, they wanted.

"A few limbs down here and there, leaves and pine needles everywhere. No major damage." he yelled back as he walked on toward the ring. He stopped and turned, squinting up at me. "And the dead frogs, along with a few fish. Just like when the remnants of Hurricane Judy hit Lake Marvin back in '55. All the preachers in Georgia back then preached for two years that the apocalypse was upon us."

He chuckled and continued his walk. By the time I had collected all the frogs off the three roofs, my bucket was nearly full. I lowered it to the ground and climbed down. I walked up to the lake and stood next to Lucille, her jet black hair almost blue in the sunshine, her long black, billowy dress spotted with moons and stars. She was watching Hector as he trolled around the lake, looking for his jugs.

"Did you see the waterspout last night?" I asked the raven-haired beauty.

"No, I was not aware of anything that was occurring. I had a nice long chat with Bob yesterday evening after dinner, then I slept like a stone until about three hours ago.

Lucille was very open, sometimes to the point of embarrassment to whomever happened to be listening, about her sexuality. Everyone at the park knew of Bob, her battery powered boyfriend who never let her down. I also knew that Hector entered her boudoir-on-wheels upon occasion for a tarot 'reading.' I wondered again: Was Johnny also getting his future read?

None of my business! Focus...

"So you heard none of the storm?" I asked, incredulously.

"Nope. Not until I looked out my window this morning and saw all these damned dead frogs everywhere. You know, Bob and I had shared the hookah for a while before our deep conversation."

I took a deep breath and was about to comment. Instead I just shook my head and turned away from her evil smile. "Well, just let me know if you find any damage around your spot." I risked a quick look back. She had pulled her rose-colored shades down and peered into my soul with those piercing, green, cat eyes.

"Why Mister Stevens. I do believe you are blushing!"

Looking into those eyes I was stricken with a memory of a misty spring morning, a couple of years back.

I had awakened with the dawn, the sun not yet cresting the trees across the road from the park. I happened to glance out my bathroom window to the lake, just in time to see a vision straight out of a fantasy novel. Emerging from the lake, just as the first rays of the sun were beginning to sparkle, was the dark-haired mystery woman from the Chevy van who had the spot next to the office. Lucille had been at the park for just a few weeks, and I had never seen her in anything other than the long, billowy dresses and wizard frocks that she wore. Until that moment I had had no idea what she was hiding underneath.

There didn't appear to be an ounce of fat on her as she climbed her naked body up onto the little pier Hector had built the past summer. She lifted her hands and her face to the sun, water dripping as she pushed her hair back and stood there for a minute. It took a lot longer than that for me to pick my chin up off the floor. She finally grabbed a towel off the back of her chair, wrapped herself, and sat down. She had a steaming cup of coffee on the little side table there, and as she reached over to get it she looked right at me, smiled, and gave a little finger wave.

I almost tripped over my feet backing away from the window. How in the world did she know I was there? No way she could have seen me, I thought...

"It wouldn't be the first time, you wild thang." I laughed at her, diffusing the tension. "Hector having any luck finding his jugs?" Yes, a quick change of subject was the plan.

"He's found a few, but I haven't seen him pull up any fish. Looks like he's struggling with one, though."

I looked out and saw Hector about 100 yards or so in the southern end of the lake, down in a little cove. He was leaned over his boat, up to his elbows with both hands in the water. I skipped down to the shed, grabbed one of our kayaks, and rowed out to help him.

Hector looked up as I approached him. "I don't know what it is, but it is not a root. I can move it but it's very heavy. I'm afraid the line will snap and I will lose it."

"Hold what you've got. I'll be right back" I hurriedly rowed back to the shop, mad at myself for not thinking of it earlier. I had a long pole with a three inch long stainless steel hook on the end. I grabbed it and headed back out to where Hector was and gently probed the hook around where he was reaching. I found a spot that felt secure and pulled up on the hook. As it broke the surface of the water, it appeared to be a half rotted canvas strap. I reached down and got my hand around it and gave a little tug. Hector reached down with both hands to feel around whatever was there. He suddenly lost his balance as his boat shifted and he tumbled head-first into the lake. He came up sputtering.

"I meant to do that," he said, smiling, brushing the hair out of his face.

"Yeah, Right." I chuckled. "Can you touch bottom here?"

"No sir. But it feels like we hooked a large duffel bag or something."

"Hang on to it. I'm a bit awkward in this kayak." I reached over with the pole and hooked Hector's john boat over to me and slowly pulled myself out of my seat and over the edge of the boat, scattering jugs as I flopped onto the floor.

"Don't hook yourself, *jefe*"

I maneuvered back to where Hector was still wrestling with the duffel, treading water as he struggled with keeping the bag steady. I reached back with the grappling hook and pulled while he pushed. It took quite an effort, but we managed to get the heavy lump out of the water and into the boat. I pulled Hector out, we tied a rope to the kayak and trolled back to the dock.

We pulled the boat and kayak out of the water and down to the shed. I cleared off a work bench in the shop and we heaved the dripping duffel bag onto it. My curiosity was at an all time high.

"I am going to shower and change clothes, bossman." Hector stated and exited without waiting for a reply. I stood there, examining our find.

The duffel appeared to be a military style thick canvas bag, and it seemed intact. It was about four feet long and a good two feet thick. Although the strap was definitely worn a great deal, the bag itself had no holes that I could see. One end was sewn together; the other end had four flaps with rusted and corroded grommets and a lump of rusted metal attached at the middle. I grabbed a wire brush off the pegboard wall and began to gently scrape the lump, which quickly revealed itself to be an old padlock, of a type and design I had never seen. I began to smell the familiar scent of sandalwood and frangipani and knew without looking up that Lucille had entered the shop.

"So what did you boys discover out there in the depths?" Her voice rattled me just a little. Although nothing had ever happened between us, she had made it very clear that she was game any time I was. She was a few years younger than me, but that didn't seem to matter.

The woman made me nervous.

I shook it off and focused on the task at hand. "I'm not sure. It looks like an old Army duffel bag of some sort, though most of the ones I've ever seen were dark green and not quite this big. The strap appears to have been red and dark gray, and the bag the same gray color."

"I think we should roll it out into the sunshine, over next to the ring." Indie chittered as she stood in the doorway. When had she come in, I wondered. "Ooo, I DO so love a good mystery! Let's let it dry out a bit and open it up." She clapped her hands, walked in and opened the two big doors. "Just roll that table right out here so we can all gather round."

I looked out and noticed the whole park had come to life, and everyone was interested in the big bag. "Damn," I thought. "'Word travels fast around here." I noticed Mary Beth holding up a hot dog bun.

"We have sausages!" she exclaimed. As if on cue my stomach gave a rumble.

Howard had strolled into the shop. "Help me get it on this wheelbarrow and we'll lay it up on the picnic table, where it can get direct sunlight for the rest of the afternoon," I said to him. The duffel was still quite heavy and solid as we grunted it off the table and into the wheelbarrow. I rolled it out next to the old picnic table that sat between the ring and the lake. Howard and I lifted the bottom and watched as more water came pouring out of it around the old padlock.

"I wonder what's in this old thing?" Howard mused.

"We will find out in a little while. Did I hear something about some sausages?" It was three o'clock and I realized I hadn't eaten a bite of any food all day. I had drank half a cup of reheated coffee several hours ago, but that was it. I wondered then about Janie, who I had left in the shower the same time I had drank the coffee, and I hadn't seen her since. She had started keeping a few items of clothing at my place, so I wasn't too worried in that respect. Just then she came walking around the corner of her RV, ribbons in her hair, sunglasses on, wearing a Jimi Hendrix tee shirt, cutoff jeans and sandals. Gazing at those smooth, brown legs, I thought back on all that had transpired between last night and this morning. I smiled. I truly was in love.

"Whatchu starin' at, Shorty?" she said, as she walked past me, brushing my shirt sleeve with a green-tipped finger. "You ain't fixed me one of them sausages, yet?"

I laughed, and thought to myself how easily she could butcher the English language, as she was one of the most intelligent people I know. She never lost her Creole roots.

I gathered myself and looked toward Eddie, grinning in his lounge chair. "They're on the grill. Buns are inside, you know where everything is. Get you a coke out of the fridge."

"Where did all the frogs go?" I asked, looking around.

"We all bagged them up while you and Hector were out there frolicking in the lake. The bags are up by your office. It's your job to take them to the dumper." Indie said, as she walked past the table, her backside testing the tensile strength of her tight cotton twill shorts.

"Great! How many bags are we talking about?"

"Twelve."

I gulped. "Dang, that's a bunch of frogs!"

"What did you do to piss God off this time, Pharaoh?" Johnny smiled as he walked past me and stuck a wad of cash into the little wooden box next to Eddie's door. Since Eddie had become the park's *de facto* chef, Hector had crafted a little oak box and attached it to their home. We all chipped in with our donations and Eddie and Mary Beth kept our bellies full. Hector had also built a small covered shelter for their refrigerator and freezer.

"I suppose the locusts will be coming next if we don't set the captives free." Johnny smirked as he smothered his sausage dog in mayonnaise, pickles, and onions.

"That is so disgusting." Janie whispered as she sidled up beside me. Johnny just looked at her and smiled, grabbing a root beer from the fridge and taking a big bite of his hot dog, white goo dripping out of the corner of his mouth.

"Different hearts beat on different strings, as my Momma always said," he said, pulling a handkerchief out of his back pocket and wiping his face.

Howard and Janie looked at each other and said, in unison, "There's a song there, somewhere!" Our laughter at the shared joke between them was broken by the sound of a loud horn blaring.

"Duty calls, chief." Mary Beth exclaimed. "Sounds like you have a customer."

William Etheredge

Johnny

"Your supper's getting cold! Get your butt in here and eat!" Mabel Coster yelled from the kitchen. "Your father's already headed over to the jail. Now come on."

Her exasperation finally got through to her young son, and he came slinking out of his room with an open book in his right hand as he pushed his glasses up on his nose with his left.

"You are not reading at the table, young man."

"But Mama, this is the *Tale of the Melungeons of Appalachia*." Johnny whined. "I just can't put it down."

"You can put it down long enough to eat," Mama chided.

"Okay." Johnny laid the book on the back of the couch and sat down to a plate of pinto beans, cornbread, fried okra, and turnip greens. "I love the ham out of these beans and greens!" young Johnny exclaimed.

His mother snatched the book up off the back of the sofa. "Well you are going to eat everything on your plate before you can have it back." She opened the book to the pages of pictures in the middle. "What in Sam Hill is a Melungeon, anyway?"

"Mama!" Johnny looked up at her. "They were the people that lived in these mountains before the pilgrims ever came here."

"I thought that was Indians."

"Well, Melungeons were part Indian, part African, part Chinese, I don't know what all. I guess they had some Viking in them, too. Nobody knows for sure."

The door opened and Chet Coster came in, stamping his feet as he hung his hat on the hook by the door. "And, they were part snapping turtle, too!" He grinned at the red-headed pride of his life sitting at the table.

"Well, they sure do look funny. Is this book for real?"

"Yes, mama. Some of those pictures are from the 1800's, the drawings are much older. But they were up in the West Virginia mountains a long long time before then. They had their own language and everything."

Mabel laid the book back on the arm of the couch. "Well, I don't ken bout a buncha Munjens or Chinese Negros from West Virginia." To Chet: "Did you get them boys fed?"

"Yep, it was that Andruss boy and his cousin. I guess they decided to go out and shoot up some stop signs again. You'll probably have to cook up some extra for the next week or so." He pulled a five dollar bill out of the zippered bib of his Liberty overalls and handed it to her. "Sheriff Duncan said it wouldn't hurt his feelings none if you came over to his house and showed Lois how to make fried okra like that. He almost ate the boys' share, too."

He took the dirty plates out of his bag and carried them over to the sink. Johnny slid out of his chair and put his plate into the sink, polished off his glass of milk and sat it next to his plate and dashed off to his room, grabbing his library book as he sped by the sofa.

"Where in the world does he find these books?" Chet asked his wife.

"I don't know if his obsession with Appalachian history is normal for a boy his age. Why, when I was eight years old I was out fishing in the creek with a cane pole, building forts in the woods, that sort of thing." He shook his head as he sat down and began unlacing his boots.

"Guess I better call Stu and see if everything's alright at the store." Chet mumbled as he reached for the phone.

"Different hearts beat on different strings." Mabel said as she began running water into the sink.

"You always say that."

The turmoil of the 1960's went virtually unnoticed in the small northeast Tennessee town of Breston. Chet Coster and his older brother Stewart owned a little General Store at the crossroads, which was actually the center of town. The store featured a single gas pump, two old wooden benches on either side of the door, and an ancient air compressor on the side of the building away from the road. Inside, the store was much the same as it was when Chet's grandfather built it a few years before the depression hit. There was an old pot-bellied stove that provided heat on the cold winter days, with several old wicker chairs nearby.

There's no telling how many times the world has been saved by the conversations that occurred around this old stove, and the lies as well. There was still a 1947 calendar hanging on the bathroom door, the year the plumbing was run and the bathroom was built on. The old outhouse still stood in the overgrown weeds about twenty yards or so behind the store. Hanging on a nail inside was about a third of a 1940's Sears and Roebuck catalog.

Young Johnny loved to sit out on the benches when he wasn't in school, listening to the old-timers talk about how wonderful things used to be. It was these palavers, which Johnny started taking in as soon as he was old enough to crawl up on the bench, that instilled in the pale, freckled little ginger boy a lifelong desire to learn everything he could about the mysterious mountain range known as the Blue Ridge, including the Great Smoky Mountains and the entire Appalachian range itself. Johnny loved the mountains and the folk lore surrounding them.

Eventually majoring in history at Appalachian State university, Johnny came back home for a little while to teach the fifteen or so students that would comprise the average senior class at tiny Breston High. Quickly tiring of this, however, he made his way back to Appalachian State after a few years, eventually becoming the chair of the history department.

Breston began to grow. By the late 1980's there was actually a traffic light put up at the crossroads. Chet took sick with pneumonia around 2010, and didn't recover. He had decided to close the store when Stu had passed away a few years earlier, about the time Chet had his first hip surgery. He died in his sleep one snowy January night.

Mabel, devastated from the loss of her soul mate, died less than a month later. It was well gossiped that she had indeed died from a broken heart. Johnny felt that that was probably true. He supposed his soul mate was the mountains, and, finally, after accepting an insanely generous offer from a foreign investor for the store property, Johnny took a hiatus from teaching to fulfill his lifelong dream of hiking the Appalachian Trail. It took him nearly a year but he went end to end, and when he got back to the small apartment in Boone, North Carolina he sat around for a few days wondering what to do. He felt like he had done all the teaching he cared to do, and he was tenured and eligible for full teacher's pension.

Watching the Travel Channel one night on the newly installed cable television, he watched a short show about the haunted cabins of the Rockies. His interested piqued, he was ripe for the picking when an ad came on during the show for a Knoxville dealership claiming to be the "Number One Conversion Van Dealer in the

Southeast." The next chapter of Johnny's life was opened; the next day he drove over to Knoxville, traded in his Mercury Marquis for a large sleeper van and headed west...

Indie

Like Eddie and Mary Beth, Indira Spector became fascinated with science fiction at a fairly young age. But, unlike her eventual Tiwanawiki cohorts, she wasn't really into space travel or aliens. When she was six years old she was hospitalized with a fever, and with her mother asleep in the chair, young Indie was changing channels on the TV one night and caught the beginning of a Twilight Zone episode entitled "Next Stop Willoughby," in which a gentleman looking to escape the rat race discovers a train that made a stop that took him into the serene, slow-paced town called Willoughby, a hundred years in the past. That show woke something in Indie's fevered young mind that she has never been able to shake. She began to look for time-travel themed books, movies, TV shows, etc. *The Time Machine* by H.G. Wells became her favorite book. She read it over and over.

As a teenager she went with her friend to the movies to see *Somewhere in Time*, and wept openly when Christopher Reeve pulled the coin out of his pocket and saw the future date on it, taking him away from the love of his life and back to his own time.

As a young woman she became obsessed with Gabaldon's *Outlander* series. She studied Ancient History at university and became an Ancient Literature high school teacher. It was a conversation she had had with a favorite student that had sparked her imagination. They had been discussing the Loch Ness Monster, and she spent some of her free time the next couple of years researching 'Nessie,' putting together a sort of data base of sightings and stories of the elusive creature.

She also became a fan of the *Jurassic Park* story, intrigued by the idea of prehistoric animals living among us. Then, one night at the park, she stumbled upon an episode of a show called *Primeval* on BBC America. *Primeval* was about anomalous passages that pop up in British forests that allowed travel to and from a prehistoric time. Dinosaurs began coming through and wreaking havoc in civilized areas. Pterodactyls began preying on cattle and pets.

The light bulb didn't just go off, it exploded for Indie.

For quite some time she had been kicking around the idea of writing a novel, and now she had all the pieces for her story. Deep in the depths of Loch Ness there exists a similar type of an anomaly, which allows the giant prehistoric lizard we know as Nessie to pop into our time every so often, swim around for a day or so, then disappear back to her own time.

She had found the Tiwanawiki RV Park through a mutual friend and began taking the Ford truck with the camper bed she had inherited from her uncle up to the park for a few weeks in the summers, while school was in recess, a year after Mike Stevens had reopened it. By the night of the storm, she had spent five years writing and rewriting her novel, mostly during her stays at the Tiwanawiki RV park.

7

*   *   *   *   *

I finished my hot dog and walked towards the parking lot. There sat what looked to be a modified Greyhound bus, like the type you would expect to see Iron Maiden traveling around in. It was bright and new looking, about a half million, I imagined. The driver's door opened and a young fellow bounded out, wearing a brightly colored tank top with a picture of a guy surfing on the front, board shorts, Birkenstocks, and a pair of $300 Oakley sunglasses. He sported a long mane of bleached blond hair, and an über tan. Rolling out of the same door was a similarly clad young lady, who stood behind the guy, bouncing on her feet and popping her chewing gum.

I opened the door to the office and motioned them inside. "What can I do for you?" I asked, maintaining my professionalism all the way. The girl motioned to the edge of her mouth as she removed her sunglasses and raised her eyebrows at me. Realization dawned on me and I reached up and wiped a big glob of mustard off the corner of my mouth, which I proceeded to lick off my fingers without saying a word.

Professionalism at all times is my motto, baby.

Finally, after looking at my freshly licked-clean hand, the guy stuck out his hand and removed his shades, letting them dangle against his chest, attached to a leather strap.

"I'm Chad, this is Darcy." Darcy popped her gum. "We are looking for a place to park our motor palace for a little while."

"How long are you talking about?" I explained our rate schedule: weekly, monthly, annual, etc. My salesman skills were becoming quite legendary.

"Hard to say, Daddy-O. We may be here a few days, take off for a month, come back and hang for few weeks, then boogie on down the boulevard for another tilt, and come back again for a while. You know, like Gypsies, man. I just want a spot to come back to and always know it's gonna be here."

"Sounds like an annual rental would be best for you, then. That would ensure you could always come back to the same spot and it would never be rented to anyone else."

"Great. You gonna give us the grand tour?"

"Come on. Let me show you around the place." As we walked out, Chad looked down at the pile of bags holding the frogs.

'Whoa!" Chad waved a hand in front of his face. "Those bags be smelling bad!" He draped his arm around Darcy. "That's not, like, a permanent deal, is it?"

I explained what had occurred during the storm the night before as we walked up by the lake toward lot number one. Lucille was sitting outside her van under her shade.

"You guys want your fortunes read, drop by anytime," she said as we passed by.

"Dude!" Chad gave his best Ted 'Theodore' Logan impression. Whether it was intentional or not, I had no idea. "The resident witchy woman, Darcy! I love it." Darcy popped her gum and grinned, her flip flops flapping as we walked on past Hector's and Johnny's places.

"This is spot number one. The edge of the park is about fifty yards that way." I pointed toward the northwest. I showed them the electrical, water, and sewer hook ups, told them about the satellite television and the free WiFi.

Legendary salesmanship.

"I'm sold, dude. Where do I sign? You want cash or credit? I can even pay you in Bitcoin, if you want that. I'm ready to park this palace and get my rest and relaxation on."

I explained the rest of the park rules and stuff as we walked back, which didn't amount to much. I'm not that much of a rules person, basically just respect for the other residents. I told them about the shower facilities, ice machine, and the nightly sunset watches. I walked them past the office and pointed out the Ring of Delight, as we referred to the Ring sometimes. Janie sat with a banjo playing some sort of classical tune that sounded amazing.

Chad looked ecstatic as we sat in the office doing the paperwork. Then he and Darcy jumped into their 'palace' and drove up to spot number one to begin setting up for their stay. Hector, always aware of what is going on, had already gone up to help them.

In the process of doing the paperwork, Chad had explained, on a rather serious note, that his grandfather had started what had become one of the three largest shipping companies on the east coast, among other lucrative ventures, and he received monthly deposits from a trust fund to the tune of $25,000 a month, until he turned thirty. At that time he is expected to assume his position on the board of directors and a one third ownership stake in the company. He explained in a low voice that Darcy either couldn't hear or didn't care-she had stood looking out the window, bouncing on her feet and popping her gum- "I've got my business mind shit together already. I graduated from Duke with my MBA last year. I have six more years to live it up and I'm going for the gusto!"

There certainly appeared to be more to young Chad than met the eye.

As I walked back around to the Ring, Janie replaced her banjo in its case and strolled toward me and fell in step. She took my hand and squeezed it. "Last night just may be the most amazing night of my life," she started. "I thought I would bust a gut when Howard sang that song to Indie, poking fun at her book she's been writing forever. I think it actually turned her on, though. Did you see how fast she jumped up and sashayed up to her place? And Howard! He didn't waste a second jumping up and following her like a drunk puppy, mesmerized and hypnotized by that big bouncing booty. Then the storm outside, the storm inside…" She trailed off, but I knew she wasn't done. "Then this morning, with you screaming at me."

I cut her off, as our hands slid into each other's. "I meant what I said. I have never in my life met anyone like you, who makes me feel the way you do. You are so smart and you are the most beautiful creature I've ever laid eyes on. But can we not make a big deal of it? I have an image to uphold." I smiled at her.

"Image Schmimage!" she sneered, squeezing my butt cheek, hard. "Like everyone in the whole Smoky Mountains didn't hear you yell how much YOU LOVE ME." She yelled that last part. I could feel my cheeks flush as I smacked her ass and pulled her in for a kiss.

"Cut that shit out." I said. "Come on." We rounded the corner of Janie's trailer as everyone in the park, with the exception of Lucille and the newcomers, were gathered around the picnic table, watching Hector cutting the lock on the duffel bag.

"Y'all need to get a room." Indie laughed, looking up at Howard. Suddenly, everyone stopped and looked at us. It may have been Hector who made the first clap, but within seconds they all gave Janie and me a standing ovation. I had never been so embarrassed, or so happy.

Hector and Indie had cleaned the duffel bag and it looked surprisingly intact. Hector had isolated the lock and was perched over it with a set of bolt cutters. The lock was octagonal shaped with a large keyhole in the front, instead of the bottom, like every other medium sized padlock I had ever seen. It was still quite crusty, but appeared to be made of layered metal, with the hook part squared off at the top, instead of round. Strange, I thought. The bar went through a rusted crusty hook that was sticking through the grommets.

"You ever see anything like this, Johnny?" I asked the old professor.

"Can't say as I have. I did take several photographs with my I-Phone, though. I will obviously have to do some research. I'm just waiting to see what, if anything, we find inside this thing. It appears to be period military, perhaps even Russian military."

Everyone looked at Johnny as Hector snapped one side of the lock. As expected, nothing moved in the lock. He cut the other side up at the hook. The lock slid off onto the table. Hector reached into his small toolbox and came out with a pair of pliers and a hammer. As he pulled on one side of the bar he tapped the other end with the hammer until it finally broke free. He pulled it out and laid it on the table next to the lock body. The flaps came apart fairly easily.

"Should we dump it out right here?" Hector asked, looking at me and then at Johnny, who was watching very intently. "It looks like it might rain again."

Johnny spoke up. "Folks, the contents of this bag may prove to be of tremendous historical significance. We need to exercise extreme caution removing the contents. We have no idea what could be in there, or how long it has been submerged in the Wakitani Taniki. Additionally, we don't know what damage the artifacts inside have already incurred."

Lucille had crept up beside me. She breathed in my ear: "I love the way he talks. Such a scholar!" Aw hell, I thought to myself. Say it ain't so! I saw the way she gazed at the buff old fellow and thought that I will believe anything from now on.

The decision was made, then, to load the duffel back onto the wheelbarrow and take it back inside the shop building, where we could put it up on the table and examine its contents one item at a time. It was a prudent decision, as a light rain began shortly after we got it back inside.

I pulled a chair around to the end of the table and looked inside the duffel. All I could see were some dark lumps. I donned gloves and reached inside, pulling out one of the lumps and handing it to Hector, who sat it down on one of the other tables that had been set up around us. A hushed silence had overcome the room. I pulled out the next lump, Hector put it on the table. Lump after lump came out of the bag until nothing was left. I stood, stretched my back, and looked at the dozen or so big lumps lying on the tables, caked with mud and slimy vegetation. Everyone was looking on in wonder until we were all startled out of our reverie by Chad, who bounded into the shed and blurted

"Whoa, dudes! I thought everyone had died, or something" Eddie had to keep Mary Beth from tumbling over the lawn mower, she had been so startled.

"Fuck, you scared the shit out of me, man. What the hell!" Howard yelled.

Janie smiled at me. "I think I may have peed my pants." I grinned back at her.

"Don't you start with me, little lady" I couldn't exactly call her young lady, as she was a few years older than me. Well, more than a few perhaps. Okay, so she's a cougar. Reaare! Sue me.

"I was wondering where I could find a couple extra chairs. Darcy and me are about to get our Kush on and check out this mythical sunset."

Dang, was it that late already? We all piled out of the shop and looked at the big fiery orb approaching the lake.

"That rain didn't last very long," Indie said as she hustled out to get her lawn chair and sunset materials.

The duffel lumps were interesting, I thought, but they would have to wait. Tradition trumps all, as Tevye would say. I showed Chad where some lawn chairs were hanging on hooks in the shed and said "Help yourself." I snatched a brewski out of my mini fridge, grabbed my chair, and retrieved my emergency stash from behind a block of wood between two studs by the door. I headed up to my familiar spot at the lake's edge and heard Janie coming up soon after. I had just sat down and popped the top on my long neck

Bud, putting fire to the end of the joint when I felt the familiar tap tap on the temple of my RayBans.

Tradition.

The sunset was spectacular, as usual. Hector strolled by and I handed him the antenna, which still had about a half-inch of the smoldering doob left on the clip. He took a big drag off it and handed it back. "I think we need to go ahead and load those frog bags onto the truck so we can take them first thing in the morning."

As I stood and folded my chair, I realized I was exhausted. It had been an adrenaline fueled twenty four hours, and I was about to crash. Eddie came by and said he was sorry, that in all the excitement time had gotten away from him and everyone was on their own for their supper tonight. I told him that was no problem, and to Hector I said, "Let's do it. Pull the truck around and I will be right there in a minute." I took my chair back to the shed and found Johnny in there, looking at the bag.

"Look at this." He beckoned me over. I walked over and looked where he was holding up the bottom of the bag. He produced a magnifying glass. "Look at the little metal plate there, that is holding the edges together." I took the glass from his hand and bent closer. I was lamenting the fact that I didn't have my readers with me when I noticed some characters stamped into the metal.

"What am I looking at?" I asked.

"These are characters from the Cyrillic alphabet." Evidently I had a puzzled look on my face. For good reason.

"The alphabet that is used in various Slavic and Russian languages."

"Hmm," I said. "Looks like you may have been right about it. I'm about to call it a day though, buddy. Make sure you turn out the lights and close up." I headed out, leaving Johnny there with his inspector tools. I really was beat.

Hector had about half the stack loaded when I got back to the shop. "Sorry Hector. I got held up a little."

"No problem." He said. By the time we finished loading the bags full of the dead lake animals it was dark. I noticed the light still on in the shed as I walked around to see if anyone had started a fire at the ring. I saw Janie standing in her doorway. She waved at me and blew me a kiss.

"See you tomorrow, Shorty." She disappeared inside her home and closed the door. She was apparently worn out, too.

I considered going back to the shed and checking on the professor, but instead went straight to my tiny house, quickly undressed and headed to the shower. I don't even remember drying off, or going to the bedroom. When I awoke the next morning, I was lying naked on top of the blanket. "Wow" I thought. Been a long time since I've done that, especially sober.

The new day dawned bright and cool. I fixed my coffee, nuked a frozen sausage, egg, and cheese biscuit, and collected the garbage from all the bins about my office and domicile. I went outside and collected the bags from all the cans around the park, replaced the liners, and headed for the dump. I drove slowly past Chad and Darcy's place, wondering how they had made out on their first night. I cracked my window a bit and heard some hip hop bass thumps and trap drum ticks coming from the palace and said a silent prayer of thanks that they were in the spot farthest from my place.

The park was showing signs of life when I returned. I did my usual morning walk-about to make sure nothing out of the ordinary was going on. As I came back around the ring, I noticed the door open to the shed. Entering, I saw Johnny standing at one of the tables, wearing the same clothes he had been wearing the day before. I looked around; Johnny had taken every folding table I had stacked in the corner and had set them up. The tables were covered with stuff.

"Have you been in here all night?" I asked him

He slowly looked at me, a glazed look in his red rimmed eyes. "This stuff is absolutely remarkable." I walked over and put my hand on his shoulder. That seemed to snap him out of his stupor a bit. "Michael." He said softly, and his shoulders slumped a bit.

"Let's get you home and you can tell me about it in a little while. I promise you, no one will come in here and touch a thing until you get a little nap and something to eat." He followed me to the door, stopped, looked back at the stuff on the tables, then turned and exited. I flipped off the light switch and did something I rarely do. I engaged the lock on the doorknob and closed the door.

We were just passing by Lucille's van when Johnny said, "Those lumps were all parts of thick, wool blankets. I don't think there is any hope for them, but they did a good job of protecting the documents and other artifacts, which are wrapped in heavy plastic as well."

"We'll talk about it in a little while." The old man was beginning to sag, I wanted to get him resting as soon as I could. "I am as anxious as you are to see what is in that bag."

Johnny stopped. "No. You do not understand, Michael. It is my belief that you and Hector have recovered the belongings of a World War Two Russian naval officer!"

That stopped me dead in my tracks. "What makes you say that?" I asked him. Johnny started to pale and sag a little more. "Come on, bud. Let's get you home and you can tell me all about it in a little while."

I got Johnny tucked in. He was snoring as soon as I had the cover pulled up on him. I let myself out of his abode and walked up to the lake, thinking about what he had told me. World War Two was over 75 years ago, and as far as I remember there were no Russian defectors or POWs anywhere near here at that time. I was at a loss. How could this possibly be true?

"How's it going, Wiki dude?" Chad startled me as he walked up behind me. "Darcy and me came around the campfire pit last night but there was nothing happening but a bunch of crickets, yo."

He did not just end a sentence with 'yo.'

"I think the whole camp was worn out." I explained about the storm the night before, how it kept everyone up most of the night. Well, everyone except Lucille, that is. I asked him how his first night went.

"Oh. Man. It is so peaceful and serene out here. Darcy got a little saucy after a few kush pulls, and after we did the chakka chakka for a little while, ya know, I just sat out here in the wild, enjoying nature, man."

Kush pulls? Chakka chakka? I think I know what he's talking about, I thought to myself. Sometimes I feel so old. "Well, we're probably all gonna be around the shed in a little bit, around lunch time." I explained Eddie and Mary Beth's cooking exploits and how the honor system works. "They never ask for a nickel, but we all chip in anyway. No one ever asked them to do it, but once they started, no one wants them to stop."

"Sounds solid, duder. I think I'm gonna play a little GTA and wait for Darce to come around, then we gonna try out your shower head. Then we'll catch up with you around the smoke ring." With that he shucked on back to his palace. I went back and stuck my head in Johnny's house. Sounded like someone was trying to crank an old lawn mower with the spark plug missing. I gently pushed the door to, smiled, and walked on.

"I need some more jugs." Hector said to me as I walked by.

"Take the truck over to *Payaso's*. They have been saving them for you and can probably fill you up." Hector gave me a thumbs up and went back into his home. Lucille was looking out her windshield and caught my eye. She sometimes sat in the Captain's chair and listened to the radio.

"Johnny okay?" She yelled through the open window, over the sound of Melissa Etheridge singing for someone to give her some water. I walked over to her door, and was mildly shocked to see her sitting there in just bra and panties. "Don't look so damned huffy. It isn't like you have never seen me naked before." My face must have started turning red. "I'm just wondering how long it's gonna take you to return the favor. If you weren't so gaga for that little hippie girl I'd swear you were gay." Now I was red, for sure.

I took a step back and told her about Johnny's all-nighter in the shed sorting the contents of the duffel. She held a lit doobie out her window. "Want a hit?" she asked. I politely declined, saying I needed a clear head today, but took a definite rain check. As I walked away I shook my head just a little and heard her chuckling behind me. Damn, I thought. There was some sure 'nuff trouble sitting in that Chevy van.

I heard Hector crank up the truck as I unlocked the shop door. I took my first good look at the duffel's contents, laid out on several tables. Johnny had piled the blankets by the door, I took them outside and draped them over the clothesline I had strung between a couple of trees. He was right, they were in pretty bad condition.

I went back in and started looking at the piles on the tables. One table had the remnants of some old uniforms, some in fair condition, others quite poor. On one of the better ones were ribbons, medals, and part of a twisted gold rope. I looked at the medals. They were very tarnished, but there were six of them and each had a different insignia on it. The cloth holders had all but disintegrated but there were a few threads in place. One had a diagram of a submarine on it. Another table had some scraps of what had once been boots and other shoes. Some other scraps of cloth were also there.

That was all that had been recovered so far, evidently. The other tables contained several lumps of plastic, which appeared to contain documents or pictures. Johnny had begun to unwrap one of them, and had uncovered a stack of very old, brittle paper, the front page of which contained type-written Russian words.

I couldn't believe what I was seeing. No wonder Johnny couldn't pull himself away. I looked at my phone and was astonished to note that I had already been in the shed for an hour and a half! "Wow." I said out loud, to no one.

I walked outside and over to Janie's coach. She opened the door just as I was about to tap on it. She grabbed my raised fist and pulled me up the steps. "Come in and have a cuppa. Don't worry, I'm not going to rape you." She gave me a sly grin.

"It wouldn't be the first time today." I murmured.

"Lucille?" she said.

"You know it. That chick is unreal."

"She knows you get embarrassed easily, that's why she does it. I'll bet if you took her up on it one day she would run."

"So you wouldn't mind? I mean, I would never, of course, but." I studied her face. "You'd be okay with it?"

"You're a grown boy, do what you want to do. We ain't wearing no rings."

"Bullshit. You are talking out of your ass, little lady. And you know it."

I sat on the little stool in her kitchenette as she handed me a hot cup.

"So I saw the light on in the shed when I got up around three. I could see Johnny still in there staring at stuff on the table when I walked over and looked in the open door."

I explained about some of the intriguing items he had dug out so far, grateful for the change of topic. "He thinks it is from World War Two, from a Russian submarine officer. How in the world could a Russian duffel bag end up at the bottom of a lake in the Smoky Mountains? This makes no sense to me."

Janie grew pensive, but said nothing.

"I'm gonna give him a couple more hours to rest and then we are gonna see if we can get to the bottom of this mystery."

I finished my coffee and gave Janie a big kiss, and went back out to continue my morning rounds. I could hear the sounds of an epic space battle behind Janie's house. I rounded the corner to find Eddie and Mary Beth entwined in their lounger, munching out on a large bowl of popcorn and drinking soda. In front of them was a 65" flat screen television perched on a table under their awning. Eddie gave me the 'thumbs up' sign.

"Battlestar Galactica. Fifth time we've seen it. Just keeps getting better." He became silent as he shoveled a big handful of popcorn into his mouth. I gave them a salute and started up to the lake.

"I have some rib-eyes I am going to start on around three-ish," he called after me. My stomach rumbled, a definite Pavlovian response. Eddie's rib-eyes were hands down the best steaks I have ever eaten. I thought of a few things I needed to get done while I was waiting on Johnny. Mundane business stuff. No time like the present.

As I neared the office, Chad and Darcy emerged from the showers, an area Hector and I had built onto the side of the office a couple years back. They were both wearing short robes that appeared to have been fashioned from spun gold. I went on and unlocked my office door and sat at my desk, turning on the computer. I heard Hector pull up outside as I opened the spreadsheet for "Tiwanawiki Income." I entered the payment I had received from Chad the day before.

I pulled the receipt from the dump out of my shirt pocket about the time Hector walked in. He handed me a piece of paper. "I had to put gas in the truck," He informed me. I looked at the receipt, pulled a zippered pouch out of my desk and handed Hector some cash.

"Keep the change," I smiled at him. He mumbled thanks as he went out. I did a little more bookkeeping and shut down the computer. Ah, the joys of operating a business.

I walked back to the rec room and got a sugar free Red Bull out of my little mini-fridge. I have those things all over the place, it seems. Going back out the front door, I found Hector sitting on the tailgate of the truck, tying fishing line to the jug handles. I have never checked into the legalities of fishing with jugs, but since Hector and I had given the local game warden a super deal on a new roof after a storm a few years ago, he doesn't pay us any attention.

I was taking the blankets down off the clothesline when I got my first whiff of smoke. I looked at my watch. Three thirty. Eddie had fired up his grill. My stomach rumbled again in anticipation. I thought about Johnny and the stuff in the shed for the first time in a while. As if reading my mind, Johnny came strolling around the corner of the shed about the time I reached the picnic table with the pile of blankets, or rather, blanket remnants.

105

"How're you percolating, ole top?" I asked the professor.
"Pretty darn good, I must say. Slept like hibernating wildebeest! What's that I smell? Is Eddie cooking already?"
"Rib-eyes," I told him.
"YES!" the old codger stuck his fist in the air and brought it down dramatically. Eddie's rib-eyes are indeed legendary, at least at this park.
"He's just getting started, so we have a bit of time if you want to give me the rundown on what you found."

We entered the shed and turned on the light. He took me over to the table with the ribbons and medals.
"You will be able to make out the detail on these once they have been cleaned a bit. But you can clearly see a submarine on this one. This one has crossed ropes, which is also a naval insignia the Russians used. These little things over here," He picked up a set of what looked like broken cuff links. "These attached to the shoulder boards of the dress uniform of a middle ranking commissioned officer, like a Lieutenant, Lt. Commander, etc. Or whatever the Russian equivalent was called. I believe this is part of said garment over here." He pointed to the tattered clothing on the other end of the table.
"These other ones have the hammer and sickle inset. I guarantee you they were red when they were put into the bag." They were black, and if you used your imagination you could see where the hammer and sickle had been etched into the metal.
"But why do you think it is from World War Two?"
"Look over here." Johnny moved to another table that had remnants of documents. "I am taking pictures of everything with my I-phone. It has a great little camera." He lifted some of the papers. "But right here, see?" He pointed to one of the pages. "Here is a date, 1938. and over here," He gently thumbed through a different stack. "1939. And look around. There is still a ton of stuff to recover, document, and catalog. This could be a major find. I am strongly considering bringing in the chair of the history department over at Asheville. He is an old colleague of mine."
"Wow, that is wild. Who knew?" I felt a presence in the room. I looked over at the door, and there stood Darcy, twisting her hair and bouncing on the balls of her feet.

She popped her gum and said, "The old dude over there said to come get y'all for some grindage." She wheeled around and bounced away.

Johnny looked at me with a little grin. "New tenant?"

I told him about Chad and Darcy. He smiled and said, "Soups on then I'd say. I suppose that is what 'grindage' means." I laughed and patted the professor on the shoulder.

"The world will soon be in their hands." I said as we walked out the door.

"Heaven help us!" Johnny chuckled. I had to chuckle myself.

The whole camp always comes out for ribeye day. Always. Janie came flouncing down her steps with two frosty long neck bottles. "Here ya go, Cowboy." She made me jump with a poke in the ribs. "Whatchu been doing all day?"

"Mostly park owner business stuff. Unlike some people I know, I have to actually work for a living."

She made a show of spewing her sip of beer out as she gave a laugh. She pretended to stick her finger into her open mouth. "Gag me," she said. "Like what you do can be considered work." She crossed her eyes at me and stuck out her tongue. I wondered if she had been hanging around with Chad and Darcy.

"I do all the work that is required to keep us all happy." I looked around at the others sitting around the ring waiting to be served by Eddie and Mary Beth. Of course, no one was paying any attention to me. Howard and Johnny were talking about something, presumably the duffel. Indie, hunched over her laptop, oblivious to the world. Lucille was actually at the picnic table with Chad and Darcy. Hector was just making his way to the group and stood next to Lucille and whispered something in her ear. She chuckled, her billowy frock blowing in the breeze. Hector and Lucille rarely took part in the nightly ring feasts, but as I have said, *every*one shows up for Eddie's rib-eyes. He makes them all the same, medium. If you like your steak rare, you get a medium steak from Eddie.

So far, however, no one has ever said anything other than superlatives regarding the steaks, which were beginning to come as the two Averys came around the end of Janie's place pushing a large cart which contained all our plates, each containing a steak and a stuffed baked potato. As we all readied ourselves to dig in, Chad piped up with "Got any A-1 sauce?"

A collective groan went up from the ring, and Hector and Lucille moved away from the table. Chad looked around and said, "What?" Eddie had marched straight over to the picnic table and leaned across it, putting his hands in front of Chad and looking him in the eye.

"Have you tasted that steak? Have you even picked up your fork? Have you noticed that there is not even a knife on your plate?" He was getting louder with each question. Chad's eyes were wide as Eddie continued, "Do you even have the slightest idea about..." Mary Beth had walked up next to Eddie and placed a hand on his arm, which was tense.

"Honey, they're new here, and they are children."

"Hey," Chad started. Mary Beth stopped him with a raised palm. She looked at Chad.

"Pick up your fork and cut a piece of your steak and put it in your mouth." Chad watched as his fork slid through the succulent steer flesh like going through pudding. He popped the morsel into his mouth.

"Now, you tell me. Do you think that there is any substance in any bottle on any supermarket shelf on this planet or any of the other inhabited planets and terraformed moons in this galaxy that could possibly add anything to the flavor of that steak?"

Chad cut off another hunk and stuck it into his mouth. "Nope." he said. "That is a pretty fucking good steak." He swallowed and chugged some of his Michelob Ultra. He looked at Eddie. "You definitely have a gift, Daddy-O. My humblest apologies." He popped another big piece into his gob and chewed contentedly.

Mary Beth and Eddie, arm-in-arm, turned and faced the rest of us. We all stared. Finally Eddie declared, "Anyone need a Coke?"

As they turned and started back to their hut to get their dinner, I saw Eddie's face split into a monster grin as Mary Beth slapped him on the butt.

The rest of the meal passed without incident. I had no clue how Eddie could make a steak so tender and perfect. I know he has a deal with some farmer down in the valley to get fresh meat. Whatever he feeds his cows is the perfect food, in my book. I savored every bite.

Johnny got up, took his plate over to Eddie and headed toward the shop. I decided to let him explore the plunder on his own for a while as I picked up a bucket and walked around the ring to let everyone toss their empty cans, bottles, and plates in. Howard stretched, patting his belly.

"Damn, I am stuffed. Time for a 'boro." He pulled a red box out of his shirt pocket, took out a cigarette and lit it, took a long pull, and blew out rings of smoke. "Y'all come back down to the ring after sunset. I got a new song to play for you."

Indie's head snapped up and around like a shot. I worried she had given herself a whiplash. "Howard Martin, Zoom Strider, or whatever the hell you call yourself these days, you do and I swear to God I will never speak to you again as long as you live," she spewed venomously at the grinning Howard. "Don't you dare, you long-haired weasel. I forgave you for *O, Nessie*." That brought laughs from those of us still within earshot. Indie, red-faced and grinning a big grin, turned back to her laptop.

"We have a couple hours til sunset, Cowboy." Janie looked at me as she tossed her empties into the bucket. "Want to go for a walk?" A couple of times a week she liked to walk the little path that meandered around the lake. I always carried a machete to chop through the places that may be overgrown, as well as a .410 shotgun. You never know when you might surprise a copperhead or a rattler.

"Absolutely. I'll go get my stuff. We need to see if that storm did any damage."

The lake was very calm and peaceful. We walked hand in hand, and were blessed with the sights of turtles basking on logs in the sunshine. We got really close to a great blue heron, and heard fish jumping here and there. I looked down at the flower-haired beauty next to me and thought, again,

Life is good.

Then I started smelling the frogs. I looked closer into the brush and spotted several dead ones. As we went around the knoll on the western edge, they stopped. "The waterspout must have just hit the middle of the lake and over to a cove where a whole city of these jokers must have been living." I mused. As we got around to the other side I started seeing them again.

"Wow. This is nuts." Janie pulled my hand and stopped.

I stopped walking and looked down at her upturned face. "Kiss me," She said. I was more than happy to oblige. "I've been thinking." I felt a little lump begin to grow in my throat as she continued. "I've been on my own for a while now. My children have their own lives and they are doing extremely well, and have no need of me any more. I like where I am in my life. I like you, too. A lot. I even love you, as much as I am capable of loving another human being. I can't imagine not having you in my life."

She looked away and started walking again, dragging me with her. She stayed silent, and after a minute or so I stopped her.

"Is that it?" I asked her. She looked up at me with a tear escaping from under her shades.

"I just don't want to give up my independence. You may be wanting to get married or want me to move into that shack house with you. I'm happy where I am.'" She looked down for a second then back up at me, tears running down both cheeks. I slipped her shades off and wiped her tears with my thumbs as I held her tiny face.

"Honey, what we have right now is perfect. I wouldn't want to change anything." I looked deeply into her eyes as crickets began to sing their melody. "The only concern I have is when winter comes and you take off again. It terrifies me, like it does every year, that this may be the time you leave and don't come back." We walked on.

She snaked an arm around my waist and pulled me close so our thighs touched as we walked in step. "About that. I've been meaning to ask you, Mister Businessman. How hard would it be to change my rental agreement to Permanent Resident status?"

"I think we can manage that with a minimum of paperwork. Call or stop by my office and my secretary will set you up with an appointment and we can go over everything. I should be able to work you in as early as next week." I gave a loud yelp as she elbowed me in the ribs. She knew all my tender spots.

"Smart ass," she laughed as we passed by Howard's place, getting back into the park. When I looked at her again, she had a huge grin on her face and the shades were back. She dropped my hand and flounced up her steps. "See you in a bit," she said over her shoulder as she disappeared into her house.

I walked back to the shed to hang up my machete. Johnny had been busy unwrapping the plastic lumps. "We need a couple more of these tables," he said without looking up.

"Let me go secure my snake shooter and I'll see if I can find some." I knew I had a couple in the office area; I would have to get the stuff off them, but oh well. Progress must come first. I folded the two up and toted them out to the shed. We were almost completely out of room in there, especially with all that unused exercise equipment. Best laid plans, and all that.

Damn. Time to add on again.

I opened the big doors, rolled the old Snapper lawn mower outside and set up the tables. Closing the doors, I asked if he had found any more treasures yet.

"I won't know how it all fits together until I get everything unwrapped, and maybe not even then. This is very delicate work, you understand. I should be working in a laboratory." I looked at what he was doing. He had found a putty knife and was attempting to separate a stack of what appeared to be pictures, or postcards, that were stuck together. He stopped, and handed one to me. "Look at this," he said. It was a black and white photograph of a striking young woman, very faded, and obviously old. But it was easy to tell that she was a beauty.

"Note the style of dress. More than likely handmade, and not a style from any region in this country, that I am aware of. Of course, I was never a big student of fashion history, but I believe I am right about this. Her dress was not made in the USA."

"Pretty girl," I said, handing him the picture. I have always had a flair for the over-dramatic. I began to unroll a lump on the table next to him.

"Take it over to one of the empty tables, where you have room to spread out."

Made sense to me. Johnny had obviously assumed command of this endeavor, and that was quite alright with me. I carried the lump over and began to unwrap it. I was a little surprised to find another plastic-wrapped bundle inside. "Are they all double wrapped?" I asked the professor, as I placed the plastic on the floor and began to search the lump for a seam to start unwrapping it.

"Nope, that is the first one." He came over to see what I had. "Here," he said, taking it out of my hands. He found the seam that I could not see.

"Good eye." I told him, letting him take control.

"Feel this inner part. Totally dry," he said, and it was. The plastic crackled as he finished its removal. Inside were several handwritten pages, in Russian, very much intact. Slightly brittle, but Johnny was handling them with all the care of an archaeologist at King Tut's tomb for the first time. It was quite impressive to watch.

There were more pictures, apparently of the same woman, a couple alone and one with a young man beside her. There was a picture of an older couple as well. They each had something written on the back, the ink badly faded and barely legible. More handwritten pages of plain, white paper, then, finally, a picture of the young man from the other photo, obviously older, with an academic looking large brick building in the background.

"This building looks vaguely familiar," Johnny exclaimed, taking the photo and walking over to the sunlight. "It's a post card. Back in the day, you could have pictures developed on postcards. Unfortunately, they were mostly printed on something like pulp paper in the forties."

He studied the picture intently for several minutes. He took out his phone, held it over the photo, and snapped a pic. He then sat down, laid the picture gently onto the table, and started tapping on his phone. He swiped on the screen several times, and stood up. He looked at the picture, holding it up next to his phone and looking back and forth between the two.

Suddenly, with a yell loud enough to startle me into an involuntary shudder, he blurted, "I KNEW IT!" I feared he may rupture an artery, he was so animated and excited. "Look!' He showed me his phone. There, on the screen, looked to be the same building as in the photo. "That's SMUT!" He practically screamed at me. "Southern Middle Tennessee State University! It's actually SMTSU but everyone calls it SMUT U, or just SMT." He chuckled. "I've been there a dozen times. No wonder it looked familiar. It is the Language and Humanities building. The Historical Studies building is next to it."

Johnny had a glint in his eyes I had never seen before. He studied the picture in his hand for a moment, then looked at the one still on the screen of his mobile phone. "I'd bet he was an exchange student, and got called home for the war. He probably met this girl at school, and she kept all his stuff after he got killed in the war." The professor's face had turned red as he paced around the shop, stabbing his finger into the air as he navigated the narrow spaces between the tables, making one wild speculation after another.

"Whoa, easy there Professor. Slow down a bit. Let's not get carried away until we've gone through all this stuff. There's still several bundles waiting to be unwrapped. Maybe we'll find some more clues and get a clearer picture of what we are dealing with here." I wasn't sure he was hearing me as he stood with the palm of his right hand flat against his forehead, his lips moving silently as he stared at his phone. Finally, he pushed a button to black out his screen and slid the phone into his pocket and said, without looking at me.

"Of course, you are absolutely correct, Mr. Stevens. It is still going take some time to organize and collate these artifacts we have already uncovered, not to mention what is yet to be discovered."

He picked up another bundle and sat it on a bare spot on the table. He started to whistle as he slowly began to unwrap the plastic wrap. I had never once, in the six years he had been coming to the park, heard him whistle. I smiled then, seeing that he was back on track and in, what my grandfather would have called, 'hog heaven,' I left him to it and silently exited the shop. I had noticed the shadows starting to lengthen and I had to go.

Tradition.

A short time later, in my customary spot as the sun approached the horizon, igniting the stratosphere in beautiful red, orange, and yellow-gold stripes, I felt a familiar tap on the temple of my RayBans. As I clipped the smoldering stick of enhancement onto the outstretched alligator clip, Janie asked about Johnny.

"Oh, my. He is definitely in his element." I went on to explain the things he had uncovered, and Johnny's excitement over the picture of the college building. "The old codger was actually whistling when I left out of there." Janie chuckled at that and began to cough a bit, having just inhaled a generous lungful of the potent wikiweed. "And I must admit it has my interest piqued quite a bit as well," I finished, taking the roachclip back from her.

"It does seem to be quite the mystery. Maybe Indie should think about writing about this instead of her time-traveling lizard." She took a big swig of her ice cold long neck. "Look over there," she said, pointing to the northern edge of the lake.

Coming over the trees was a small flock of Canadian geese, landing in the water and splashing their wings with the sunset in the background. I looked down the ridge and saw Eddie and Mary Beth with their phones up, snapping pictures.

"I want a copy of that, you guys." Janie hollered at them.

"I'll text you the best ones." Mary Beth yelled back.

We both settled back into our chairs and admired the wonderful view for a while longer.

113

It was more than a while. I awoke in that same spot, the sun long since gone, twilight waning into darkness as the stars were already visible. I tilted my mostly-empty beer bottle and let a few drops hit Janie's nose and lips. She shook her head and looked up at me.

"I was dreaming you and I were riding on the back of a giant goose, heading towards a magnificent castle that I knew, in my dream, belonged to us. We were the King and Queen of Gooseland."

"Maybe you and Indie should get together and collaborate. You can write the next *Game of Thrones*. You can call it *Throne of Goose*." Janie slapped me on the butt as we both stood to pack up out chairs and collect our trash.

"You really are a smart ass, sometimes," she said.

"Better than a dumb one, is what I always say. Hey! It could work. Have the geese breath fire and converse in English. You could be the next Alan Dean Foster."

"Shut yer hole. Don't you think you should go check on your buddy? I'm going to take a shower, unless you want to join me, Cowboy?"

"As tempted as I am, I will take a rain check right now. You are right though, I do need to see about Johnny and the duffel. And, believe it or not, my steak has started to wear off. I could eat a little something."

Janie looked up at me demurely. "I'm a little something." She cocked her head and stuck her finger to the side of her mouth, swaying from side to side.

I said, "Who's Johnny again?"

I did go back to the shed a little while later. It was good and dark by then and the crickets were very noisy. Howard was all alone at the ring, playing *Turn to Stone* on his bass. I told him I was sorry I missed the new song, and asked how it was.

"I didn't play it yet. After everyone got their bellies full and their sunset haze on, I guess they all fell out somewhere. Ain't seen nobody out here."

When I walked into the shed I was surprised to find Lucille side by side with Johnny, lifting pieces of paper while he snapped away with his camera phone. Neither of them noticed me standing there as Lucille put her hand on Johnny's arm and said, "Check this one out, sweetie."

Sweetie, huh? Oh well, I thought. Stranger things have happened. "Have you found the Ark of the Covenant yet?" I said, a little more loudly than I needed to, striding into the shed. Lucille made no move to take her hand off Johnny's arm. Johnny stuck his phone into his pocket and looked over at me, then placed his hand on the small of her back as he squeezed around her and walked toward me. I looked at Lucille, knowing full well what she was hiding under that billowy old wizard frock she wore, and back at Johnny. I smiled to myself and thought, "You old dog."

"There is so much to learn here. I have no idea how all of this fits together. There are some old newspaper clippings, which are mainly about Russia's involvement towards the end of the war, and their ultimate smashing of Germany out on the tundra."

Lucille brushed by me. "I'm going home. See you fellas later." With a polyester and rayon whoosh, she was out the door and gone. My stomach grumbled a bit. After my tryst with Janie, I realized, I still had not eaten any real food. I looked at Johnny.

"I know you must be hungry. Let's go over to the Awful House and get some chili cheese hash browns."

Johnny smiled at me. "Scattered smothered chunked chilied and cheesed. That is a terrific idea. I can there impart to you my revised and updated *Theory of the Duffel*.

I chuckled at that as the fit old fellow followed me out into the darkness. He had quite a spring in his step as he hopped into the passenger side of the truck. The Waffle House was a good twenty miles away, and about halfway there I couldn't contain myself. I uttered the one word that I had been thinking since we walked out the door. "Lucille."

Johnny smiled; even in the dark of the old truck, I could see that smile. "There is a lot more to that young woman than meets the eye." No more was said on the subject, by either of us. I wanted desperately to pry the facts out of him, but let it go.

None of my damn business.

We sat in a booth, gave the waitress our order, and Johnny started. "There is so much to ponder from that duffel. About 50% of the papers and clothes in there have been totally destroyed by the water and time, but there were several of the packets that were double wrapped. I suppose the owner of the duffel thought them important. There are many handwritten pages that are intact, many that aren't. All in Russian. I did find this, however." he pulled out his phone and scrolled through his pictures until he found what he was searching for. He held it out for me to see: A name: Samuel MacDougald. The paper was torn underneath the name, but there was what looked like a 6 visible underneath the S.

"Could have been a phone number under the name, we'll never know. But I intend to wear out Google to find this Samuel MacDougald." Johnny became silent as he dug into his mound of chili and cheese covered wonderfulness. He took a long sip of his cola. "This is simply divine." He kept at it until the last morsel disappeared into his mouth. "I believe I shall have a slice of apple pie," he declared to the waitress as she gathered his empty plate. She looked at me expectantly.

I waved her off. "I'm good," I told her, as I still had half my meal to go. Johnny had wasted no time polishing off his meal, then his pie. We sat in virtual silence until we were both finished. The waitress came with the check, and Johnny snatched it from her before I had time to react. "My treat." He peeled a fifty off a small wad of bills he pulled out of his pocket, and handed it to the waitress. To her he said, "Keep the change."

"All righty then!" she exclaimed, strutting over to the cash register and opening the till. "Y'all come back soon. I mean it! Real soon!" she yelled as we walked out the door. She waved a stack of bills in her hand before sticking them into her pocket. Johnny was beaming as we got back into the truck.

"You really made her night," I told him.

"Just spreading the good cheer." He looked over at me. "It's what I do." I couldn't contain my laugh as I cranked up old Betsy. A quick glance at the clock on my Clarion in-dash CD player revealed that it was 10:30 pm. "Wow, where did this day go?" Johnny said, following that sentence with a small belch.

"I know, time has certainly seemed to speed up. We can get an early start tomorrow. I am as curious as you are to see where this is going to lead." I didn't have any idea at that moment how portentous those words would prove to be.

I dropped Johnny at his house. I noticed Lucille sitting outside in the darkness, looking up at the stars. It was a clear night, the lights of the truck the only unnatural light around. The park was dark as I parked the truck and walked around to the shop to make sure everything there was secure. I went home and settled into bed, another long, busy day in the books.

The next day dawned cloudy and overcast. There was a definite nip in the air as I noted that we were just a few days from the official start of Autumn. I popped a couple of blueberry waffles into my toaster and started the coffee brewer. I was startled out of my reverie by a tapping on my glass door. I looked up to see Lucille. She smiled as she looked me up and down. I ducked back into my bedroom and pulled on some pants and a shirt as she walked through the door.

"You don't have to get dressed on my account, stud muffin," she said coyly.

"Behave," I said, as the toaster popped. "Care for a waffle and a cuppa?" I asked, hoping to ease the tension I felt.

"I love what you've done with the place. Two cream, two sugar. Ixnay on the Afflesway though."

"I have hazelnut creamer. Come on in and fix it however you want." I filled two cups. "So, what brings you slumming on my side of the tracks?" We sat at the table as I poured syrup on my waffles.

"Johnny's been up all night, staring at his computer. Even I couldn't pry him away." She stuck one leg out straight, causing her wizard frock to fall off it a bit, revealing a smoothly muscled, alabaster calf. I coughed a little and looked at my waffles, afraid to meet her eyes.

"Well, he is pretty excited to try and find out the history of this bag." I continued to study my fork.

"This is two nights in a row, though." She pulled her leg back and stood up. She took a step towards the door and whirled around. She finished her coffee and sat her cup on the table. She glared at me. "I don't know what you're so afraid of. You are not that much older than me. In fact, Hector's older than you are." She tapped her foot.

"Well, you see," I started, taking her cup and my plate to the sink. "There's Janie, and I..."

She cut me off. "You know you can bring her, too. I'll bring Bob, and we can have a double date."

I had no comeback for that. She called over her shoulder as she walked out, "Just check on Johnny. I worry about his heart." I heard the storm door close and stood there, flabbergasted.

I looked down and said, "Calm down, Rover. It ain't gonna happen." But Rover and I both felt there was little confidence in that statement.

117

Johnny was just closing his laptop as I tapped on his door. "Come on in," he said. He stood and stretched with a loud moan. "I must urinate profusely. Have a seat and I'll be right back." He disappeared into the little water closet. I looked on the table at a stack of yellow paper filled with writing, torn from a legal pad. I heard water running, then the old professor came back, drying his hands on a towel. He laid the towel on the table, picked up a sheaf of notes, and looked at the cup in my hand. "Got any more of that?" he asked slyly. I stood and we headed over to my place, where there was a bit more room. He sat at my table as I put some more coffee on and popped two more waffles into the toaster.

"I couldn't find much of anything on the name Samuel, or Sam, MacDougald. In fact, the name 'MacDougald' is quite uncommon, with that spelling, and with the 'd' on the end as well. There are many, many listings for the name with different spellings, for instance beginning with 'Mc' instead 'Mac,' and ending with 'le' or 'al,' but hardly any at all with the 'd' on the end."

I sat a plate and cup in front of him, refilled my cup, and sat down. He took a sip of his coffee and rifled through the stack of papers. He pulled out a sheet and sat it on top.

"However," he began, as he took a fork to his waffles and shoved a good sized chunk into his mouth. "There was a Duncan MacDougald, a Scotsman, who was the British Ambassador to Russia in the teens and twenties."

That got my attention. I emptied the last of the carafe into our cups. Johnny dabbed the corners of his mouth with a napkin after he polished off the first waffle.

"You know, of course, that the stock market crash of 1929 didn't only affect the United States, but crippled all the major economies of the world. Duncan must have had a premonition, or just damn good luck, but he relinquished his position in 1927 and went home. In 1928 he emigrated to the United States. It seems he had made the acquaintance of a young lady, whom he met on an absolute twist of fate. They were both vacationing at the same time in Goteburg, Sweden, and met at the restaurant of the same hotel where they had rooms on the same floor. She was a debutante, the daughter of a tobacco executive who owned a large farm in..." He raised his eyebrows at me and held up a finger.

"Chattanooga?" I asked, totally enrapt in his story.

"Close. Actually a little burg near there called Englewood, about fifty miles away or so." He drained the last of his coffee, clanked his fork on his empty plate and chewed the last of his waffle, as I chewed on the tale of Duncan MacDougald.

I waited expectantly for the rest of the story. After a long pause, and it appeared that he wasn't going to finish the story, I finally blurted out, "Well? What next?"

"I have no idea. The trail ends there. I have to assume he married the gal and moved to Tennessee. I have dug and dug but can find nothing else on the interwebs. I suppose I will just have to go to SMUT U and dig through their archives."

"Whoa," said, filling the sink with hot water. "What are you saying?"

"You suddenly have a problem comprehending spoken English? I am taking my notes and heading west. Not today, of course. It is Sunday, and arrangements must be made. I still have several piles that I haven't examined and cataloged. Perhaps in a few days."

"Wow, that gives us a lot to think about."

"Thanks for the breakfast," Johnny said as he gave a big yawn and headed for the door. "I believe a short nap lies in my immediate future."

I watched as the spry old scholar bounced down the steps and disappeared around the corner. I followed him out, but turned the other direction, to the shed, where I looked over the tables full of stuff. Gazing at the piles and the spread, I wondered how in the world all that had fit inside that bag, especially considering the pile of blankets as well. The duffel looked quite small in comparison, crumpled in the corner.

It was still very cloudy, and I felt a few drops of rain as I watched Hector out trolling around, checking his jugs. He pulled up his stringer from the side of the boat and put on a nice sized bass. It looked as if he had a half dozen on there. I suddenly heard a loud whine, and turned just in time to see Chad and Darcy whiz by on a crotch rocket, their long blond manes flowing in the wind. Chad gave out a yell and stuck one hand up with his pinkie and index fingers raised. "They're about to get wet," I thought as I looked up at the gray, overcast sky. Didn't look like there was a magic sunset in the cards for us tonight I thought as a big rain drop hit me square in the eye.

"Hey, Chicken Little." I looked over at Janie, sitting under her awning. "Don't go all turkey on me and drown your damn self." I walked over and sat on her step. "What's on your mind, Cowboy?" She adjusted her chair so she could look at me straight on. I looked deep into her eyes, temporarily mesmerized. Her pupils were ringed with a light brown, surrounded by a bluish gray hue I have never seen anywhere else. "What?" She smiled, making her eyes dance. "Cat got your tongue? Why you looking like a lost boy all of a sudden?"

I snapped out of my trance, and spent the next twenty minutes bringing her up to speed on Johnny's discoveries. She tapped her toes on the concrete block that served as her footstool, looking down at her feet. She looked up at once, ribbons swishing.

"When are we going?" She smiled.

"What are you talking about? You have a mouse in your pocket, or something?"

"You know for a fact that we can't let him go by himself. And what's he going to drive? That metal beast he sleeps in that probably hasn't even been cranked in two years?"

"Oh, so we're all gonna pile into old Betsy, or in your wheeled home here? You have so many guitars and keyboards I'm surprised there is even a place to sit and eat, much less carry a couple of passengers a few hundred miles. Besides, Betsy probably wouldn't even make it to Maryville. She's good for about thirty miles at a time. I was worried Johnny and me wouldn't make it back from the Awful House the other night, it was rattling so bad"

"I know. All that damn money you're sitting on and you won't even get a decent set of wheels."

"I have a decent set. Two of the nicest wheels you've ever seen."

"Okay, so you and I will ride the Moto Beasty, and what, are you gonna put a sidecar on it for Johnny?"

I looked up then and saw Lucille sitting in the rain, perched on the picnic table, staring at us. Her raven-hair hanging in dripping ringlets. She hopped off, and when she raised her hands to push her hair back out of her face, it was very obvious that she wore nothing under her light blue starry nylon frock. Of course, Janie saw me blushing. "Get over it, already," she said as Lucille walked over.

"I heard everything," she said. "And, of course, Madame Lucille has a solution. It is written in the stars." She shook water off her dress, making other parts shake, as well. She walked over and patted me on the shoulder, shooing me out of the doorway. "Whatcha got to drink in here, Janie Shanie?" she bubbled.

"Budweiser and Perrier."

"Then this Bud's for me!" She popped the cap off a frosty long neck and sat down on the threshold, letting her dress slide off her shapely thigh. I was not going to let this minx get to me, I told myself.

Yeah right. I should tell another lie. Even Janie seemed entranced by her. Uh oh, I thought. There could be trouble a-brewin'. "Well." Janie started. "Do tell."

Lucille adopted a rare, semi-serious demeanor. "You two could go with us, of course. We would have to take turns in the bed, you know, because there are no seats in the van except for driver and passenger." She took a small sip of her beer. "I know you two wouldn't mind spending six hours in a cozy bed going over bumpy roads and around mountain curves."

Janie and I looked at her. I could see how she had been so successful on the festival circuit. This lady oozed charisma, as well as other...she cut my train of thought. "Or, Johnny and I can go in the van and you two lovebirds can follow on your two wheels of fire."

Johnny appeared then, looking rested and sporting an umbrella. I said, "I thought you would still be snoozing."

"I slept about two hours. More than enough. More than Einstein ever got at one time. What are you three plotting over here?"

Lucille got up and linked her arm into his, sharing his umbrella as the rain had picked up a bit. As she related her plan to him, he nodded and pulled out his phone. "I suppose we will need an accurate weather forecast and see how long this rain is going to last." He touched her shoulder. "Come on, you need to get on some dry clothing. You'll catch your death of cold in this rain."

Lucille wiggled her fingers at Janie and me, saying "Toodles!" as they walked away, huddled together under the umbrella.

"Say it ain't so," Janie murmured as she watched them go, mesmerized.

"I said the same exact thing." I told her.

"I believe I will have a Bud myself and drink to that."

"Grab two," I told her, grabbing her seat when she got up, my mind in a whirl.

Janie and I sat and chatted a little while longer, listening to the rain. "What are y'all expecting to find in Chattanooga?" she finally asked me.

"Well, I wasn't planning on going until you volunteered us," I retorted. "I don't actually know. Maybe someone who can translate Russian text? And someone who has any knowledge about a man named MacDougald who may have lived in the surrounding area 75 years ago? That's all I can think of."

She walked over and began rubbing my shoulders. "I guess Hector will be in charge while we're gone." I closed my eyes and relaxed. She definitely still had the nurse's touch.

"Ooh yeah. I suppose so. He always did it before when I would take off." I purred like a cat. "I will give you twenty minutes to stop that." She continued my massage for a good while, then stood and walked up the steps and through her door. She turned toward me and stood still, lifting off her tie-dyed shirt to reveal her sheer bra. As she reached behind herself to unsnap it, she winked at me. "My turn," she said breathily as she shrugged out of it. I nearly twisted my ankle getting out of that chair.

It had stopped raining when I woke up, spooned with Janie on her sleeper sofa. I pulled my arm out from under her and rolled off, standing and pulling on my pants. I watched out the door window as Hector backed the truck toward his place, a load of firewood stacked on the tailgate from the big stack we had out past Howard's place. I guessed he was going to be smoking some tamales. He must have caught enough fish.

"What are you doing, handsome?" Janie asked sleepily, as she rolled over to face me.

"I was just watching Hector. He has a load of firewood on the truck."

"Tamale time!" she sang. "Love those succulent bass tamales."

"I guess I had better go see what Johnny has come up with," I said as I sat on the edge of her bed and began to put on my shoes.

"Oh, hit and run, huh? I've seen your kind before." she pinched the back of my arm.

"Ouch!" I cried. "You are going to get a spanking for that!"

She rolled over on her stomach and squirmed. "Promises, promises."

I smacked her bare buttocks a little harder than I meant to. "OOO- That stings!" I saw her hand slide underneath her pelvis. What the hell, I thought. Johnny can wait a while longer. I smacked her ass again as she twitched and moaned...

I found Johnny back in the shed with Lucille. I stood there dumbfounded. Lucille was wearing Guess jeans and a Fleetwood Mac tee shirt. She got up from a stool and walked over to one of the tables opposite Johnny. Wow. She was really wearing those jeans. I nipped that thought in the bud and said, "What are you kids working on?"

"I think I may have some of this figured out. I found a translation app on my phone. It can do nothing with the handwritten stuff, but the typewritten pages it does a little better. They are mostly remnants, only a few whole pages, but so far they're just mundane military papers. Nothing top secret or anything like that. But one name keeps coming up." He passed a note pad over to me, where he had written a name.

Nikolo Slesarevich.

"That is more or less the consensus spelling. Sometimes it ends in just the *c*, and sometimes Nikolo ends with a *j*."

Lucille held up her phone. "I've been looking on my Android, but so far no luck." She had sat back down on her stool and looked at her phone. She caught me looking at her and smiled. I couldn't get over how she looked in normal clothes. I wondered what had hurt her so badly in her past that made her feel the need to hide. Or, maybe in her world normal meant something completely different.

"This stack here," Johnny said, bringing me back to the here and the now. Lucille popped her bubble gum. I snapped around at her; I hadn't ever known her to chew gum.

"Have you been hanging around with Chad and Darcy?"

"Wouldn't you like to know?" She hopped off her stool. "I'll see you boys later," she said, and she and her jeans were out the door, just like that.

"Anyway, once you can get your chin off your chest, come over here and look at this." Johnny was grinning. He pointed to a stack of papers. "I believe these written pages, here, are these newspaper articles," he pointed to the other stack, "Translated into Russian. Now, I know that throughout history, there have occurred some remarkable coincidences, but let's take a look at what we know. We have a duffel bag in a mountain lake in Western Carolina." He held up a finger to make each point. "Said duffel possibly belonged to a Nikolo Slesarevich, who was possibly a naval officer aboard a Russian submarine." He was running out of fingers on his left hand.

"Inside the bag is a picture of a man in front of a building on the campus of SMUT University, and remnants of a flier from the same school with the same building printed on it." This was news to me; I had not seen this item. Not surprising, since I hadn't been in here while he was cataloging the majority of this stuff. The index finger of his right hand shot up.

"The Scotsman who was the British attaché to Russia gives up his post, and moves close to Chattanooga, just prior to the crash of '29, and has the same last name as a name found in the contents of this duffel bag." He stopped, turning his head, looking at all the loaded tables. His hands fell to his sides.

"There has to be something connecting all these things." He suddenly looked a little older. He looked at me with red-rimmed eyes. "I have to find this link. You know this, don't you?" He was almost pleading. I walked over to him and put my arm around his shoulder.

"Have you checked the weather forecast?"

"Lucille is supposed to be checking that for me. Let's go see what she has discovered."

The next few days passed by in a blur. I went over everything with Hector, which was pointless. He could probably run the park better than me, truth be told. Janie and I each packed a small suitcase. I made reservations for the two of us, Lucille having informed me that she and Johnny would be driving their sleeping quarters. Johnny organized some of the papers, medals, and badges into an old briefcase, first polishing up the metal pieces until they gleamed. We planned to stay Thursday and Friday nights, and come back Saturday.

Johnny had a lengthy discussion with the head of the History department at the college, and he was expecting us with a similar level of excitement as our Johnny. I took the old Moto and had her professionally serviced, as she had seen little use lately. We loaded our bags into Lucille's van, and before sun-up on Thursday morning we were on the road.

After about two hours of winding roads we finally hit the main interstate, Janie and I leading the way. I had forgotten how much that Italian iron horse loved the mountain roads. I also realized how out of riding shape I was. But my jacket still fit, so I was happy about that.

The Bluetooth in my helmet chimed. It was Johnny, telling me to be on the lookout for a Cracker Barrel restaurant. We all got our bellies full, hit the bathrooms, and we were back on the road. GPS said we were about three hours from our destination, putting us happily ahead of schedule. We arrived at the Sheraton, and Janie and I went up with our bags. Johnny and Lucille followed, wanting to see what our room looked like. Then it was off to SMT. Professor DeLaval was waiting on the steps of the History building when we pulled up.

I parked my bike at the curb, and Lucille pulled in behind me in her wizard mobile. I shook my long, salt and pepper hair out of my helmet as Janie removed hers, revealing all her colorful ribbons and flowers. We shook ourselves and followed Johnny and Lucille up the steps. DeLaval's smile wavered a little as he looked at us. Me, with my black leather jacket, half finger studded gloves, and RayBans. Janie, with her faded bell bottom jeans, Jefferson Airplane Volunteers tee shirt, rainbow tipped fingers, the ribbons and flowers in her wavy dirty blond hair, not to mention yellow framed shades. Next was Lucille, in her black and gold ankle length frock, with stars and moons all over it, complete with a long draped shawl with fringe, and all the rings and bracelets, black nails, and round, rose colored glasses accenting her blue-black raven mane. And our Johnny, smiling, resplendent in gray houndstooth jacket, maroon turtle neck, and black slacks, looking very professorial.

DeLaval quickly regained his composure, shook hands with everyone, and invited us in. He led us into a room with a long table.

"This is our conference room," he said. "I have cleared my schedule for the rest of the day and am at your service." He looked over at Johnny, who had laid his briefcase on the table and was unsnapping the lock. "Of course, I am anxious to see your artifacts, Professor Coster. I suppose that is a perfect place for us to begin." Johnny slid his briefcase up and began removing things from it, giving a running commentary on each item.

"Do you have a snack machine or something in this place? I'm feeling a mite peckish." Lucille stood, producing a small handbag from somewhere in her robe.

DeLaval stood and, looking a bit flustered, said, "Of course. Please excuse my ignorance. You have traveled far. We have a wonderful cafeteria just around the corner and…" Lucille was out the door like a shot.

"Thanks. I'll find it," she said as she disappeared. Janie and I looked at each other.

"We'd better..." Janie started, as she stood up.

"Yes, we had," I agreed as we both disappeared out the door, leaving the professors to their academics.

There was a buzz of conversation that ceased as we entered the cafeteria. All 75 or so sets of eyes were on us as we walked toward the counter. A preppy looking fellow in the line looked at me and said "Are you guys a band? Is there going to be another concert on the quad?" Lucille was looking around, enjoying the attention.

"Order me a cheeseburger, fries and a coke," she said to me, as she flitted over to an empty table and sat down, pulling a deck of tarot cards from her frock.

I thought, again, "Where does she hide that stuff?" I looked at Janie, who must have had the same thought as me. She shrugged and pointed me towards the order counter. I told the attendant, "Four cheeseburgers, four fries, four cokes."

"That'll be $12. You can can get your drinks right over there." She pointed to the soft drink machine.

I handed her a twenty and said "No change necessary."

She smiled at me and said, "I'll bring it out to you." I asked her to make one of them to go, and looked over to where Lucille had sat down. She had already drawn a small crowd, and was holding the hands of a young coed, palms up, sitting across from her.

"Will I ever understand algebra?" the girl asked, seriously.

I sat Lucille's drink in front of her and said, "We'll just be over here."

As we dug into our surprisingly tasty institutional lunch, I stopped and said softly, "Dammit."

Janie looked at me and touched my arm. "What is it?" she asked, very seriously.

"I forgot to ask for a damn receipt. This is definitely a write-off."

She smacked my arm and gave me a kick to the shin. "It's less than twenty friggin dollars! Here I thought you were really upset about something." She kicked me again. "Can you think of anything other than business for a change?"

"Ouch. Kick me again and I will beat your ass," I told her.

"You promise?" She smiled and kicked me three more times.

We finished our meals and refilled our drinks. Lucille was still giving free 'readings' and we could hardly see her for the crowd of students around her. Janie said "What are we? Chopped liver?"

The professors walked in then, and Johnny sat down beside me. I handed him his Styrofoam box. He opened it and said, "God bless you. I'm famished." He gestured toward the students thronging Lucille. He looked at me with raised eyebrows-he wouldn't dare speak with his mouth full. Janie raised her hands to either side of her face.

"Your little girlfriend," she said, tilting her head. That seemed to embarrass Johnny a bit, as he looked at DeLaval.

"She is NOT my girlfriend," he protested.

DeLaval just beamed at him, and gave a little head nod. "I'll be in the conference room. Just come on in when you're finished." He turned and walked to the door, stopped, and looked back at us, and especially at Lucille. He smiled and shook his head a bit, and stepped out into the sunshine.

"I guess he's got something to talk about for a while," Janie laughed at me.

Johnny, seemingly oblivious to everything but his lunch, took a sip of his drink, wiped his mouth and announced, "This burger is delicious," and stuck the last bite into his mouth.

I got Lucille's attention and pointed at the door. She nodded and stood, gathering her cards and making them disappear into her robe. She held her hands out, palms down, until her admirers were silent. Then she rotated her palms upward and said, "Remember, around the tenth of next month Saturn will be in Pleiades and the moon will be aligned with Jupiter and Neptune. Then will begin the season of love and Eros will reign in the heavens for the next seven moon cycles. Peace and joy and happiness to you all. I must leave you now, but one day I will see you again." With a flourish of her robes and a tilt of the head, she breezed past Janie and me and out the door, leaving the students flat-footed, staring at the door.

At once, the cacophony of voices started again, and I tapped Johnny on the shoulder and said "We ready?"

On our way back to the History office building, Johnny spoke. "Professor DeLaval told me the school has boxes of records in the basement of the Administration building. After the blizzard of '93 they moved them there after the roof caved in on the storage building where they had been keeping them. An effort had begun to digitize them all, and that is still ongoing. They have gotten to

1956. The school has not dedicated any funds to this project, and it is being done exclusively by students seeking extra credit in certain classes. I figure we can start in 1944 and go forward."

The other three of us looked back and forth at each other, with frightened looks. "What exactly are we looking for?" I asked.

"We will know when we find it."

When we got back to the office building, Janie said, "Lucille and I will be right in. She wants to show me something in the van." I looked at her, and she shooed me with a wave of her hand. "Go on in. We'll be fine."

I turned and followed the professor up the steps. We went into the conference room, and DeLaval looked disappointed. "Where is the rest of your entourage, Professor Coster?"

"Please, call me Johnny. I believe the ladies are currently holding palaver out in the mystery machine." I couldn't stop myself from bursting into laughter. I left the room to find the toilet. Mystery machine indeed!

Johnny met me in the hallway as I came out. "DeLaval has phoned the Admin Assistant over in the admin building. She's expecting us. It's at the other end of the campus." We went outside. "If you follow this road, it circles around. You can see the flag, there," he pointed. "That is the building. I'm walking." I could barely make out the flag, but I had no doubt it was there. He handed me his briefcase. "Give this to Lucille and have her follow you over in the van. I will meet you there." With that he turned and began walking.

I went down to the curb and tapped on the window of the van. The sliding door opened and a small cloud of smoke escaped. "Hookah time." Lucille sang, holding a wooden tipped plastic tube toward me. "Here ya go," she said.

I looked around, thought "What the hell, one won't hurt," and stuck my head inside.

The girls followed me around the loop. Johnny was nowhere to be seen. We entered the front door, and the lady behind the glass partition pointed and said, "The stairs at the end of the hall. The door marked *records*." She sat back down and watched us over her glasses.

"Miss Congeniality herself," Janie remarked. That got a snort out of Lucille.

"Voted most likely to have a stick up her ass!" she declared as we all laughed.

The fun ended as soon as we opened the records room door. Row upon row of metal shelving that stretched to the ceiling and seemed to disappear into infinity greeted us in the dimly lit, dusty room. Each shelf was jam packed with boxes.

"Good grief," Janie said. "This looks like the freaking Vatican archives."

Johnny, looking nonplussed, said in his usual dry tone, "With any luck, the boxes will be clearly labeled and it won't take us long to find the answers we seek."

Lucille said, "What is it again that we are looking for?"

"We'll know when we find it!" Janie and I said in unison.

I walked around the gloomy room. I noticed tables in the corners and a couple of ladders on wheels. The ends of the shelves were labeled with months and years. Janie had begun exploring as well, in the other direction. Johnny walked down a row titled Jan, 1941-Aug, 1945. He was pulling a dusty box from a one of the shelves onto a rolling cart when Janie screamed, "Hey! Come look at this!"

We followed her voice to the end of the room and saw her about midway down, looking up at the top shelf. We went to her, and there on the top were boxes marked *Yearbooks*.

"Eureka!" Johnny shouted. "Grab one of those ladders, Mr. Stevens, if you please. I think we are in business."

It didn't take long until we hit pay dirt. We had wrestled a box titled '1935-1951' over to the table. It was very dusty, and very heavy. Johnny jumped up after about ten minutes of looking through one of them.

"Aha!" he said, pointing at one of the pictures. There, looking out from the pages of history, page 117 of the 1947 SMTSU annual to be exact, was a dapper looking fellow, mid-30's possibly. Below the picture, the caption read "Samuel MacDougald, Instructor Per Diem, Russian Language."

Johnny was in a frenzy now, pulling out yearbooks and flipping through them quickly. "1947, 1948, 1949," he said, as he would find the man in each yearbook. "1950. He is not in the 1951 book." He turned and headed back to the stacks. I knew where he was headed.

"Allow me, professor." I pulled the steps over and pulled down the box labeled "1952-1966." I brought it over and sat it on the table. Lucille had her phone out, thumbing through the 1946 book and snapping pictures. Johnny started pulling out books and looking through them in a frenzy. He had a half dozen stacked up, and sighed.

"It would appear that 1950 is the end of our trail here for Mr. MacDougald. And, there was no mention anywhere, that I saw, of a Nikolo or Slesarevich, either."

About that time Miss Ratchett, the Admin lady, came in. "We are closing in thirty minutes. You folks are welcome to come back tomorrow morning. I open the door at 8:00 a.m. sharp." She turned and marched out.

Johnny, deep in thought, did not appear to have heard a word she said. He pushed back the stack of books. Janie and I began putting them back into the boxes. "Lucille. Please open that 1946 annual to the freshman class photos." Lucille sprang into action as Johnny pulled out his phone and began snapping pictures as she turned the pages. He had just finished with the 1950 book when Miss Ratchett came back.

"Five minutes." she said.

"We may have everything we need. Thank you so much. You have been very kind."

We blinked as we exited the building into the bright sunshine. "Let's head back to your suite," Johnny said. "I believe the sign in the lobby said free WiFi."

It was hard to believe we had spent four hours in that basement. As we headed back uptown, my Bluetooth chimed. It was Lucille. "We are ordering pizza, right? And I am going to use your shower." The line went dead. I laughed to myself. She was something else.

We got back to the hotel. Johnny sat at the little table and had me call the desk for the WiFi password. He pulled out a note pad, and began downloading pictures from his phone to the laptop. I knew he was going to be there for a while, and neither wanted nor needed any help. Lucille came out of the bathroom wearing a thick pink robe, her hair wrapped in a towel. "I'm next." Janie jumped up and shot into the bathroom.

I plopped on the bed and turned on the TV, grabbing up the booklet for room service. I picked up the phone and ordered a large supreme pizza with breadsticks and a six pack of long neck Budweisers. Lucille had opened her suitcase on the bed next to me and stood over it. Our eyes met as she dropped her robe. I gulped and tried to look away. She smiled and looked down at my groin. I quickly laid the room service menu in my lap. She shrugged into a tee shirt and pulled on a pair of shorts. Totally commando. She closed her case, leaned over and whispered in my ear, "You know, Janie is more older than you than you are older than me." She brushed her lips against my cheek and walked over to where Johnny sat, scribbling on his note pad and looking from his phone to the laptop.

"I'm going to need my phone plugged in before long. Can you dig out my charger?" Lucille handled that task, and came back over to the recliner next to the window. She snatched the remote out of my hand, sat down, and started flipping channels.

Janie came out of the bathroom wrapped in a towel, drying her hair. She grabbed some clothes and her little bag and went back into the bathroom, closing the door. I looked over at Lucille, which was a mistake. She was staring at me, a sardonic grin on her face. I was saved by a knock on the door,

"Room service," came the voice from outside the door. Lucille jumped up and ran to the door. She accepted the beer and the two boxes and waved the porter into the room. She sat the boxes on the bed and looked at me, expectantly.

"Oh, right," I said, digging my wallet out. The charge was going on my bill, but the bellhop needed tipped.

"Allow me." Johnny pulled a wad of cash out of his pocket and peeled off a fifty, which Lucille snatched and handed to the grinning delivery boy.

"Thank you! Enjoy your meal." He bowed and backed out of the room, closing the door.

"You know that was just the prom night promise, right? The room service is charged to the bill for the room." I said to Johnny.

"Prom night promise?" Lucille asked me as Johnny looked from me to her.

"Just the tip." I said, grinning. Lucille burst into laughter, and I do believe she may have blushed just a little. Johnny simply went back to work.

I heard the hair dryer in the bathroom, and Janie reappeared a minute later, fully clothed, no ribbons, hair pulled back in a pony tail. Johnny continued to be focused on the business of the duffel, clicking keys and jotting down notes.

Janie said "I smell pizza," and walked over to the bed.

After we had our fill, Janie went over and opened the curtains. Our room had a westerly view, and Janie said 'Uh, Ahem!" to get our attention. I looked over and saw the sun approaching the horizon. Janie raised her eyebrows at me.

Tradition.

I pointed at my toiletry bag. She tossed it to me and climbed up beside me on the bed. "What is Gobekli Tepi," she said as I pulled out the doobie and struck fire to it. I noticed that Lucille had stopped the TV on *Jeopardy*.

Some time later, the sun having long since dropped from the sky, and my mind in another dimension, Johnny stood up and announced, "I hope you saved me a slice of that pizza." We looked at him with droopy eyes. "And I might accept a bit of the other if you pass it my way every now and then."

Janie opened her eyes. "I'm so sorry, Johnny. There's some left though for when you finish your slice." I could sense a change in her demeanor. She was awake. "You know that pizza is the world's most perfect food. All five food groups are represented, in a convenient, easy to hold delivery system." Johnny opened the mini-fridge and grabbed a beer.

"I couldn't agree more, Janie dear. The ancient Chinese invented many things that are still widely used today."

"I thought pizza was Italian," Lucille said.

"The Sicilians did perfect the pie we all know today. But the idea was stolen by Marco Polo and brought back by him. Spaghetti as well."

The professor grew silent as he chowed down on his pizza. He finished quickly, wiped his mouth and hands, downed his Bud and sat the pizza box and the six pack of empty bottles outside the door. We all watched him as he sat back down and, looking at his notepad, picked up his phone and dialed a number. We could hear a faint voice on the other end say hello as the connection was made. Johnny introduced himself and said, "Am I speaking with Carl Danforth? I am? Good. May I ask if you were a student at Southern Mid in the 1940s? Oh okay. So you must be Carl Junior, then. Would it be possible to speak to your father? Oh my. I am so sorry to hear that. No, I am just doing some research on the school around the time of the war. Not at all, thank you for your time."

He drew a line across the paper and punched in another number.

"I believe there is a bar downstairs. Anybody game?" Lucille hopped up, grabbing her bag and heading into the bathroom, the towel still on her head. "Be out in a jiff," she giggled.

Johnny looked over at me as he crossed another name off his list. "I know the chances are slim. All these folks would be well into their nineties by now, of course. But I must do my best." I told him I understood completely.

I stood up as Lucille exited the bathroom, looking like a real girl in a floral button up blouse, jeans, sneakers, and her hair pulled back in a ponytail. I had a moment of *deja vu*, remembering how I felt as a teenager when I saw *The Breakfast Club* the first time, when Claire gave Allison the makeover. She grabbed Janie by the hand and linked her other arm in mine and we were off. "Don't wait up for us John," she yelled over her shoulder as we went out the door.

The bar had a little bandstand with a small dance floor in front. A few tables were scattered around the dark room, with a long bar on the side. Lucille plopped onto a stool and told the bartender, "Give me a sloe, comfortable screw." He nodded and went to work. I must have had a look, because Janie elbowed me in the ribs, making me jump.

"It's like a screwdriver, but with sloe gin and Southern Comfort." She pinched my cheek and said, "Grow up." She ordered up a tequila sunrise and I asked for a draught as the band cranked up a great cover of *Dance*, the old Ratt tune. The band was good.

We turned around on our stools and watched the band, and checked out the crowd, which seemed to be very good for a Thursday night. Janie, looking at all the twenty-somethings, leaned over and said softly in my ear, "Damn I feel old."

I told her she put all these wanna-bees to shame. She grabbed my hand and kissed it. "You're so sweet," she said.

The band finished with a flurry and went into *Hot Blooded*. A guy who looked like a bank teller walked up to Lucille and nodded toward the dance floor, holding out his hand. She downed her drink and looked at the bartender, getting his attention and holding up a finger, then pointing to her empty glass. He went to work on another one as banker boy led her out on the dance floor. Janie hopped down, pulling on my arm. The bartender looked at us. Janie nodded and held up a finger. I waved him off. I already knew someone was going to have to keep a level head this night, and that someone was me. I let Janie lead me out onto the floor and did the 'white boy shuffle' as she shook her little booty in circles around me. After about ten minutes of guitar soloing I was about danced out, but I stayed with Janie as the band transitioned from *Tush* to *Get Down Tonight*.

I kept my eyes on Lucille and her banker boy partner. She had ducked over to the bar and downed another drink and hit the bartender for another before going right back out onto the floor. She was shimmying her body to *do a little dance,* hunching her partner's outstretched knee to *make a little love,* and dropping into a very suggestive squat in front of him to *get down tonight."*

Janie pulled my head down and yelled in my ear "There may be trouble brewin'." I nodded and led her back to the bar. We kept our eyes on our friend as the song ended, the band took a break, and Lucille headed back to where we were sitting. A few locks of hair were out of the pony tail and stuck to her red cheeks. Her partner had followed close behind, his eyes never leaving her butt as she made her way back through the tables.

"Whew, that was fun!" She said as she picked up her drink. Banker boy put his hand on her butt and leaned over and licked her neck. "Whoa," she said, moving his hand and hopping up on the stool. Undeterred, banker boy tried to slide between her knees, reaching for her waist.

"Hey, come on. Lets go out and get some fresh air."

She spun around to face the bar and showed him her back. He was persistent, sliding his hands around her waist. Janie elbowed me. I had seen enough. I slid off my stool and looked down at the preppy fellow.

"Go away, geezer. I saw her first." he said, trying to nudge me out of the way.

This was unacceptable. "I think the dance is over, and you need to go back to whatever rock you crawled out from under." Banker boy looked at me, thought about it, and swung a fist towards my face. I caught it with my left hand and squeezed, putting him on his knees.

"Ow ow owie!" he screamed, as the bartender looked on. I released the idiot and he scampered away. I looked over at the bartender. "Another drink for the lady, please." Janie held up her empty glass.

"Me, too," she squealed, grabbing me around the waist.

"I was handling it," Lucille said.

I caught a glimpse of banker boy heading out, flexing his right hand. I looked over at Lucille. "I could tell. But I don't think we need to worry about that imbecile anymore."

We stayed in the bar for a while longer. Lucille and Janie danced with a couple more guys, and with each other. There was one more minor incident, but I didn't have to get involved this time. Another little pup followed Lucille back to our perch and tried to get fresh.

"Sorry, you're not my type," Lucille said, grabbing Janie and giving her a big smooch. To my mild surprise, Janie played right along, putting her hand on Lucille's cheek and wrapping the other arm around her waist, giving it right back to her. The pup turned and walked away, shaking his head.

"Fuckin' dykes," he was heard to mutter as he disappeared. That brought peals of laughter from the three of us. Lucille smacked her lips.

"I might try one of those sunrises. That tastes pretty good." The band finished *Flirting with Disaster*, which I thought was appropriate for the moment. The singer announced they were taking their final break and would be back in fifteen for the last two songs. I thought that was a good time to call it a night, and the girls agreed with me.

The elevator ride up was fun, with both of the girls wobbling. Janie slurred, "What happens in Nooga, STAYS in Nooga!" They both held up a hand and went "WOOOOO" as the elevator door opened on a stoic looking Asian couple, who stepped back as we staggered out. Well, the girls were staggering, anyway. They each had one of my arms, yanking me along with them. I caught the eye of the gentleman as we passed.

"Woo girl convention going on downstairs. Proceed with caution!"

"I gotta peeeeeeee!" Janie proclaimed as we entered the room to an astonished Johnny. Lucille followed her to the bathroom, kicking off her shoes as she undid her pants.

"I'll take the tub."

I had to go too, but not nearly that urgently. Johnny grinned at me. "Interesting evening? I think you all were gone about four hours."

"You don't know the half of it." I told him. The girls came crashing out of the bathroom and plopped on the bed, both of them talking at once and looking at the ceiling.

"Lucille pissed in the bath tub!" Janie said.

"Why is the room spinning? Make it stop!" Lucille said.

I have been around enough to know what was coming next. I grabbed the ice bucket, as it was the closest container to me, and prayed it would be big enough. I made it to her side of the bed just in time to hear her say "Uh oh." She rolled over and spewed a multicolored conglomeration into the bucket. She took a break, and I took the waste basket from Johnny, who had followed close behind. Lucille hovered for a second over the ice bucket and said "Is that a carrot? I don't remember eating any carrots. Urp epp."

I managed to make the switch in time to catch the next load. Then she fell back onto the bed and was snoring within minutes. Janie was already there, taking in deep breaths and blowing out puffs of tequila-scented air. Johnny shook his head as I headed for the bathroom with my presents. "Be right back," I told him.

When I came out, Johnny had removed Janie's shoes and lain a blanket over the two partied out woo girls. He dampened a washcloth and dabbed at Lucille's face. I sat in the chair and took off my shoes. Johnny said, "In the morning, we are going to the town of Red Bank to meet with a gentleman named Bill Oglesby, Jr. His father, the senior, graduated from SMT in 1948, and spoke to Junior quite a bit over the years about Mr. MacDougald, and a mysterious Russian fellow he met.

I looked over at him, obviously agape. "Oh, it gets better." The old professor looked about ready to jump out the window.

"Junior has his Daddy's memoirs!"

He stood and stretched, looking at his phone. "It is quite late. I am taking Lucille's keys and heading to the mystery machine to sleep. I will get cleaned up in the morning." He disappeared into the bathroom with his toiletry bag. When he came out, he looked over at the slumbering females. He smiled as he grabbed Lucille's keys off the dresser and went out the door "I believe they are down for the count," he said. He was wrong about that, and said "Goodnight, Mr. Stevens," as the door closed behind him.

I grabbed the remote and found Forrest Gump kneeling with Jenny in the cornfield, praying for God to make her a bird, so she could fly far, far away. That's all I saw of the movie.

It was still dark outside when I awakened. I looked at my phone. 4:17. On the television a grinning overweight man sprayed some black gunk onto a hole in the bottom of an aquarium and filled it with water. As I switched it off, I noticed Lucille not in the bed. I looked around and noticed a light under the bathroom door. I heard the toilet flush and some water running, along with the sound of teeth being brushed. She finally came out and walked over to me, her hair a mess. "I had to brush my teeth. It tasted like an ocelot had taken a shit in my mouth." She sat on the edge of my chair and kept going, sliding onto my lap. I didn't try to stop her. I noticed she had changed out of her jeans and had on shorts and a tee shirt. My hand on her back revealed that she did still sport a brassiere, however.

"You know, I really had a blast tonight. I haven't been that drunk in a long long time, though. It was wonderful being able to cut loose knowing you had my back." I could see her eyes in the soft light coming from outside. I thought she had never looked so vulnerable and lovely. "I really appreciate the way you make me feel so safe. But now you can maybe understand a little bit why I dress and carry myself the way I do in public." She raised up, draping an arm around my neck.

"I choose who I want to lust after me." She lowered her lips down to mine and kissed me. I kissed her back as my hand drifted over her shirt. I pulled back.

"I can't," I said, slightly out of breath. "I mean I want to. I have since I saw you in the lake that day, not long after you came to the park." Janie shifted, and her breathing changed into a light snore. I nodded her way. "But I won't do that to her. I had it done to me and it hurts. I know we aren't married, but we are committed."

"I know." Lucille sat up. "I think that is why I am so attracted to you. You are one of the truly good men. That and you are so damned good-looking." She hopped down and lay back down on the bed. "Janie is great. I love her to death, and y'all are really perfect together." She said no more, rolled over and went back to sleep.

I would sleep no more that night.

The sky was getting bright about around 5:30, and I decided to hit the shower. I was just getting rinsed when Janie slid in behind me, wrapping me in her arms as the warm water went over us. I turned around to face her, and wrapped my arms around her. I helped her soap up, and we rinsed and got out. I glanced out the door and saw Lucille still sleeping. I walked back over to Janie and sat her down on the edge of the tub, and I sat on the closed toilet. I looked Janie in her eyes.

"I have to tell you something. I kissed Lucille last night. I know it was wrong to to it and nothing more happened then or will ever happen. But you need to know."

Janie looked at me, her eyes moving from one eye to the other. "Actually, she kissed you. I saw and heard everything, you big lug. I was awake the whole time. I love you!"

"Yeah, but I did kiss her back."

"I suppose that makes us even, then. I kissed the girl, and I liked it." She got up and straddled me, on my lap. She kissed me long and deep, as her hand slid down between our naked bodies. She drew back as she eased up and slid a little closer.

"I love you, too," I murmured into her ear as she lowered herself onto me.

We all had breakfast at a place called 'The Blintz Room.' I looked at Johnny. "What do you think Mr. Oglesby is going to think when we all come pulling up in a wizard mobile and my big loud Moto? Maybe we should hit up the Avis down the street and rent a sedan or something?"

"Why don't you boys do that?" Lucille spoke up. "Janie and I have found some hippie shops we want to check out. You two go talk to dude and we'll meet you back at the room later on this evening." Johnny and I looked at each other. I shrugged. He nodded.

"You need to get your bike back to the hotel, anyway. They can drop me off at the rental place and I'll come collect you. Junior isn't expecting us for another two hours."

I pulled out my wallet. Johnny waved me off. "I know you have more money than Davy Crockett. So do I. Put your damn wallet up." I smiled and did what he commanded, but not before putting a c-note on the table for breakfast.

Mr. Oglesby lived in a well kept split-level brick home with orange shutters in the end of a cul-de-sac. He was outside as we pulled up. The professor got out and held out his hand. "Mr. Oglesby, I presume."

The neat little balding George Costanza look-a-like grabbed his hand and shook it vigorously. "Please, please, call me Bill. Do come in, do come in." He ushered us into a quaint, fairly large eat-in kitchen with rooster wallpaper, and rooster figurines all around. "This is so exciting, so exciting." Johnny introduced me, and Bill grabbed my hand and started shaking it vigorously. "Mr. Stevens! Mr. Stevens! SO nice to meet you!"

"Call me Mike," I said as he released my hand and led us into the living room.

"Have a seat, have a seat. Make yourself at home. I'll be right back." He disappeared through a doorway. A very attractive older lady with shoulder length gray hair and an olive green pantsuit appeared from somewhere.

"May I get you two gentlemen some coffee? I must apologize for Bill. He has been waiting for years on top of years for someone to show up asking about his father's memoirs."

We both told her yes on the coffee, and Johnny smiled at her. "It is certainly an amazing twist of fate that has brought us here today."

"Well, actually it was a Toyota Avalon we rented from Avis, but who's keeping score?" The lady sat down on a kitchen chair, she was laughing so hard as Johnny punched me in the arm.

"Janie's right about you! You are quite the smart ass sometimes." We both were still smiling when a few minutes later, the tension broken, we were presented with a tray containing a small silver pitcher with steam rising from it, flanked by two ceramic cups and containers holding real cream and sugar.

We were stirring our cuppas when Bill came back into the room, huffing and puffing, carrying a clear plastic box with an interlocking, split hinged red lid. He sat it down in front of his chair and sat, saying "Good, good. I see Sophie has taken care of you." He looked up at his...wife? Housekeeper? It's never prudent to assume, you know. "Thank you dear." She came over and leaned down for a little smackeroo on the lips. Okay then. Wife.

Bill began talking as he brought folder after folder out of the box, stacking them on the coffee table. "My father was a history major at University," he started, looking over at Johnny and smiling. "He went on to teach history, as that is what one does with a history degree in most cases, am I correct, Mr. Coster?"

"Call me Johnny, please. And yes, that is certainly the career path many of us take. Do continue, if you may."

"Of course, of course. He taught high school, you know, world history. He was a student of the great wars of Europe, and loved to teach about them. But I digress.

"When he was entering his third year at SMUT, he was advised that he needed a year of a foreign language. Now mind you, in those days, Spanish was not nearly as ubiquitous in this country as it is now. Most students took French or Latin. However, this was right after the war, you see, and the entire Western Hemisphere was scared to death of Stalin and others like him. The government was offering incentives to colleges to begin teaching Russian, and would send certain officials there to learn the language. States were encouraged to educate some of their officials, as well.

"The problem, you see." He lifted a large album from the box. "Ah yes, here we go." He sat the album on the floor and began replacing the folders into the box.

"The problem was that there were very few people in the country who had the credentials, and the fluency, to teach it, especially at the university level." He flipped open the album and sat it on the table. He put his hands on his knees and leaned back in his chair, his face beaming. This was obviously a major event for him, the most fun he had had in a long time. Sophie had taken a seat on one of the kitchen chairs, and was perched on the edge, as intent as Johnny and I were on what Bill was saying. He continued.

"As luck would have it, or perhaps it was kismet, you see, the secretary in the math department, a Miss Snow, had had a boyfriend in school. She had gone to Vanderbilt, you see, in Nashville. She went to the head of the languages department, a Mr. Sloan, I believe, whom Miss Snow had been to dinner with a few times, and explained to him about this fellow she had dated in college. A lad named MacDougald."

He took a breath as Johnny did the same. I realized that I had been holding my breath as well.

"It seems that this Mr. MacDougald's father had been some sort of British diplomat or something of the sort, prior to the war, and lived in Moscow for about twenty years, which is where our Mr. Macdougald was born. The elder MacDougald met with heartache, as his wife was stricken with scarlet fever and died quickly, before they could get medicine to her. Young Master MacDougald was at the tender age of four when this atrocity occurred, and the ambassador considered returning to England then. Encouraged to stay, young Samuel spent the next decade or so being tutored in the evenings but his father insisted he be educated in the Russian schools as well. By the time he was fifteen,

Samuel was very fluent in both Russian and English, being an extremely bright and intelligent lad.

"When the elder MacDougald decided to win the love of the young lady from Tennessee, he resigned his position and emigrated, along with his teen-aged son, *and*." He emphasized the 'and' and stopped for a moment, taking a drink from the cup Sophie had set on the table next to him. Johnny and I looked at our cups, which were still three quarters full and no longer steaming. Sophie came over.

"Do you gentlemen need a freshen up?" she asked.

"No, ma'am," Johnny and I said at the same time, as we looked at Bill to continue, even though we thought we knew this part of the story. Some of it, any way.

Bill stood. "Forgive me, gentlemen. But nature has called, and I must respond." He went back down the hallway. Johnny and I sipped our coffee, now lukewarm but still delicious. Sophie got up and started, but I waved her to sit back down.

"We're fine, really. Thank you," I assured her.

Bill returned after a short time, and sat back down. He was silent for a moment as he collected his thoughts. "So sorry, so sorry," he started. "I had to search this old brain to remember where I was in the story. It has been years since I have even thought about it. My father has been gone for over twenty years, you see." He took a sip of his drink.

"Anyway, you see, the ambassador, or whatever his title was, had, in his personal employ, a Russian peasant woman named Olga who was their housekeeper as well as nanny to young Samuel. When they came to the United States, Olga came with them. She had learned some English during her employ, but Samuel could converse with her fluently in Russian. She remained Duncan's housekeeper after moving here. But, as for Samuel." He stopped, took another sip, and stretched. "Please forgive me. As for Samuel, the schools here were a bit different than he was accustomed to, and he was placed in the eighth grade. The first year was slightly difficult, but he quickly caught on, and by the time he reached senior year he was making straight A's and was captain of the football, baseball, and basketball teams. Of course, he was a bit older than his classmates, but that wasn't his fault. He received a general scholarship to Vanderbilt, and that is where he made the acquaintance of our Miss Snow.

"They dated a few times, but nothing ever bloomed from it. But what stuck in the mind of Miss Snow, however, was a spring break trip in which she accompanied Samuel to his home. She was astonished to hear him conversing in Russian with the housekeeper. So it was, several years later, that upon her recommendation to Mr. Sloan that Southern Middle Tennessee made contact with Mr. MacDougald, and it was a match from the start. So that is how it happened that SMT had the only university level Russian language program in the entire Southeast."

"Wow," I said. "How can you possibly remember all this?"

"As I told Mr., um, Johnny, on the phone. My father took this course, and talked about it to my mother and I, as well as anyone else who would listen. But we are only scratching the surface of the things I have to tell you."

He looked at Sophie, and at his watch. "We are having chili and grilled cheese sandwiches for lunch. We have more than enough if you would care to join us. My Sophie makes the best chili east of the Mississippi."

"That sounds terrific." I nodded at Johnny. "I need to make a couple of calls anyway." I stood, pulling out my phone.

"Yes, by all means. You may sit out on the back porch if you wish. We have a wonderful view of the forest." Bill nodded toward Johnny and looked at the open photo album on the table. Johnny was up like a shot.

"Yes, I would love to look at them."

I went out back and called Eddie to check on things at the park. He said he had some chicken on the grill, and that Howard and Indie had gotten into a tussle the night before, then disappeared into his trailer, where Indie stayed all night. "So, a typical Thursday night," I laughed.

Next I called Hector, who informed me that Darcy had accidentally flushed her underwear and backed up the toilet, but he had everything flowing. He asked how Lucille was doing, I replied, "You know Lucille."

He laughed out loud at that. "*Si señor*. I am well acquainted with that *mamacita*" At that I chuckled and signed off.

I rang Janie and asked how her excursion was going.

"We are having so much fun. This riverwalk area has some great shops. Lucille even found some sort of an occult super shop or something. She is still in there and it's been over an hour! I'm sure we will be seeing her in some new high priestess garb." I laughed and told her to have lots of fun, and don't be in any hurry.

"We are getting into some deep water over here." I said.

"Well, just so you know," she said ominously. "We have been talking about you." I closed my eyes and shook my head.

"Please don't ruin your time talking about me. Enjoy yourselves and spend lots of money."

I came back in to find the table set with four bowls of steaming chili and a platter full of grilled cheese sandwiches. Sophie said to have a seat, and called the other two to the table. It was the best chili I had ever tasted, hands down. I looked at our hostess.

"I seriously doubt there is anything this good west of the Mississippi, either."

"You are too kind. It is an old family recipe that has been passed down through the centuries using an extremely selective process. There exists only one written copy, on a parchment scroll, and it is in a triple locked safe in a small European country with round the clock armed security."

I smiled at the grinning woman with the sparkling brown eyes. I supposed there was a good deal more to Mrs. Oglesby than I first imagined, as well.

We finished the meal, and I asked if I could help with the dishes.

"Absolutely not. Get in there for the rest of the story while Bill has his wind up."

I looked at her inquisitively. "He's had two heart surgeries. He does very well, but in short increments. I wasn't kidding when I said he has been waiting for decades for someone to show up asking about Nicky the Russian. You have no idea how thrilling this is for us." I looked over at the nice old gentleman, who was sitting next to Johnny on the sofa. He motioned me over to sit next to him. He had the photo album in his lap.

"This is my Dad," He said proudly, pointing to a picture. He flipped a few pages and stopped on a page with an open trifold flier, like you would see in a medical office encouraging you to try the latest expensive drug. It was an advert for SMTSU, which was very worn, and proclaiming that they were now teaching Russian, which was written in English as well as Russian. He flipped back to a picture with his father and a thin fellow with baggy clothes, holding a duffel bag. Even through the expanse of time, and the faded picture probably taken with a cheap camera, the eyes of the skinny fellow pierced into our souls.

"This is my father and Nikolo, later called Nicky. Taken the day after they met." I looked over at Johnny and noted his eyes were beginning to water. I looked back at the old photograph.

"Is that?" I started. "No, it can't be." I looked closer. Johnny pulled his magnifying glass out of his inner jacket pocket.

"Look at the lock." He held the glass over the bag so I could see it. It had a squared off hasp and an octagonal shaped body.

"Oh my gosh!" I exclaimed, getting up and beginning to pace back and forth. "How in the world? I don't..." I was on the verge of hyperventilating. I was speechless. "I am speechless," I said as I sat back down, my heart beating about ninety miles an hour.

Bill closed the book and went back over to his chair. "The year was 1947. The university was on the quarter system then, three 11 week quarters with a two week break in between. They had a limited summer session, mostly make-up classes to get students back on track. Dad was in his second quarter of Junior year, about midway through. Also in his second quarter of Russian with the enigmatic Mr. MacDougald. The school had a lake on the back side of the property then. I think it has since been filled in and paved over to make room for the football complex. But in 1947 it was very picturesque, surrounded by woods and with a walking track around the entire circumference. It had many benches here and there, and a few little tables where students could do their homework, or just sit and watch the ducks and other water activities." He paused, taking a sip of his drink.

"And, as you can well imagine, it was also a very popular make-out spot. Dad had begun to see a young lady in his Russian class." He pointed to a picture of a smiling older couple on the wall. "My mother, Ellen."

He smiled then, and as I studied his face as he looked at his parents on the wall, I could see in his eyes a glimpse of the younger, dashing man he had been.

He gathered his thoughts and continued. "Mom and Dad were walking around the lake one afternoon around four o'clock. It was mid January, which around here can be very temperate. It was a nice day and they sat on a bench to study. Suddenly Dad heard a rustling sound from the woods behind them and a voice. He turned to see a very disheveled looking hobo peeking from around a tree. He did not feel the least bit threatened, something about the man's eyes, he always said. Instead, his thought was how long the man must have been in the woods, he has to be starving. Dad scooted over to make room, and motioned for the haggard gentleman to join him on the bench. The man shuffled over and sat. Dad spoke to him, but the man only looked at him. Then he reached into his pocket and pulled out a flier. The same flier in the photo album. He pointed to the Russian words written on the flier and then to himself.

"My father, who knew a few words and phrases but could never get a full grasp of the language; he was a solid 'C' student in most things, you see. And this class was no exception."

"It is a well known fact that the world is run by C students." Johnny interjected as Bill took a sip of water. A moment passed, and he continued.

"Yes, he got enough of it to pass, but that was about it. My mother had a better understanding than he, however. She asked him if he could speak any English. "Fish Stew, Hamburger, Coke." She asked him if that was all, and he just nodded.

"Dad was perplexed, sure that Mr. MacDougald had gone for the day. He felt that the man couldn't stay out there and they couldn't just take him with them. He looked at the glossary in his textbook, took off his jacket and offered it to the bedraggled Russian. The man shook his head and disappeared back into the woods and returned with a blanket. He said something that Mom was able to decipher.

"I am from Russia. This is like summer to me."

"Dad found the words in his book, and told the man to meet him at that very bench in the morning."

Bill stopped then, and took a folder out of the box and laid it on the table. "I'm almost finished, but first I must answer the call of nature again."

Johnny and I looked at each other like two children on Christmas morning. Sophie spoke up. "We have a guest bath over by the stairs." I thought I could add mind-reading to her list of talents. I thanked her and walked over to the door. When I came out Johnny was waiting and went right in after me. Bill had not returned when I sat back down on the sofa. My head was spinning; I had a thousand questions about this duffel bag and the man it belonged to. Number one: How in the world did it end up in my lake?

Bill returned about the same time Johnny came out of the bathroom. "Whew," he said. "I haven't talked this much since I don't know when." He stretched, sat in his chair and opened the folder. "The next morning Dad caught Mr. MacDougald as he was getting out of his car and convinced him to follow him down to the lake. They got to the same bench Dad had sat on the previous evening, and Dad began saying 'Hey,' gradually getting a little louder. After a few minutes, they had gotten no response and were about to give up when they heard a rustle from the woods. They both turned to gaze at the haggard figure peering at them from the edge of the woods. Nikolo emerged and sat down on the bench, next to Samuel MacDougald, who began speaking to him in Russian. Nikolo's countenance changed immediately, as he became quite animated. Tears streamed down his face as he embraced the professor."

Bill pulled a sheaf of paper from the folder, about a hundred pages worth from the looks of it, and held it out to Johnny. He took it and looked at Bill.

"Gentlemen, I apologize, but I can say no more. The rest of the story is here, in my father's memoirs." I glanced out the window and saw that the day was almost gone. We had been there more than eight hours!

Johnny asked him, "Bill, will you trust us to take this back to the hotel and make copies? I will gladly leave you $1000 as collateral."

"That will not be necessary. Take it, make as many copies as you want, and return it at your leisure. I do ask one thing, however." He nodded at Sophie. She came over with a document and a pen. The document stated that if any part of the memoirs of William Oglesby, Sr. were published, or cited in any other publication, that Bill would receive credit for the content and 10% of all profits. Johnny couldn't sign it fast enough, and handed me the pen to sign as well.

Johnny and I were mostly silent on the drive back to the Sheraton. The clerk at the desk pointed to a room past the elevators marked *Media*. "Just scan your room key," the clerk said. "And you can make all the copies you want. Let me know if it runs out of paper. It will charge your room a nickel per page." I looked at the stack of paper and figured we had about five dollars worth. What a bargain, I thought to myself.

We made the copies and went to the elevators just as Janie and Lucille breezed back in, overloaded with boxes and bags. Janie saw me and laughed. "There are this many more in the van." she said breathlessly as we piled into the elevator.

Room service that night was chicken alfredo with garlic toast and Caesar salad. And, of course, the obligatory six pack along with a large bottle of Coke. I also asked for a replacement for the ice bucket. I rinsed ours out and sat it outside the door.

The girls excitedly showed off their finds: Various tie dyes, ribbons, sandals, dresses, etc. for Janie; Wizard clothes, naturally, for Lucille, along with various wraps and shawls, incense, and new-agey looking occult stuff.

"I don't know where we will put all these new things," Lucille stated. "I suppose some stuff will have to be thrown away." Janie nodded; the facts of life when you live in tiny spaces.

The food arrived, with another large tip from Johnny. We ate until we were full. Finally Janie said, "Well, did you boys find out anything?"

Johnny said, "You start, Michael, while I take care of business in the shower. I'm sure I am quite gamy by now." He held out his hand and Lucille tossed him the van key. I began to tell the story as he went to get his suitcase.

Johnny came out of the shower wearing khakis and a polo shirt, which for me is dressing up, but for the dapper old professor is dressing down. He sat down with the papers in hand and started reading.

William Etheredge

Nikolo

"Full reverse, full reverse!" came the frantic call from the bridge. The submarine shuddered then came to a stop. Nikolo and his mates in the engine room were slammed against the bulkheads, holding on to the grab rings in the ceiling for dear life. Nikolo thought to himself "This is it. This is the day I die." He held on as the boat started moving the other direction. "And for what."

Nikolo was a gentle, peaceful person. He had been a graduate student in St. Petersburg University and had planned to go to medical school so he could go back home and help the people in his village. Then the war came to Russia, and he was conscripted into the Russian Navy as an engineer, as that had been his undergraduate major.

The sub suddenly rocked back and forth. Nikolo held on until the swaying stopped. The sounds of shouting and alarms blaring were deafening. He said to himself, "I am prepared for this. I know what I must do." He had worn his inflatable vest under his work clothes every day, in spite of the uncomfortableness of it. "Yes, it is hot," he would think, but so what. It may keep him off the bottom of the ocean. He had kept his bag packed; the important stuff waterproofed. He had maneuvered his quarters until he had the state room closest to the torpedo tubes. He looked around the engine room and saw all he needed to see. Water was building up in the bilge, and bubbling up through the grating in the deck. He abandoned his post as the speaker blared "GENERAL QUARTERS, GENERAL QUARTERS. ALL HANDS TO BATTLE STATIONS!"

The boat started rocking again, more severely this time. Nikolo struggled up the ladder. His room was just on the next deck. He made it there and grabbed his seabag, heading for the torpedo room. He went from tube to tube until he found an empty one. He struggled over to the equipment room and found one of the little compressed air modules. He put it between his teeth and bit down, feeling the air enter his mouth. Good. He said a prayer then, and thought of Iliana, whom he had not spoken to in over a year. He removed his overshirt, inspected his vest, and went back to the torpedo tube. He was walking the narrow passageway like a drunken sailor staggering back to the ship after the club had closed, the boat was rocking so badly.

He had rehearsed the next steps in his mind at least a dozen times. All he had to do was hold on and withstand the pressure from the rush of water into the tube when he opened the outer hatch. It should only last about 3 seconds, and he could float out with the air bubble. He took a deep breath and entered the tube, closing the inner hatch behind him. Just then another depth charge exploded, seeming to stand the submarine on its end and slamming him back against the hatch. He made his way to the end of the tube, looped his arm through the straps of his seabag, and put his hand on the inflation pull of his vest. He made sure he had a good clamp on the small air tank in his mouth. He slowly began to turn the wheel that would release the outer hatch, noting where he had to be when it slammed open. One more turn would be the point of no return, as water began to spew in through the small crack. He popped his ears several times to equalize the pressure, which was increasing rapidly. He closed his eyes and lowered his head, protecting his mouth. He tightened his grip on the wheel. It was now or never.

He made the final turn. The hatch slammed open so hard it wrenched his wrist, hard, but he held on as he felt the bones crunch in his wrist. The water pressure yanked his shoulder out of socket, but he held on to his bag. Then all at once the air was forced out of the tube and he was catapulted out into the icy depths of the North Atlantic Ocean, tumbling end over end. His left wrist and right shoulder were screaming in pain, but he did not lose consciousness. He knew he had to find the rope with the wooden peg tied to the end so he could inflate his vest. He briefly chastised himself for not doing that before he opened the hatch. He felt around the bottom of his vest until he found it and pulled. Nothing happened. He bit down on his air tank and took a deep breath.

Don't panic! Grip it again and pull down steady and hard. He snaked his right hand down, shoulder grinding and sending flashes of light into his vision, threatening to pull him into unconsciousness. The pain was excruciating. He got his right hand on the rope and pulled toward his feet, giving it all he had and wanting to scream, but knowing if he did he would lose his air. Finally the rope gave with a pop and the vest filled with air. He could feel himself rising. He blew out a bubble and watched as it hovered in front of his eyes. *Too fast. I will get the bends if I don't slow down.* He remembered his training, and adjusted the ballast on his vest. The bubble zipped upward. He recited the Motherland Creed to himself and released the ballast, He counted *one Siberia, two Siberia,* all the way up to fifteen, trimmed the ballast again, and stopped. He took a breath and popped out another bubble, watching it float upward.

He heard another concussive blast that rattled him, but it seemed far away. He had no idea how far it was to the surface, or what he would find once he got there. He went through his routine and slowly continued upward.

He knew it had been late afternoon when he had started his watch, so it had to be night by now. He went through his repetitions and made it to eight Siberia just as the air in his mouth tube gave out, and his head broke through the surface of the water. The darkness was complete. It was a cloudy night, and there was no sound but the water sloshing against his head, the weight of his pack kept him submerged up to his chin, but no way he was letting it go now. He switched it to his left arm to give his aching shoulder a rest.

Just then he noticed how cold the water was, even this late in the spring. He did not know his position or what he was going to do next, but he was alive. That was what counted. He closed his eyes and stayed still, finding his balance with the neck support on his vest. He must have slept; when he opened his eyes, dawn was beginning to break to his right. He knew Europe was that direction, but he was sure he was much closer to North America. He turned away from the sun and looked, but could see nothing but endless ocean. He floated, thinking about his Iliana, hoping she had waited for him, wondering if it would matter. He pushed the negative thoughts away. He had made it this far; he would make it all the way. He floated all that day until the sun sat in the west. He had seen no sign of the ship that had sent the charges that sunk his submarine. His vest was holding up, keeping his head above water. He could not feel much of his extremities, but continued to float through the night and the next day.

Finally, on his third day at sea, he thought he saw a bump on the horizon to the west. His luck held, as he caught sight of something floating in the water to his right, he struggled to get to it, using the last of his meager supply of energy. Finally reaching the object, he found it was a large plastic tank covered in a net, bobbing in the water. He climbed and pulled, able to get his upper torso onto the tank, with only his feet and legs in the water. He looked at his right shoulder and saw it out of the socket. Laying his bag on the flat surface of the tank, making sure it was secure, he cinched the pull cord from the vest through the net.

He raised his right arm, moving it as far in front of him as he could. He reached as far as he could reach with his aching left hand and, wrapping his fingers around his right tricep, sweat breaking on his brow as he huffed and puffed, pushing himself through the most excruciating pain imaginable, he yanked as hard as he could. The pain was like a shotgun blast. He screamed as loud as he could. Then, as fast as it came, it was gone. He looked at his shoulder, which now looked normal, and reached up, grabbing the net and pulling himself the rest of the way out of the water and up onto the bobbing tank. He curled into a fetal position, linking his arm through the strap of his bag, and slept.

Barely conscious three days later, dehydration almost ending him, he thought he was dreaming when he heard shouts. He couldn't raise his head or even a hand, but he did manage to lift a finger.

"He's alive!" came a shout, but Nikolo couldn't understand it. It was English.

They were fishermen out of Terence Bay, Nova Scotia. They managed to haul Nikolo and his bag onto their small boat and got him alert enough to swallow a mouthful of water. He coughed for a minute and a half, then fell still and silent. The fishermen feared him to be dead until, finally, he raised his hand a centimeter off the deck and barely moved his fingers. "Give him some more, Derek," one of them said. Derek raised Nikolo's head off the deck and put the jug to his lips. This time Nikolo took a gulp, and only coughed for thirty seconds. He opened his eyes and looked around. Derek handed him a small flask filled with some cheap Canadian whiskey. Nikolo smelled the flask, then poured some of the liquid into his mouth and sloshed it around a bit before he swallowed. Then he turned up the flask and coughed again. Derek snatched the flask from him.

"Go easy, eh. Think you better rest a bit and get yourself some warmth." One of the others had gotten a blanket and draped it over Nikolo, who was beginning to shiver. He slept, and when he awakened, he wasn't sure how long he had been out. He wasn't sure of anything. He was dry and warm, he knew that. The sun was beaming through the small porthole above his head. He sat up on the edge of the small cot he was lying on, and was glad to see his seabag on the floor next to him. He felt under his shirt; the key was still there, attached to the small chain he wore. He noticed his flotation vest had been removed, but that was okay with him. He would not be needing that anymore. He tried to stand up, but was quite unsteady so he sat back down.

He looked up at the porthole and saw the sun bobbing up and down. "I'm on a ship," he thought. He noticed a water jug on a small table above his bag. He took it and removed the lid and smelled the contents. Satisfied, he took a long gulp from it. His left wrist still pained him but not quite as badly. He was pleased to check his right shoulder and find it to be relatively pain free. He stood again and felt much better. He took a few steps and sat back down, thinking about what he had gone through the last day or so.

The door to the little room opened and a gruff bearded man came through it. "Oy! You're awake! You look like a man just back from the dead."

Nikolo just looked at him. He had no idea what the man was saying, and felt it wise to remain silent. The man rubbed his abdomen. "I bet you could stand a bite." He smacked his lips. Nikolo felt his stomach rumble, and rubbed it, nodding his head as he did.

The bearded man disappeared but soon returned with a steaming bowl of savory meat and vegetables. "Fish Stew," he stated.

Nikolo looked up at the man and took the bowl and the spoon.

"Feest tool," he said, tasting the hot liquid, then starting to shovel spoonfuls into his mouth.

"No, repeat after me." The man pointed at his mouth and said "Fish."

"Feest."

The fisherman shook his head. "Fish."

"Feess."

They continued this back and forth until Nikolo said the word correctly. As he polished off the bowl, he looked up at the bearded man, let out a loud belch, and let go with a string of Russian.

"Guess you like fish stew, huh."

Nikolo looked up, his chin dripping, and handed the bowl back to the man. "Fish Stew!" he announced.

The burly man left and came back with another bowlful and a shank of stale bread. Nikolo accepted the food gratefully and ate it all. As the burly man took the bowl back he looked at Nikolo and raised his eyebrows questioningly.

Nikolo shook his head and lay back, rubbing his stomach. He had no idea where he was or where his rescuers were from. His belly was full, he was alive, and things appeared to be okay so far.

Up on deck, the men were in deep conversation amongst themselves.

"Well, he must be a Russkie or a Polack according to that writing on the vest we took off 'im"

"So?" another one chimed in. "They're not at war with us, eh. He probably got blown out of a u-boat or something. He seems pretty harmless to me. Didn't have a knife or anything on him"

"Hell, he can help us clean fish until we get back to the island in a couple weeks. We can decide what to do with 'im then. Maybe you can take 'im home with you, Eddo, let 'im sleep in your barn." They all laughed at that.

Nikolo proved to be a welcome addition to the crew, not only cleaning fish, but helping with the nets as well. Eddo did let him stay in his barn and help with his cows when they weren't fishing. His wrist healed quickly from the protein-rich diet he found himself on; in addition to the fish Eddo also brought him hamburgers and cokes, prompting Nikolo to learn those words as well. The captain of the fishing boat put him on the payroll, and he was able to build up a little stash of cash.

One morning, as he arose from his sleeping pallet in the barn, he heard voices outside. He looked through the boards towards the house and saw two men in uniform talking to Eddo, the lights on the top of their patrol car visible behind them.

Nikolo panicked. "They have found me." he thought. "They will send me home to face the firing squad for desertion." He grabbed up his bag and fled out the back of the barn as Eddo's cousin and his partner followed Eddo into the house for the purpose of their visit: breakfast.

Nikolo had been with the fishing crew for about four months through the mild maritime summer, and had built up his strength considerably. He walked all day and all night and all the next day, until he reached the other side of the island and, as he stood in the shadows of late evening looking at the bridge to the mainland, he thought he would collapse if he tried to go any farther. Then he saw something that lifted his spirits: a blinking sign on the road past the bridge with a picture of a hamburger above it. "Hamboorgur!" he said out loud, and walked out of the shadows toward the diner, his fear of being captured pushed to the back of his mind.

As he entered the nearly empty diner the lone waitress waved her hand and said "Sit anywhere you like." Nikolo was confused but found a booth and sat down. The waitress brought him a glass of water which he immediately drained. "I'll get you another. Do you need a menu?" She stood looking down at Nikolo, holding the empty glass.

He looked up at her. "Hamboorgur, coke."

"You want that all the way, and with French fries, hon?"

"Hamboorgur, coke."

"Got it." She popped her gum at him and spun around. She brought him another glass of water and sat a pitcher next to it. "Thirsty, huh?" she said as he downed the second glass. "Whatcha got in that bag?"

Nikolo looked up at her. "Hamboorgur, coke." he said, pulling a roll of bills out of his pocket.

She laughed. "Coming right up, hon. Ain't you just a hoot and a half." She walked over and leaned on the counter. "We got a live one over here, Danjo." The cooked smiled at her as he handed her the plate. She brought the plate over to Nikolo; the burger piled high with the works and a heaping mound of fries, along with a large glass of coke.

Nikolo devoured the burger in about four bites, and started shoving fries into his mouth. "Whoa, slow down! You look like you ain't ate in a week!"

He sucked down his coke and let out a big burp. Danjo looked around from the grill and grinned. "The sound of a satisfied customer if there ever was one!"

Nikolo picked up the roll of cash from the table and looked at the waitress. She came over and pulled a couple of bills off and wrapped his hand around the rest. "Thanks for the tip sweetheart." she said to him as he stuck the roll back into his pocket. He got up, grabbed his bag and headed for the door, letting rip with another window-rattling belch.

"Must be some kind of retard or something," Lindy the waitress said to Danjo the cook.

Nikolo walked across the bridge and kept walking, day after day. He had no idea where he was or where he was going. Instinct told him to head south and stay off the roads; the nights were beginning to get cooler and he knew winter wasn't far off. He passed by a beautiful waterfall and stopped to admire it for a few minutes before continuing on, staying to the woods far away from the roads. He realized it had been a long time since he had heard a car, but he kept going until he finally found a small path going south.

He got on the path and occasionally his hyper awareness would lead him to a small creek, and he would cook fish he caught with his net. His supply of matches was beginning to dwindle, however, and as he rounded a curve one afternoon he was startled when an older blond man stepped out of a thick stand of pine trees. The two men stood looking at each other. Nikolo noticed in front of him a little ways down the path was a small fire. The man said "Damn, buddy. You scared the living shit out of me. Where the dickens did you come from?"

Nikolo, wide-eyed, took a step backward. "Hey, its okay. You're safe." The man held his hands up, palms facing Nikolo. Nikolo let out a breath, dropped his bag beside the fire, and sat on it. The blond-haired man looked at Nikolo then, at the burrs in his hair and embedded in his clothes along with several sticks and twigs. He was dirty and had a reek to him that furled the man's nose. "Damn, boy. You look fit to be tied. You must be hungry as hell." The blond man patted his stomach.

"Hamboorgur, coke." Nikolo croaked. It had been a while since he had spoken, and his mouth was dry.

"Well, we ain't got that on the menu here at Chez Bobby, but I can share my venison jerky with ya." He handed Nikolo a hunk of jerky. "I was just about to cook up some beans, which you are welcome to as well."

Nikolo chewed the jerky and watched as Bobby opened the can of beans and sat it on a flat rock near the fire. As soon as they started steaming Bobby donned a thick glove and lifted the can, digging some beans out with a spoon. He took a few bites and handed the can over to Nikolo. "It should be cooled off enough for you to handle." he said. Nikolo took the can and spooned some of the beans into his mouth. He nodded then wolfed down the rest of them. Nikolo slid his bag a little closer to the fire, curled up with his head resting on the bag, and was asleep before he took three breaths.

It was dark when he awakened to Bobby kicking his feet. He snapped awake and sat up. "I don't know who you are or where you come from, but dawn is around the corner and I'm bugging out. You are welcome to walk with me if you want." With that Bobby produced a small spade. Nikolo recoiled. Bobby laughed and started shoveling dirt onto the fire. Nikolo stood and Bobby handed him the jug of water. Nikolo grabbed it, removed the lid, and started guzzling, like he was trying to suck the bottom out of the jug. Bobby snatched it from him. "Whoa there, Hoss. That's gotta last us til we get to the creek."

Pushing his hair back, Bobby took off walking down the trail. Nikolo scrambled to his feet, grabbed his bag, and followed after him. Bobby had set some traps on the way up and checked them on the way back south. The two travelers dined on a diet of squirrel, raccoon, possum, rabbit, and gopher, which Nikolo learned to skin and spit. Although the two couldn't communicate with words, they got along swimmingly and complemented each other until finally, after about four weeks of walking, Bobby said "This is where I get off the trail. My sister is coming to get me as soon as I call her. I am ready to get home, and she will have a fit if I try to bring home a stray."

He shook hands with Nikolo and disappeared into the tourist station. Nikolo slowly entered the building and looked around. After locating and utilizing the men's room, he did a little exploring around the center and found a large display of tourist fliers and pamphlets, touting local attractions and other regional locations. He picked up a sample of each one, having no clue what the words meant. *See Rock City, Biltmore House,* and *Ruby Falls* had no meaning for him. Finally reaching the bottom row, he felt the first ray of hope he had felt in months. It was an advertisement for the Southern Middle Tennessee State University. When he opened the first flap, he almost began to cry when he saw words written in Russian. He had to find out what this place was.

He had been away from the fishermen long enough and had gotten so far from them he felt safe being back among civilization. The next several days, however, were rather harrowing for him. He still tried to stay away from major thoroughfares, but had no idea where to go. He just kept walking, occasionally seeing police cars driving fast with their lights flashing and sirens blaring, sending him scurrying into the woods.

He came out of the woods one day to find a young man leaned into the open hood of a pickup truck. He tried to walk past him, but the young man jumped down and ran in front of him.

"Hey Buddy! Do you know anything about a Ford truck engine?" the fellow said, gesturing back to his truck. "It quit on me and I can't get it to start back." He pulled Nikolo along back to the truck. He jumped into the seat and turned the key. The engine spun once, then disconnected, giving a loud roar as the pitch decreased. Nikolo looked into the engine well. He grabbed a wrench off the front bumper and leaned way into the truck's engine compartment. He tapped the engine starter hard with the wrench, and looked back at the young fellow, motioning to him to turn the key again. The engine caught this time and roared to life.

"Hot Damn!" the young man whooped. "That is amazing!" He slammed the hood shut and grabbed Nikolo by the hand. "Let me give you a ride. Where you going?" Nikolo just stared at the fellow.

"Dang, you can't speak, can you? Well, don't that just beat all I've ever seen." He gestured down the road and pantomimed turning the steering wheel, then pointed to Nikolo and back to the truck. Nikolo's eyes lit up, and he smiled, reaching into the back pocket of his dirty and nearly threadbare dungarees and pulling out the flier for SMTSU. He pointed at the picture of the college, and opened the flap and pointed at the Russian sentence printed on it, and spoke to the man in his native language. Smiling, the young man nodded. "So, you're a Russian! And, you want to go to Chattanooga to SMT. That is a pretty good ride, you got some money for gas?" He rubbed his thumb and forefingers together, in the apparently universal symbol for cash. Nikolo knew immediately what the young man was asking him, and pulled the wad of bills out of his pocket. Nikolo was no dummy, and had stashed rolls of cash in several different places on his person and in his bag. The truck man took the roll Nikolo offered him and unrolled it.

"Canadian, huh. Damn if this day don't just keep getting more interesting by the minute. They's about fifty dollars in here, I'm not sure how much that is in American money, but it should be enough. Let's go find out." He snatched up Nikolo's bag and tossed it into the back of the truck. "Damn, you got a house in there or something? Dang thing must weigh a hunnerd pounds." He clapped Nikolo on the shoulder and said "Let's ride, Clyde." Walking to the driver's seat, the man saw Nikolo head to the back and jump in beside his bag.

"No. Up here with me." The young man shook his head and pointed to the passenger seat. When Nikolo still didn't seem to get it, he went around and opened the passenger side door, gesturing to Nikolo to get in. Nikolo nodded finally, jumped down, and got into the cab.

They drove down a dirt road for a while then on a gravel road, and ultimately smooth black top. Along the way the young man got Nikolo to say his name, Randall, and Randall learned his passenger was Nikolo.

"Russian, eh?

"Da, Rooshka" Nikolo answered.

"Well, it don't make no never mind to me. You are A-OK in my book." Randall pulled into the parking lot of the Sevierville First National Bank. Nikolo looked frightened by the official-looking edifice, and slunk down in the seat. Randall held out the money, and said "Relax. They can exchange it for real money in here." Nikolo stared out the window. "Just stay put." Randall patted the seat and hopped out of the truck and sauntered into the bank.

A few minutes later Randall came out of the bank and got into the truck, and counted out the green paper money on the seat between himself and his passenger. Nikolo didn't understand what had happened, but when Randall tried to start the truck the starter ground again and let out a high pitched whine. "Show me what you did," Randall started, but Nikolo was already out of the truck with the big wrench in his hand. Randall opened the hood, and looked quizzically at Nikolo, who took the bait and pointed at the starter and looked at Randall, who nodded. He leaned in and reached way down and gave the starter a couple of hard whacks with the wrench. He nodded at Randall, who jumped in the truck and fired it up. Nikolo closed the hood and got back into the truck, smiling.

Randall handed the stack of bills over to Nikolo. "Here's your money. We're fixing to need some gas though, so I will need some of it back." They pulled into a Texaco station and Randall leaned out the window and hollered to the attendant, "Fill 'er up!" The attendant did, and came up to the window after cleaning the windshield.

"That'll be seven bucks and a quarter."

Randall held his hand out to Nikolo, who just looked at it. Randall rubbed his thumb and fingers together. He understood then and handed the money back. Randall pulled a tenner out of the stack and paid the attendant, who gave him back his change. Randall handed it back to Nikolo, who was very confused. He didn't know why the man kept taking his money and giving it back to him.

The rest of the ride passed without incident. Nikolo kept looking at the flier, wondering what awaited him at their destination. The Cyrillic symbols on the flier only said *Learn a New Language* so he supposed he was headed for some sort of indoctrination center or school. Finally, after a few more stops for food and gas, Randall pulled onto the SMTSU campus. Nikolo looked from the flier to the sign. He looked over at Randall, then at all the people milling about on campus on the late fall afternoon.

"Oh, I get it. You must be looking for someone and don't want to be seen walking around!" He pulled onto the campus and went around a loop that circled around all the buildings, until he finally got near a lake which lay at the edge of a forest. He pulled the truck into a parking spot. Nikolo was way ahead of him. He had been on high alert as soon as they had entered the campus, and he jumped out, grabbed his bag out of the back and headed for the woods. Randall stood there, arms akimbo and mouth agape, finally shaking his head and saying, "Damnedest thing I ever seen!" as he climbed back into the truck.

It would be a couple of days before Bill Oglesby, Sr. happened by, and Samuel McDougald ended up taking Nikolo home with him, where he stayed for the next two years. Samuel taught him passable English and helped him with all the news he could find about Russia. Nikolo determined that the war ended very soon after his boat was sunk, and he was sure if he showed up in Russia now he would surely face a firing squad for desertion. Samuel's father, now considerably up in age, and Olga, older as well but still the picture of health, lived nearby. Working in tandem, they created a new identity for Nikolo, and tried, unsuccessfully, to locate Iliana, as Stalin had locked down communications into and out of the new Soviet Union.

Duncan McDougald called on an old friend who had a sizable sheep farm in Scotland who was willing to take in Nicky Solara, and help him find his Iliana, while Nicky learned sheep farming. They found a private pilot in Chattanooga who had his own plane, and could make it to Scotland with a couple of refueling stops, who agreed to fly Nicky to a private airstrip in Scotland. The last they saw of Nicky Solara was him getting on that plane and disappearing into the bright blue Tennessee sky.

William Etheredge

Everyone sat in stunned silence around the ring as Johnny finished the tale. Even Chad and Darcy, who hadn't popped her gum once. We had gotten back to the camp late and tired Saturday night after taking Bill's memoir back, and lingering for an amazing Sophie breakfast of country culinary delights. Biscuits that melted in your mouth. They were both charmed to no end by our female companions, asking questions of them, how they came to live in an RV park and such. Janie and Sophie turned out to have much in common, as Sophie had also been a nurse, as well as a stage singer and dancer at the Grand Ole Opry. Her eyes glittered as she related her story, and Bill beamed as well.

I knew she was more than just a simple housewife!

She and Janie had lot to talk about, and it was afternoon when we pulled out, my Moto leading the way.

Sunday had dawned bright and cool, and we had a special breakfast at the ring: Grilled sausage, egg, and cheese burritos, courtesy of Eddie and Mary Beth.

After Johnny's story of Nikolo/Nicky, Darcy actually hopped down and helped Mary Beth gather up the dishes. Howard said, "Wow. There is a whole concept album here." He tapped Johnny's folder. "It'll be bigger than Tommy!" he boasted.

Slowly everyone moseyed back to their respective homes. Everyone, that is, except Indie. She sat in her customary spot, staring straight in front of herself, at nothing. Conspicuously absent was her laptop. For all the years she had been vacationing or retreating here, I had never seen her without it.

She caught my eye, and, as if she could read my mind, said, "I finished it."

"Really?" I walked over and gave her a big hug. "Now what?"

"Now I need to find an editor and an agent, preferably one who has contacts with a reputable publishing house." She took my hand

and led me up to the lake front and stood, looking at the sun reflecting off the tiny ripples. "I will be going home in a couple of weeks. When I do get published, I am dedicating my book to you and the people of the Tiwanawiki RV park. I'm not sure if I will be back."

"What about Howard?" I asked, genuinely curious.

"Oh, Howard," she grinned. "He is a one of a kind." She had a mischievous grin on her face as she turned and headed down the little ridge going to her camper. I watched her step down the hill and suddenly had an image of two basketballs bouncing in a net bag.

"You are going straight to hell, Mikey ole boy." I thought to myself and chuckled a bit as I looked back out over the lake.

"Hey!" It was Indie, coming fast up the hill, curves bouncing. I was afraid she was going to give herself a black eye.

"I just had an epiphany. My next book. Fiction based on the true story of the wandering duffel bag." She had me by the arms. "I want you to give me exclusive rights to write the story!"

"I see no problem with that, whatsoever." I smiled as she let me go and went skipping away. Actually skipping. I wondered how hard basketballs had to hit each other before one of them burst. I laughed and went back down to the ring.

Howard had brought out his bass and strummed on it. He sang

"Nicky was a young man."

"Sounds like the next hit," I said. He nodded, and scribbled on his notepad. Hector came around the shed just then and motioned me to follow.

"I couldn't tell you this last night, bossman," he started as we walked around my digs. I saw the truck with the hood open. We reached the front and Hector produced a flashlight. He pointed with a stick to a spot under the left valve cover of the big V-8.

"What am I looking at, Hector?" I couldn't see anything odd.

"Come around over here and get your head down there, right where the stick is." I saw it then. A crack in the block and the tip of a piece of metal sticking out.

"*El Fordo esta muerte,*" he said. Yep, old Betsy had finally bitten the dust. I knew a new motor would most likely cost way more than the truck was worth, but it had been my Daddy's truck, and it was hard to let go.

Janie sidled up beside me, handing me an ice cold sugar free Red Bull. "I figured it was too early for *you* for the hard stuff," she grinned, holding up a frosty long neck. "Not for me, of course. It is currently five o'clock in Khartoum, so here's to all those slaves who built the pyramids!" We clinked our containers together.

"So, what are you two hunky fuckers looking at?" Hector shook his head, crossed his chest with his right hand, and looked toward the heavens.

"Betsy finally gave up the ghost, eh? Good. I hated riding in that smelly old bitch. I always smell like grease and armpits when I get out."

"You never ride with me in that truck." I told her.

"For good reason!" she retorted. "But I will definitely ride in the new one."

"What new one?" I turned to face her head on. I had actually already decided to get one, but I was going to have a little fun with her.

"The one you are going to buy first thing in the morning. You are *not* going to pour any more money into this damned hunk of junk. You are rich as freakin Croesus, and besides," She grabbed my arm and pressed herself against me. "We need something comfortable to ride in when we go off on your little expeditions now. My butt is sore as shit after being on that big hog of yours all those hours."

"If you think you can persuade me to buy a new truck using wiles, then you have some learning to do about me, little lady."

"What wiles? I have no clue what you are talking about," she purred into my ear as her hand went under my shirt.

"Get a room already!" Hector said, as he walked towards the lake.

After I finished my morning rituals, I went into the office to enter the receipts from our trip. I had finished the Red Bull, and walked back into the rec room to grab a bottle of water. I glanced over at the pool table and said out loud, "I need to find a billiard service company to come clean this thing."

I sat back down at the desk, opened a web browser, and began looking at trucks. I heard a high pitched engine whine and looked out the window in time to see Chad and Darcy go by on their crotch rocket, Darcy's legs straight out and her hands up in the air.

"Damn, be careful girl," I said, to no one. She certainly didn't need a head injury to deal with.

The rest of the day went by in typical fashion. The entire park was out for the sunset, and the ring was abuzz as Eddie and Mary Beth served hamburgers. Even Johnny and Lucille had grabbed a log. Chad and Darcy perched on the picnic table, as usual, watching the rest of us and poking each other. It was odd to see Indie without her laptop.

Howard brought out his bass and began chording it, and sang the ballad of Nikolo. Janie jumped up, went into her house, and came out with her mandolin and accompanied him, joining in harmony on the chorus. We all clapped and whistled when they were finished.

Chad stood abruptly. "Wait just a damn minute." he said loudly. Everyone fell ominously silent as Chad verbalized the question that had been niggling at the back of my mind, and I'm sure I wasn't the only one. "That is a whale of a damn story. But you still haven't figured out how the bag got in the friggin lake." He pointed at the now darkened lake behind him. For whatever reason, everyone, myself included, looked at Johnny.

"That, my good man, is the $64,000 question," the professor muttered. "There is one more mountain yet to climb." He said no more.

Monday opened with Hector checking his jugs and me doing my rituals. I called him over and said, "Grab your helmet," as I took the cover off Moto. We rode into the big city of Asheville and went to the largest truck dealer we could find. I gave Hector carte blanche in picking out the truck he felt would be best for the park. He followed me back to the park after I had signed all the requisite paperwork, and gotten a cashier's check sent over from the bank.

Everyone at the park except Johnny came to see what all the ruckus was, as Hector and I did a couple of loops around with the engines revving and horns blaring. Hector finally pulled up at the ring and hopped out, leaving it running. Janie squealed, "You actually bought this?" She smacked Hector on the arm. "How on earth did you get this world renowned tightwad to come off the hip for this?" She was running her hand along the smooth, flat military gray paint. She was about to have a meltdown. "Four doors? Huge knobby tires? A big roll bar with floodlights pointing in both directions and a winch on the front? Oh my goodness, I love this!" She clutched at me and shook.

"Thank Hector. He picked it out." She looked over at the ole fisherman and gave him two thumbs up. "But you haven't seen the best part yet." I went over to the tailgate and opened a secret compartment. I pulled a thumb drive out of my pocket and stuck it into the USB port and twisted a knob. Almost immediately the surrounding woods began to echo with the sound of *Godzilla*.

"Hell yes! That's what I'm talking about!' Howard jumped up, playing air guitar and banging his head.

After the song stopped, I turned it off and closed everything up. I held up an envelope. "This is definitely a write off." I proclaimed and headed for the office. Janie laughed her head off.

"Some things will never change." She swatted my rump as I passed by her.

Later I found Johnny in the shed, seemingly oblivious to what had been going on outside. He had a small filing cabinet, and was putting the contents of the duffel into labeled folders and organizing them in the cabinet. He had his phone and laptop on the table.

"What was all that about? It sounded like we were being invaded by a heavy metal band," he said, looking up. I told him about the truck. "Four door, you say? Well, I suppose we can break it in on our trip back to Chattanooga."

I looked at him for an explanation. He started, "You realize, of course, that after we found Mr. Oglesby, we stopped looking. We still have a lot to learn about the good Mr. MacDougald, and the archives may contain a clue or two." He stuck a folder into the cabinet and turned, placing his hands on the table. "We have only half the story, I intend to make it my life's work, if need be, to find the other half."

He held his magnifying glass in front of his right eye, making it appear comically large. "What says you to that?"

I looked at the professor and thought for a minute. "Okay, I'm game. What's the plan?"

Professor DeLaval looked like he was about to pee his pants when we crawled out of the truck Wednesday morning. We had left about 3am so we could make a day of it. The professor stuck his hand out to the shaggy Howard, who had insisted on coming along to help. DeLaval invited us all into the conference room and Johnny gave him a brief rundown of what we had learned so far.

"Well, that is very exciting indeed. I let Miss Stokes know you were coming back and she is expecting you."

Miss Stokes looked up when we entered the admin building. "I'm glad you came back to replace the boxes you left down last week." I looked at Johnny.

"Oops," he said. "I am terribly sorry Miss Stokes. I assure you it will never happen again."

She waved us away. "You know where you're going."

"Woman has the personality of a bowl full of ramen noodles," Lucille muttered as we walked down the hallway.

"So, what are we looking for again?" Howard asked as we entered the records room.

"WE'LL KNOW WHEN WE FIND IT!" everyone except Johnny shouted in unison, laughing. Johnny wasn't laughing, however.

"What we are looking for," he began, "is anything that will give us a clue to the whereabouts of one Samuel MacDougald, after his tenure here ended in 1950." He looked each of us in the eye. "And any mention of Nicky Solara."

"Okay, let's get to work then," I said. "We are burning daylight here."

Howard and I took down all the boxes that pertained to 1945 to 1952. There were 13 in all. Howard helped me replace the yearbook boxes, and we began the tedious process of pulling out each folder and examining every piece of paper in them. The folders were labeled by month, and contained class schedules, rosters, attendance sheets, and so on. After about four hours we had made little progress. Miss Stokes appeared. "The cafeteria will be closing in about 30 minutes. I thought you all may be getting a little hungry."

Janie looked over at Lucille, who thumped down the folder she was looking through and headed for the door. "Come along, my minions," she ordered.

Again, we blinked like moles emerging into the brightness of the outside world after spending hours in the tomb of the archives room. And, of course, Madame Lucille was mobbed when we entered the cafeteria. Howard looked a little confused. "It's a long story," Janie told him.

We ate our burgers and got up to leave. "Come along, Madame," I said. Lucille got up amid protests from her fans.

"Pleeeze come to Octoberfest!" one coed begged her.

"I shall try my best," Lucille assured her as she made her cards disappear somewhere in her garments. When we got outside, I asked her where she hid all that stuff. I regretted it as soon as the words escaped my lips. She stopped, whirled on me, held her arms out, and said "I'll give you twenty minutes to find them!" She was beaming like Arnie Grape.

I must have blushed. Janie, laughing, yanked my hand. "Come on, Shorty, before you bite off more than you can chew. We have work to do."

It was getting late as Howard and I replaced the boxes that had been thoroughly searched. There were only two boxes left to examine, and a feeling of tiredness and despair was beginning to creep into our group. So far we had only found routine clerical stuff with MacDougald's name. Janie stood and stretched, stating, "I need to stretch my legs a bit." She began walking around the room and down the aisles. She had been gone about ten minutes when she let out a yell.

"Hey, come check this out."

I looked until I found her in the far corner of the room, her phone torch shining on a group of dusty old boxes on the top shelf in the gloom, as the bulb was burnt out in that corner of the room.

"I can't read it," I said, and started to climb up the shelves.

Janie put her hand on my arm and said, "That's what they make those ladders for, super duper man." I shook the shaky shelf and said,

"Good call, Janie Lou."

I came back with the ladder, and took her phone light up with me. I immediately came down and handed her phone back to her. "Turn the light out and save your battery," I told her. I went back up and came down with a box. "Grab the cart over there," I motioned to Janie with my head. "This thing is blasted heavy."

I put the box on the cart and pushed it over to where the exasperated and dejected looking professor stood. "Move that crap out of the way," I told him, gesturing to the boxes and folders in front of him. He pushed them back and I sat my box down in front of him. I thought the old man was going to cry as he began to tremble after reading the writing on the side of the box.

>Faculty: 1936-1958

Johnny rubbed his hands over the top of the box as the girls began replacing the folders in the other two boxes. Howard and I took them back where they belonged as Johnny removed the top of the box and thumbed through the folders.

"They could have put them in alphabetical order," he mumbled, to no one in particular. Finally he let out an "Aha!" and pulled out a folder labeled,

>MacDougald, S.

In the folder were his personnel records, tax withholding slips, vacation requests, performance reviews, etc. There were two different addresses attributed to him, in different years. Occasionally Johnny would lay a page on the table and snap a photo.

"Look here," he said, pointing at a line on a page. A document with '1950' in the heading had a line that listed 'Emergency Contact,' and the name handwritten beside it was 'Olga Volkov,' with a phone number. Johnny snapped a picture and replaced it in the folder. He reached the end, clearly disappointed that we couldn't find more.

Howard had been steadily looking in the box while the rest of us were watching the professor look through the MacDougald folder. He tapped the dejected professor on the shoulder as he closed the folder. Johnny turned and looked at him, as Howard held another folder out to him.

"It was in the very back," he said sheepishly. Johnny looked at the tab and noted it, too, was labeled 'MacDougald, S.'

Johnny reverently opened the folder. It contained more of the same as the other, and we all began to share his let-down feeling. He removed each page from the folder until he finally lifted the last page, revealing an unopened, yellowed envelope. He picked it up and turned it over. Written on the front was:

>Macduggle
>SMTSU

USA

In the upper left corner:

> Solara
> Iverly
> Scotland

The envelope looked fairly thick.

"I need to sit down," Johnny said, weakly. In the gloom of the dim, dusty records room, of the Southern Middle Tennessee State University, it looked like all the color had drained from his face. Lucille was behind him in a flash with a chair, just as Miss Stokes popped her head in.

"Thirty minutes," she informed us, and closed the door. Johnny found his reserve strength and was up and out the door behind her, envelope in hand. The old glue crackled faintly but offered no resistance as Johnny slid his finger under the sealed edge, and pulled out a folded sheaf of paper, about 6-8 pages by the looks of it.

"I wonder if I could impose on you to make a copy of these documents, please," he asked, looking through them as he walked. "They appear to be written in Russian."

Johnny returned shortly with the letter and a stack of papers in his hand, He stuck the letter back into its folder and replaced it in the box. As Howard and I put the box back onto the cart and began to push it back to where it belonged, Johnny said, "I made three copies." The girls helped tidy the place and we were ready to go.

We exited into the unseasonably hot sun of an early October afternoon. The professor had sweet talked Miss Stokes into giving him a blank folder. It was obviously less than new, but served the purpose.

"This will have to be translated quickly," the professor said as we climbed into Godzilla, which Janie had christened the new truck. The name had caught on immediately. I liked it.

Howard convinced us to take a short detour on the way back, in Knoxville. His old road manager from the 80's had opened a theme restaurant in Nashville, and it had done so well he had opened a second one in Knoxville. Called *Paradise 57,* it featured an actual 1957 Chevrolet convertible parked facing the road, with

171

Laverne and Shirley look-alikes in the front seats, honking the horn and waving at cars as they drove past. The place was shaped like a big 'Y' with the long base of the 'Y' being the indoor, main restaurant. The forks of the 'Y' were for curb service, and had a circular riser in the middle. Wonderful old 50's rock and roll played loudly; the waitresses (dolls) wore pink poodle skirts and roller skates, the waiters (guys) had slicked back hair, jeans with the cuffs rolled up and white tee shirts with the sleeves also rolled up. Every so often a siren would go off and a DJ's voice would boom from the speakers that it was 'Time.' Then Chubby Checker would blast out *The Twist*, and the staff would all start dancing. Out at the 'Y' they would get up on the riser, and kids would jump out of the cars and dance with them.

We sat at a booth and had burgers, fries, and real fountain drinks. Johnny had a root beer float. There were album covers stuck on the walls from the era: Chuck Berry, Elvis, Jerry Reed, Duane Eddy. I loved it, along with everyone else.

"I love this place," Janie said breathlessly as she sat down after doing the twist for about three minutes.

"I must say," Johnny started. "The gimmick will get you here once, but it is the flavor and the size of these burgers that will have folks coming back for more. I give it five stars."

Howard, in obvious heaven in the back seat between the two dolls, started singing Elvis style as I hit the highway, but that didn't last long. With our bellies full and the smooth lull of the highway, by the time we pulled into the park, everyone but me was snoring. It was after midnight, and as the lights came on in the truck there were a few protests, but soon everyone staggered to their abodes to sleep the rest of the night.

The next morning I awakened after a strange dream about a Russian couple water-skiing behind a large boat that was really a truck. I shook my head and rubbed my eyes as I stumbled over to my coffee maker and looked out the window. This time, instead of seeing a raven-haired goddess emerging naked from the water, I saw that a gaggle of geese had taken residence on the ridge between Hector and Lucille. I chuckled to myself. "Folks will have to mind their step up there."

I pulled on my clothes and filled my insulated coffee mug, grabbed a cinnamon raisin bagel and headed outside. I did my morning walk-about, and noticed Eddie and Mary Beth out, enjoying their outdoor theater. Eddie motioned me over, as he hit the pause button.

"We are watching *Game of Thrones*. I don't know how we never watched it before. It is terrific."

Mary Beth said, "Tell him."

"I'm getting to it." He looked at me. "We're leaving."

I must have looked hurt. Mary Beth chimed in.

"Just for a couple of weeks." She elbowed Eddie in the gut. She was in her customary spot, on his lap.

Eddie stated, "We are going to hit Dragon Con in New Orleans in three weeks."

"You finally going to don plastic yellow aprons and gas masks, and be Walter and Jesse?" I asked, renewing an ongoing joke that never got old, for me anyway. The two lovebirds had never once taken the bait, however. They both just gave me blank stares,

"Have you really never seen *Breaking Bad*?"

Ignoring me, Eddie said, "I am dressing as Khal Drogo and Mary Beth will be Dany Targaryen."

"I've decided to show off my legs," Mary Beth said, opening her robe a little to reveal her scar-mapped left lower limb.

"You will be a shoo-in for first place," I told her. She smiled at that, and I was struck by what a beauty she still was.

"Everything here will be kept just like it is while you're gone," I assured them as I took my leave and wandered on. The park was otherwise quiet, only Hector was out, trolling the lake. As I found nothing that required my immediate attention, I decided to go back inside and put my feet up. I had just settled into a nice doze when I was startled awake by a tap on the door.

"Come on in. It's open," I yelled. Johnny walked in and took a seat on a kitchen stool.

"I have scanned the letter into my computer and emailed it to a lady named Sonia Godoranskaya, somewhere in New York. Professor DeLaval found and vetted her for me. She assured me she would have an accurate translation for me by next week. She adamantly assured me that she would adhere to the utmost discretion, regardless of what information is in the letter."

I thought that was a little extreme, but said only, "That sounds great. Hopefully it contains the key to the mystery."

Johnny had a pensive look. "It is amazing that the letter ever made it at all, the way it was addressed. Goes to show you what a different world we are now living in. No way that much effort would be given today to deliver such a letter." He stopped for a moment, then continued.

"Professor DeLaval opined that Mr. MacDougald must have been gone by the time it arrived, leaving no forwarding address."

"That sounds plausible," I said. Oh God, I thought to myself. I am starting to sound like him!

"I also think I need to clear something up for you." He grew serious. I sat up and looked the old professor in the eye. "In the matter of Lucille and myself. We have become quite close, as she shows me a side of herself that she normally keeps hidden." I have seen that side, too, I thought. I must have had a look, because he continued.

"Not what you are thinking, so you can stop grinning. I refer to a side of her personality, her soul, if you may. Yes, she is a physically gifted and stunning woman, and I have seen the way she torments you."

"Oh, goodness," I thought. "Where is he going with this??"

"I don't know how to put this delicately, so I am just going to say it. Contrary to popular theory, Lucille and myself have not been carnally intimate. We do have a special friendship and enjoy each other's company greatly. But I am old enough to be her." He paused. "Much older brother." He laughed. I was afraid he was going to say grandfather. He gathered himself and continued.

"But she is definitely a remarkable young woman, and lucky will be the man to tame her."

He rose and walked out, gently closing the door behind him. I propped my feet back up and thought, "Yes indeed, he will be a lucky man."

The next few days passed in typical Tiwanawiki fashion. Janie and Howard had apparently teamed up to write some songs in the afternoons. I noticed Lucille had begun to visit Chad and Darcy's motor palace a bit.

Janie and I put a new stain on the pool table. I finally broke down and called Stone Billiard Supply and Service, and they said a guy would come out sometime in the next month. I told them that was fine, I would be here. Sometime in the next month? Customer Service at its very best.

The following Tuesday morning found Johnny going door to door around the park, calling a meeting at the ring at 11:00 a.m. sharp.

We all assembled on time, and waited expectantly for the old professor to come. He walked around the corner at 11:05. "Printer jammed," he said, holding up a stack of paper. He sat down, took a deep breath, and imparted to us the amazing tale of Nicky Solara.

William Etheredge

Nicky

Apparently the pilot had not been fully briefed on his passenger. Shortly after take-off, he noticed something off in his readings. After tapping the glass on a few gauges, he thought "Something is amiss here." He was pushing the limit of his range as it was, but he knew he had enough fuel to make it with the weight of himself and his passenger. He set the plane on autopilot and walked back to where Nicky was strapped in his bench seat. Looking around, he spied Nicky's bag and hefted it.

"This is it!" the pilot exclaimed. "This fucker must weigh as much as you do! It has got to go!" As he moved toward the door, realization hit Nicky, who had been daydreaming. He unsnapped his seat belt and stood.

"No!" He cried out, distraught. "Please do not do this thing that you are thinking!" The pilot punched him hard in his solar plexus, buckling Nicky's knees and leaving him gasping for air. The pilot opened the sliding door and tossed out the bag.

"We have just enough gas to make it, and I ain't going into the damned ocean just for a few souvenirs." he said as he took his seat and resumed control of the plane. "Quitcher damn crying, you'll live."

Nicky did weep as he thought of everything he had been through with that duffel bag. He suffered through the rest of the long, bumpy flight in silence.

The plane landed on schedule on a grassy runway in the Highlands of Northern Scotland. Nicky was met by two men, one wearing coveralls, the other a spry old white-haired gentleman sporting a very impressive mustache. "You must be Nicky!" Shaking the hand of the glum Russian, he looked around and said, "No luggage, eh? No matter, we'll get you fixed up. Come along with me as Clive here takes care of your pilot friend and gets him back on his way."

Nicky spent the next year and a half as a sheep farmer, and tried his best to locate Iliana through whatever channels he could find. He finally discovered that she had given him up for dead, and had married an old friend who had been his chief rival for Iliana's affection. They had two children. Nicky was crushed beyond belief. *What can happen to me next?* he often wondered as he tended the sheep. *I am about as low as you can go.*

    He began to visit a local pub after a day of hard work on the farm, but did not become a drunk. He did enjoy a frothy pint, but tempered himself and refused to drink more than one. He rarely spoke to anyone, and usually sat by himself in the corner watching the other patrons carry on. He drew the attentions of a comely young barmaid named Anna, who was drawn to him because he was so different from all the others. He never once helped himself to a pat or pinch on her backside when she walked by, which was indeed a rarity among this lot.

    They began to talk a bit, which seemed to perk Nicky up a little, and he started staying past closing to walk Anna home. When they finally kissed, it was like Nicky had experienced a rebirth. After a six month courtship, they were married by the vicar of a little church and went to live in the small cottage that had been given to Nicky by his benefactor at the edge of a small forest close by the farm. Of course, Nicky would not allow Anna to continue working in the pub, as the thought of his lovely wife getting pawed by a bunch of drunken Scotsmen was unbearable.

    Nicky named his first son Samuel, and their daughter Olga, after the friends in Chattanooga who had taken him in.

9

❋   ❋   ❋   ❋   ❋

"And that, my friends, concludes the story," Johnny said, and spoke no more.

"So when the pilot tossed the bag out the door, they were right over the lake! Wowie, zowie, That is amazing." Eddie shook his head.

"That's right," Indie said. "And seventy years later a waterspout slings bullfrogs everywhere and dredges up the bag, to be snagged by Hector's fish hook!"

I looked over at Johnny, who was staring at me. I had seen that look before, and knew there was something else. He was going to take his sweet time to drop it though.

Janie looked at her phone and hustled back into her home and closed the door. I went into the tiny house and whipped up a can of mini raviolis. Yum. I flipped on my television and watched Headline News for a minute, disgusted at the way that channel was no longer true to its title, now just talking heads bashing politicians and cops.

I became curious of Janie's quick departure, and decided to check on her. I tapped on her door. She opened and put a finger to her lips, keeping me silent. She was wearing a Bluetooth headset and her laptop was open. She spoke into the microphone,

"When you push down with your finger, does the skin stay dented in when you pull your finger off, or does it spring back? Okay, how long does it take for it to smooth back out?" She typed '2+' on the screen. "Okay. Do you know how to feel his pulse? Good. Let me know when you have it and count the beats when I say go, and when I say stop tell me what number you're on. Okay." She pressed a button on her laptop, and said "Go."

I waved to her and backed out, closing the door behind me. Janie refused to let her nursing license lapse, and had to work a certain number of hours every couple years to maintain it. She worked freelance for an insurance company call center every now and then, triaging patients for their nurse call line. The patients were instructed to call the line before seeking treatment. Janie entered symptoms into the computer, which would respond with instructions, usually one of four options: do nothing and monitor and call back if it gets worse; hang up and call 911 immediately; go to the nearest Immediate Care office or hospital Emergency Room if the Immediate care centers are closed; or call their physician when their office opens in the morning. She usually does a twelve hour shift when she does this, so she must have gone on duty at 12 today.

    I looked at the monster truck sitting outside my office and shook my head. How had I let Hector talk me into that? He had assured me that we would need the four-wheel drive if I ever wanted to clear out more space and add more spots. I had recently purchased a 35 acre tract on the south side of the lake; a few years back I bought 85 acres bordering the northern edge. I really had no desire to expand, I just don't like neighbors. I hope to eventually own all the land around the lake.

    Movement to my right caught my eye. Indie, laptop in hand, approached from the road. "Come on in," I said, opening the office door. I sat at the desk and motioned for her to sit in one of the chairs. Instead, she walked right over to me and set her laptop down in front of me. On the screen was an outline of *The Fellowship of the Sunken Duffel*. That reminded me; I opened a drawer and brought out a piece of paper, and put it into my fax machine to make a copy. Yes, I still have a fax machine.

    When it finished its whirring and the copy slid out, I put the original back into the drawer and handed Indie the copy of the contract Johnny and I had signed with Bill Oglesby. "I like what you have written here, and you certainly have my blessing. I wish you the best."

    "Thank you Mike, that means so much. It is such a wild and true story that everyone needs to know about." She studied the paper and looked up at me with watery eyes. "I love it here so much. I wish I could just live here. Maybe one day I will. But one thing I know for sure. I will be back next spring!"

    I pulled her folder out of my little file cabinet. "Hopefully you will be on a worldwide book signing tour." I smiled at her. "But you will always have a home here. You are such a special lady, and I miss you when you're not here. What day are you pulling out?"

"Day after tomorrow. I've already spoken to Hector, and he will help me unplug everything before he gets in the boat."

I couldn't stop myself. "And Howard?"

"Oh, we have some plans." Her eyes sparkled as she thought of the shaggy guitarist.

And that was that. One of the colorful characters of the Tiwanawiki, like the geese that leave their droppings all over the lake ridge, going south for the winter.

The next several days saw the departures of Indie, Eddie and Mary Beth, and Chad and Darcy. Chad had popped into the office one morning to say he and Darcy would be leaving for a little while, and would I mind keeping an eye on his palace on wheels, keeping it aired out and such. He tossed me the key. He didn't elaborate on how long they would be gone or where they were going, or even how they would get there. I wondered if they were just going to take off on his Ducati. That question was answered about two hours later when a long white Hummer limousine appeared to collect them. I didn't see very much of Janie, either, for about a week, as she put some hours in on the triage line.

Sunset was coming earlier now, and I had broken out my light jacket for the evening show. Hector had recently harvested a new crop, and I applied some fire to the first fruits. I inhaled a generous lungful of tenth generation Wiki, and felt a tap on the left temple of my RayBans.

"Don't forget your old partner over here, Shorty." I hadn't even heard her come up.

"Finished with work for a while?" I asked her. She coughed.

"Yeah, for a little while I suppose. Need about 200 more hours in the next fifteen months." She drew in another puff and passed it back to me. "This the new stuff?" she asked, taking a drink of her long neck. I nodded. "Gets better every year." She settled back into her chair, and after a few minutes she said dreamily, "I don't think I have ever seen that shade of purple before. Simply beautiful." And beautiful it was, I mused. The best one yet.

Lucille had become a bit of a recluse, only coming out to use the shower. She had conspicuously cut down on her flirtatiousness with me. I kinda missed the attention, but I had made my decision.

She came into the office one day while I was doing some spreadsheet stuff and sat down. She was in jeans and a Hobbit shirt. "That's new, isn't it?" I asked her.

"Yep, got it in Nooga." She informed me that she had left her email address with a couple of the students there, and it had been shared. Now she had been inundated with correspondence and requests. "I plan to go down for Frightfest week in a few days, at the end of the month. They won't leave me alone," she laughed. She grew silent, and serious. She couldn't meet my eyes now, and said, finally, "I wish things were different. I believe you are the one man I could trust with my whole heart." My eyes burned, and I looked away quickly. The tears streamed down my cheeks when I turned back at the sound of the door closing, and she was gone. I was stunned beyond words.

The next day was met with bad news. Hector had received word that Pancho had passed away suddenly from a heart attack, and his Mama had been hospitalized with pneumonia and was herself in dire condition. "I must go," he said.

"Of course, you have to," I told him. He assured me he would definitely be back, but he didn't know when. We went into the office and got onto the Charlotte International Airport site. They had a non-stop to Veracruz leaving at eight in the morning. I showed it to Hector.

"That is perfect." I told him to go get packed and take care of his business. I booked his flight and bought him an open-ended ticket for the return flight, good for a year. I also got him a Toyota 4-Runner for a month, with an automatic renewal if he should need it longer, at Aztec Auto Rental at the airport. I printed all the necessary forms, details, and itinerary for the trip, and delivered them to my friend. We sat in his trailer and he looked at everything, as I explained it all to him. Everything paid for, he had only to think about getting to his mother.

Hector got choked up, "Bossman, I..." I cut him off.

"You owe me nothing, and never will. Go, take care of your mother. Stay in touch when you can, but don't worry about a thing here. You know we are more than just friends." Hector clasped me in an embrace and held tight for a moment, his tears dampening my shoulder.

"Thank you," was all he could get out.

182

"Be ready to go at five," I told him, and exited his camper. I went back to the office to tidy up and get something going for dinner. With Eddie gone, it was every man for himself. Some nights Janie and I would drive to a restaurant, others it would be frozen dinners or sandwiches. I had just walked back into the rec room when I heard a horn bleat. I turned around and headed back through the office and went outside.

It was Indie! She had been gone all of three weeks.

She bounded out of her Winnebago and wrapped her arms around me, pressing her thick self into me and twisting back and forth. She stopped and held me at arm's length. "You haven't rented out my spot already, have you?" She grinned real big and hugged me again. I must admit, it felt pretty damn good.

"No," I told her when she finally let go. "Its just like you left it."

She yelled "YAY!" and pointed toward the door. We went inside and sat. "I just felt so alone when I got home. It was different this time, for some reason. I couldn't sleep, nothing felt right." I just sat and smiled at her, letting her go at her own speed.

"Then after about a week of that, I got a message." She beamed at me with damp, glittering eyes. "I'm being published!" She squealed. "Its a small, independent fantasy imprint of a larger publishing house, but they sent me a $10,000 advance. They love it."

She fumbled in her purse. "Print me out the annual contract. I took a leave of absence from the school; I have tenure, so they can't fire me. I phoned a realtor friend of mine and put my house on the market. She told me that the way the housing market is now, and with all the equity I have in it, the house should sell quickly and I will net over $200,000" She squealed again and pulled out her phone. "This has happened so fast, Howie doesn't even know I'm here."

Hector came in then, and Indie jumped up and grabbed him. "I'm so glad to see you!" Hector gave me a slightly confused look over her shoulder, but he, like me earlier, was in no hurry for the buxom beauty to let him go and hugged her back.

"She's back," I told him. "Do you have a few minutes to get her hooked back up in number 8? I hate to ask, but..."

"No, it's okay! Of course." He smiled at Indie as she released him. "I am very happy to see you. Come on *mamacita*, let's get you connected." He put his arm around her shoulder and led her out the door.

In all the goings-on the past few days, I realized that I hadn't seen Johnny since, well, I couldn't remember the last time I had seen him. I made a mental note to check on the old codger in a little while. As I walked outside, I glanced toward the lake and noticed the sun beginning to get low. I locked up the office and made my way around to get my chair and other items from the shop. I could see Hector guiding Indie into her spot, Howard looking on, beaming. As she bounced out of the driver's seat, I thought about a song lyric from the 80's. *I like big butts, and I cannot lie.*

Janie came out with a frosty long neck in her hand; she saw me and stopped, eyebrows raised. I nodded, and she went back in for a second, coming back out with two. We sat up on the ridge in silence, admiring nature's wonder. Then...tap, tap.

Tradition.

We had a roaring fire that night at the ring. Howard and Indie had some long sticks and roasted hot dogs. They picked and giggled with each other like school children. Hector had cooked up some meat he had in his refrigerator, which would surely spoil in his absence. He had made a big platter of quesadillas, which were incredibly good. I was into my second helping when I caught movement beside me. Lucille was leading Johnny to the ring.

"Luckily for him I found him before he started to decompose," she joked.

"Okay, I have become a recluse the past little while, I know." Johnny reached for a quesadilla and took a bite. "Wow, this is delicious," he said. He munched until it was gone, and looked around. Janie handed him a Bud.

"Just opened," she said. "Knock it out."

Howard and Indie finished their dogs and disappeared, whacking each other with their sticks and giggling. "My money's on number eight. Hope you got that foundation secure, Hector," Johnny said, grinning at our surprised faces. "What?" he said. "I know you were all thinking the same thing. I may be old, but I'm not stupid." I chuckled heartily at that. There was no end to the old professor's surprises, it seemed.

Hector stood. "Sleep time, if I can. See you in a few hours," he said to me. He headed back to his trailer.

"What was that all about?" Janie asked. I explained everything and told her I would be gone until about noon the next day. Johnny asked if he could ride along, I told him sure, but 5:00 would get here in a hurry. He assured me he would be up and ready.

"Not me. You boys have fun, I may be up when you get back," Janie said with a chuckle as she got up and gave me a kiss. "Good night sugar."

Hector talked all the way to the airport, telling of his father, the fisherman; his mother, the gardener and cook; how he learned from them. He told of Pancho, how he had taken Hector and his mother out of the dirt and treated him like a favored son. He told us of meeting Eduardo, and about how thrilled he had been reading about Tom and Becky hiding from Injun Joe in the cave. I looked at Johnny.

"*Tom Sawyer*," Johnny smiled.

Hector told how that book had taught him to read and write in Spanish and English at the same time.

We got him to his gate with time to spare. We embraced and I told him again to call me as soon as he had a chance and let me know how things were going. He could call collect if he needed to, I didn't mind. He had tears in his eyes as he turned to check in and enter the boarding area.

Johnny and I took our time getting back, stopping at, of course, the Cracker Barrel, evidently the professor's favorite restaurant. "These biscuits taste just like my Mama's," he said. We ate heartily, and after a trip to the restroom, headed back to the park.

We had been on the road for about twenty minutes in silence, letting our food settle, when Johnny began to speak. "I suppose you have wondered as to my whereabouts the past little while."

"I know I haven't seen much of you since we returned from Chattanooga a month or so ago," I told him.

"Well, you should know me by now. I am like a doberman with a raw steak when I get hold of something. I can't turn loose until I'm sure it's finished. I sent Bill a copy of the translated letter from Nicky. He was so excited I feared he would rupture one of his coronary artery grafts." He fell silent for a few miles. Finally, he resumed.

"I have been scouring the interwebs, utilizing different search engines, and running up a substantial telephone bill." He looked out his window for a bit, then turned and looked at me.

"I have located Samuel Solara."

I almost stopped the truck, but managed to hold it in the road. "How on earth…" I started.

"It wasn't easy. But it is him. I spoke with him last evening. I texted him some pictures of Nikolo. He confirmed that the man in the photograph is his father."

I considered what I had just heard. Finally I said, "So, are you planning a trip to Scotland?"

"No, not hardly. It wouldn't do any good to go to Scotland. Samuel lives in Halifax. And he is coming here."

I was, again, without speech for the next fifty miles.

Samuel

Young Samuel and his sister Olga were about a year apart, and each totally believed their Daddy loved them more than the other. And, in turn, knew that they loved HIM more than the other did. Papa was obviously the smartest man in the world, as he knew how to fix all the machines on the farm where they lived, from the largest tractor to the smallest pair of sheep shears. He knew the answers to all their questions.

Every day at dark Papa would come home, scoop up his little munchkins, and eat his supper with one on each knee. They grew to love the smell of their Papa, as the smell of his clean sweat mingled with that of the farm machinery and the sheep was very unique. He devoted his evenings to them, then he would wash after they were in bed, and give the rest of his time to Mama.

By the time Samuel was five years old, he could not wait for his Papa to get home to tell him stories. Olga, too, grew to love hearing her father talk about his life. Their Mama would stand just outside the door as Nicky would regale their two youngsters to sleep, sometimes with tears running down her cheeks.

Samuel and Olga were very bright children, and they learned both English and Russian from their Papa. Sometimes Papa would get a faraway look in his eyes when he was telling the stories and he would lapse into Russian without even realizing it.

He told them about his young days, raising pigs and goats. He told them about his school days, about being chosen for University. About the vast differences in Russian culture and his dream of becoming a doctor. He told about being an Engineering Officer on the submarine, how it was sunk by the Germans and he was the sole survivor. Samuel loved that story the most, as well as the fishermen who rescued him. He made up his mind at that young age that he would visit that place. Nova Scotia, named for the place they lived; New Scotland.

Samuel grew and became a man. He went to University and was set to apply to Glasgow Medical College. Papa was an old man by then, the years of hard work and hardship finally catching up to him. Olga had taken his place running the farm; she was a natural with the animals and the machines; she actually loved the animals more than she did most people. She had been born with a cleft palate, and had been ridiculed relentlessly in school. Her reluctance to speak had been taken as a sign of an inferior mind, which couldn't have been farther from the truth.

Samuel had decided early that he wanted to become a surgeon so he could fix his sister's affliction, but he was also desperate to see the place his father had lived after his rescue from the ocean. So it was that, before he sent his application to medical school, he took a trip to Nova Scotia.

He fell in love with the land. He loved the bridges, the beautiful green hills and lovely flowers, the waterways and rivers that dominated the landscape. He loved the old forts, the modern buildings. He was fascinated by the history there, visiting the Titanic Museum and graveyard in Halifax. He discovered the university there had a world renowned Medical College, and the University Hospital had a surgery residence. He kept that fact in his mind when he returned home to find his Papa stricken, unable to speak or move one side of his body from a massive stroke that happened on his flight back home. He lived one more week and died peacefully, going to sleep and just not waking in the morning.

Anna was completely devastated; Papa had chosen her, and she loved him more than life itself. So, of course, did Olga and Samuel. Weeks went by, and the pall of misery was very slow in lifting. Samuel missed his deadline to apply to the Glasgow Medical College. Compounding things severely, the owner of the farm informed them that the farm had been sold, and they could live there for another year but they would have to relocate, as the new owners had different plans for the land.

Samuel wrote a letter to the Saint Elizabeth Medical College in Halifax, a very long letter detailing his father's life as well as his own, and also Olga and his Mama. He told them of his dream of becoming a great surgeon so he could fix his sister's deformity and others like her. A few months went by without a word, until finally a letter came for him from the college. They had spoken with his university professors from the Inverness College, where he had gotten his undergraduate degree. They had spoken with the owner of the farm where he lived and verified the story of his father and Olga.

Samuel was offered a full scholarship to the school, which would also provide housing for his mother and sister, should they wish to accompany him. He wrote them back immediately to ask if they had an agricultural or veterinary program, telling them of his sister's love for animals. They sent back word straight away that she was welcome to take the entrance exam, and his Mother could work in the school cafeteria if she wanted. In the meantime, the school had an animal farm, and Olga could work there while she was waiting for the exam. That sealed the deal, and the three of them relocated to Halifax.

Olga was happy as a clam on the animal farm, and although she missed passing the entrance exam by just a few points, she never bothered with retaking it. The variety of the work she was doing with the different animals there was very rewarding. Samuel studied hard, and, graduated with flying colors. He became one of Canada's pioneers in cleft palate surgery. He repaired his sister's deformity, and she became an extremely confident and vibrant young woman, and ended up falling in love and marrying one of the veterinary interns she met at the school.

William Etheredge

10

*   *   *   *   *

I pulled into my parking spot and got out. Johnny had looked at his phone the rest of the drive, which we made in silence. I got out and saw Lucille standing outside, looking at me. Our eyes met, and I got the message. I saw a sad little grin on her face, and winked at her. She laughed and the sadness was gone, if it was ever there to begin with.

"Forget it now, bud. You had your chance. I will never be someone's second choice." I must have made some kind of face. "Relax, duder. I'm just funning you." She gave me a punch in the arm. "How did it go at the airport? You didn't spring for one of those $20 breakfast burritos, did you?" I laughed.

"Cracker Barrel," Johnny licked his lips and patted his belly. "Best breakfast stop in the nation."

I went into the office and tried to figure out a way to claim Hector's plane tickets and car rental as a business expense. I was snapped out of it by a honk. I looked outside. The billiard people were here.

A large burly fellow with muttonchops and a 'Dirk' patch on the left chest of his shirt walked over and tried to squeeze my hand off. "Let's take a look atcher pool table." I noticed a missing tooth as he gave me a big smile.

I watched Dirk as he examined the rails and felt the cloth on the pool table, running his fingers over the stained areas. I stifled a cough. "Spill something on there?" he asked. I almost lost it when he leaned over and sniffed at the stains

"Was like that when I bought it," I lied. I grabbed a sugar free Red Bull out of my little glass-doored cooler. "Care for a drink?" I asked, quickly changing the subject. Dirk was already turned toward the door. "Nope, got sumpin in the truck." he said as he walked outside.

He came back in with a spray bottle, a brush, some rags, and a bucket. I left him to it and wandered outside. I was taken aback by the scene at the ring. Howard had his guitar out along with Janie, who sat across from him. Indie was over by the picnic table shaking her ample booty. Next to Janie was a guy with a ten-gallon hat and a handlebar mustache, who was beating on the bottom of a bucket, using it like a bongo. At first I thought they were playing *Beat it,* but when they got to the chorus, Tex the bucket banger sang out;

Meet it, Seat it.
Open up your mind and seed it

The dude could sing, I must say. And he could play a mean bucket, to boot. They went into the solo, which Janie played note for note as the original. Tex was visibly impressed. They finally wrapped it up, and Indie squealed and clapped, running over and giving Howard a big smooch, Howard's arm around her, um, hip. Tex jumped down and fell to his knees in front of Janie, bowing his head and hands to the ground repeatedly.

"That was awesome! I doubt if Eddie could even play it on an acoustic guitar!"

Janie waved him off. "Up, up. There's no need for that." She stretched out her arm, fingers down. "But, you may kiss my hand," she remarked dramatically. Tex shuffled over on his knees and slobbered on her hand, and started up her arm.

"*Cada Mia*," he said, in his best Gomez Addams imitation. Janie jerked her hand away.

"Just the hand, you miserable cur." She slapped the hat off his head, which looked like an onion with hair growing out of the sides. Howard noticed me as Tex gathered his hat and stood, turning my way.

"Allow me to introduce mister Wild Dog Donnie Dew, the original drummer of the Penetrators." Tex removed his hat, clicked the heels of his pointy-toed snakeskin boots, and bowed majestically towards me.

"The pleasure is all mine, guv'nor," he said, in a ridiculous British accent. Smiling at Janie, he said "AKA Buster, if ya know what I mean." He gave her a wink. She even looked a bit embarrassed at that, which was something new for me. I had never seen her so much as blush.

Tex got busy back on the bucket. "1,2,3,4," he counted off, and Howard began playing the chords for *Godzilla*. Janie had slipped a glass tube over her little finger and played the 'wee ooh' parts, perfectly wiggling that slide. I nodded, and turned to go, running smack into Lucille, chest to chest. She didn't budge. "Lil competition, huh?" she smiled, as I tried to breathe. "Who, Tex?" I gestured with my head as I walked around her. "He does have a good singing voice," I said as I rounded the picnic table, trying desperately not to think of the sensation I still felt on my chest.

I passed by Janie's spot and gathered up a few stray twigs and some brush from where Eddie's Fleetwood had sat. His grill was there, covered well, but the electrical cord was sticking out from underneath, so I tucked it in to keep it protected.

Venturing on past Indie's, I noted a bronze colored Aztek parked behind Howard's motor home. "Tex's wagon," I thought, and walked on. Out past Howard's place I saw an elm that must have been hit by lightning during the frog storm, and was split in two. I would have to get Hector to saw it up and add it to our firewood stack. Thinking of Hector, I wondered if he had made it in safely. I looked forward to hearing from him with an update on his mother's health. I thought about his story and all he had been through. I knew he had lost his wife to cancer a dozen or so years ago. I also knew that he got 'readings' from Lucille from time to time. But he must still feel the hurt every now and then. I used to think it would have been better for me if my wife, whom I had loved above all others, had died, instead of finding a better lover than I had been. Yes, it had taken me a while to move on, but I hadn't had to watch her wither away.

As I passed by the ring, I noticed the concert had wrapped up with Tex's last scream of *Go, Go, Godzilla*. Janie was putting her Taylor back into its case, Tex on the bucket, watching and talking to her. I walked on.

Dirk was putting his stuff back into his truck as I came around the corner. "All spick and spanky," he grinned. "That was a tough one, but good as new, almost. You are getting a little thin in places, and you have a couple of soft spots on your long rails. Nice table though. You may want to get it recovered sometime down the road. Be tournament ready, then." He held out a ticket.

"Hang on, I'll bring you a check." I took the bill into the office.

A little later I heard from Hector. He texted me that his mother was conscious when he arrived, but had fallen into a deep sleep, with respirations down to about eight per minute. I had zero medical training, but I knew it should be at least double that. He told me she looked old and frail, and he was going to be forced to make a decision soon about mechanical ventilation. I told him to follow his instincts about what he thought she would want, and to ask the doctors very specific questions. Questions regarding quality of life, etc. I realized then that what I had told him earlier was true. Hector is more than just my friend. We are indeed brothers.

I went out to find Howard, Indie, and Tex sitting around the ring, a small fire already going in the cool autumn afternoon. I had to admit that I was secretly pleased that Janie was not out there with them. Indie saw me looking, and pointed to her door, which was closed. I went over and tapped on it. She opened it with her finger to her lips, headset on. I started to leave, but she pulled me in.

"So he has one pupil larger than the other, and can't speak or move his left arm? Hang up and call 911 RIGHT NOW and tell them your husband is having a stroke. Do not wait. Do it NOW! Goodbye." She clicked off her headset and typed for a couple minutes on her laptop. "I thought I would go ahead and get a few hours in," she said.

"Man, you guys were rocking out there," I said.

"Hmm," she eyed me. "Not feeling insecure, I hope." She came over and kissed me full on the mouth. "Not to worry, lover. He's queer as a three dollar bill." She gave my butt a squeeze, then stood straight and tapped her headset.

"Thank you for calling the nurse line. I'm Janie, how can I assist you today?" I gave her a little pat and exited.

I decided to go check on Johnny. I walked along the ridge to find him at Lucille's, the two of then sitting under her awning, her hookah on the table between them. She held up a wooden-tipped hose. "Join us?" she said. I grabbed a chair from Hector's place and joined them, but declined the offer.

"Still on duty," I said, which elicited laughs from around the table, myself included.

"Oh, that's rich," the professor said, with a hint of British drama.

I questioned Johnny about Samuel's impending visit. He told me he was making arrangements and hoped to get away in a few weeks, just after Thanksgiving here. Lucille informed me she was leaving tomorrow for Frightfest, which wasn't due to start for another few days, I thought. Seems she had formed a sort of bond with one of the fellows she had met through her emails with the students. She assured us both that it was not what our dirty little minds were thinking. I didn't say a word.

That evening around the ring, Wild Dog regaled us all with tales from the road with the Penetrators, getting Howard wound up a few times. Indie gave him a look that would melt glass at one point, to which Howard just shrugged.

"It's rock and roll, baby. What can I say? Gross out competitions happened all the time. At least it wasn't like Ozzy, licking another guy's piss off the concrete by the pool." That brought a chorus of yucks and ughs. "Well, what can I say? Right, Dog?"

Tex howled and went into a chorus of *Long Live Rock and Roll*.

About one I was awakened by a tapping on my door. I got up to find a haggard looking Janie. "Can I use your shower? I feel like shit and don't want to walk around the building." She drug herself in and collapsed on the pool table. "This smells different," she said.

"Yeah, I had to have it cleaned. You keep leaving stuff on there." She laughed an evil laugh.

"I'm not the only one, buster." I informed her that 'Buster' was currently sleeping one off in a Pontiac Aztek parked behind Howard's RV. "I'm too tired to joust with you right now. Will you carry me into the bathroom and scrub the filth off me?" She sat up.

"I've decided that nursing is hard work whether you are doing hands-on patient care or just talking on the phone. This dude from Sacramento argued with me for twenty minutes about going to the ER with a mildly twisted ankle. I finally told him 'Do what you want, but be prepared to get billed, because your insurance company will not pay for a visit to the ER.' Then I hung up on his dumb ass."

I didn't know what to say. But I have learned that most of the time in these situations its best just to listen. She jumped down, or rather, fell off onto her feet and wrapped her arms around me, burying her head against my chest. I rubbed her scalp, underneath all the ribbons. "Mmm, that feels good," she purred. I eased her into the tiny house and onto the bed, removing her shoes as she pulled off her shirt and fell back. As I pulled off her socks, I noted a change in her breathing. She was asleep, and soundly. I walked around, hooked my robe onto the headboard, and slid in bedside her. She rolled over and nuzzled my neck, murmuring something that sounded like "I love my Cowboy." I pulled the blanket up over us and closed my eyes.

She was gone when I woke up. I rolled over to the other side of the bed and sat up. The sky outside was just turning gray, but it was still dark. I heard the shower running and laid back down. Too early yet, I thought. I wasn't alone in the bed for very long...

I was curious about Howard's friend and his intentions. Was he just passing through, or was there more than that to his visit? After my coffee and a sausage on a stick wrapped in a pancake, I went out for my morning rounds. I went ahead and drained Hector's tanks, as there was no telling when he would be back. All was quiet until I finally got up to Howard's place. He and Tex were sitting outside, having a cuppa. Howard motioned me over and waved for me to have a seat on the stool, which was actually a bucket. I sat on the bucket, declined a coffee, and asked how it was going.

Both of them started at once, clearly excited about something. I waved them silent and said, "One at a time." They looked at each other, and Howard started.

"You know, we had a huge hit with *Ride the Bull*, and everything that happened after that, right?" I didn't know everything, but I knew enough. "After Nirvana hit, flannel shirts, dirty jeans, and depression music took over the rock and roll scene, man. It was brutal. Party rock just died, you know. The record company pulled the plug on us. We already had nine songs recorded for the next album, with the new single already in the box."

Wild Dog cut in. "It was gonna be bigger than *Bull*, man. We were gonna be headlinin' arenas and shit, man." They both nodded, and checked out for about thirty seconds, lost in the land of 'what if,' I assumed. Howard finally looked up.

"What Dog says is true, man. *Shakin and Bakin* had it all. Great groove, great hook, kickin' ass solo; hell it even had a melodic rock bridge man, that was like Jeff Beck or something." He stood up, clearly adrenalin-ized. "Tell him the rest, Dog, man."

Tex was bouncing his leg like he was trying to shake a snake out of his pants. "I got a message from Dee Snider about a week ago. He wants to do a five minute segment on his *House of Hair* radio show, like a 'Where are They Now' kind of deal."

"Yeah. 'Whatever happened to...blank'" Howard jumped in.

"So, yeah, he is gonna do that, then play the song. It could be a huge freakin deal, man. But I'm having a hard time finding Lucky and Storm, and who knows, man, we could end up getting a new deal or something out of this." Tex grew silent.

Howard picked up the narrative, "Part of the deal when the record company broke our contract was that we got all the master tapes and rights back for any unreleased material, but we had a ten year waiting period that we could do nothing with it."

"That ten years is long gone, man," Dog said. "The Penetrators are a four headed dragon, man. We need all four heads to move on this."

"We gotta find Storm and Lucky, soon," Howard said solemnly.

We sat in silence for a few minutes. Finally I said, "I sure would like to hear the song."

Howard sighed. "See, that's where the problem is. The master tapes consist of four separate reels of ¾ inch 16 track tape. Each of us got one. Mine is in a safe deposit box at a bank in Indiana. Dog's is with him. We need the other two for the complete record. Lucky has the one that has *Shakin and Bakin* on it."

"We recorded all our stuff analog, man. So we have to get the tapes and get them digitized so we can get the song to Snider in time for his Christmas special."

"Wow," I said, standing up. I had had enough of the bucket stool. "Let me know if there is anything I can do to help."

At least now I knew why Tex was here.

I walked back to my house to find Janie playing pool. I picked up a stick and joined her. While we knocked the balls around, I told her what I had just learned. She propped her stick on her foot and looked at me.

"What?" I asked her.

"Are you really that thick? Who do you know that just found, not one, but a whole slew of people who have been missing for 70 years?"

I hung my stick back in the rack and headed over to Johnny's.

After my meeting with the old professor, who seemed excited over Howard's plight, it was time for a grocery store run. I had installed a drop box for long term residents to drop requests, so I gathered them together and created a master list. I would add everything up from the receipt and give everyone a monthly invoice. Plus my Red Bull stash was beginning to get a little low.

Just another of the many exciting perks of life at Tiwanawiki.

I returned to find the two Penetrators, along with Janie, out jamming again at the ring. Of course Indie was there spectating. They stopped, and Howard said to Janie, "Right here we go C Sharp, E Major, A sus to A and then to the B. After two bars, the guitar solo starts on the B."

Janie nodded, and said, "From the chorus."

They played, Tex on the bucket, Howard singing:

"We start it in the bar
And continue in the car
By the time we hit the door
Its already gone too far

By then I'm achin'
Shakin and a-bakin'
Wearin snakeskin
Shakin and a-bakin'
When my baby starts the lovin'
Ain't nothin we're forsakin'
Through the night and all the day
We are shakin' and a-bakin."

Indie had her eyes closed and her head was turning back and forth. The song was really good, it had a nice beat, and you could definitely dance to it. After they wrapped it up, Tex/Dog clapped so hard he must have bruised his hands.

"Damn, Janie. I believe I like your solo better than Lucky's!"

"It's a cool tune," she said, giving me a sly grin. "I like shakin and bakin." Then she gave me a wink, to which Dog whooped.

"I know what time it is now! AAAAHHHOOOOO!!!"

I shook my head and said, "Y'all's stuff is on the pool table." That got everyone moving, collecting their beer and victuals.

I should mention here that I had also purchased a vinyl cover for the pool table.

We had another magnificent sunset that evening, which would be the last late one for a while. Daylight savings time was coming to an end tonight. As we were folding our chairs I saw headlights lighting the trees across the road. Lucille was back, quite likely with wild stories of her escapades in Chattanooga. I was sure I didn't want to hear some of them.

Johnny made it to the ring that night. We had a roaring fire going as he settled on an empty log. I had not said a word to Howard or his band mate about my talk with Johnny, but by the way he was smiling at me, I felt confident he had found something. He sat quietly for a while, waiting until everyone was silent. He finally spoke.

"Howard, Donnie, Mr. Stevens spoke with me this afternoon about a dilemma you have. I may have some good news for you." That got everyone's attention.

"Lucky Longfellow no longer exists." Dog nearly fell off his bucket, but quickly gathered himself as the old professor continued. "He is now known by his given name, Ernie Blevins. Mr. Blevins is currently on tour with a singer known simply as Pink. I believe she is quite famous. They are probably wrapping up a concert as we speak, in Frankfurt, Germany. Next is Munich for two nights. Not sure what their itinerary is after that, but they are all over Europe for the next couple of months."

Everyone waited silently for more. "Storm Geiger, sadly, has suffered a debilitating stroke and resides in a long-term care unit in Scranton, Pennsylvania. He has been there for several months." He paused for a long moment.

"Dammit," Dog muttered.

"Seems that Storm, real name Walter, has a congenital defect in his brain, something called an AVM."

We all looked at Janie, as the fire crackled. "Arterio-Venous Malformation. You know those areas in major cities where there are roads stacked on top of roads, with traffic coming and going in all directions? They are known a lot of times as 'Spaghetti Junction', because that's what they look like from above." Everyone nodded or murmured their assent. "Well, that is sort of how you would describe an arterio-venous formation, with veins and arteries together in a space. Now, imagine a giant reaching down onto a spaghetti junction and twisting it in his hand."

"So the blood coming in has no place to go." Howard said.

"Not all of it, but a lot. It depends on how severe it is, of course. If it is bad early, severe headaches can alert doctors to the problem. Mild cases can go unnoticed for a long time."

Howard mused, "He did complain of headaches some, when we were on the road. A few shots and he would even out."

"What may have happened was that he developed a clot, that eventually got big enough to occlude a major artery, if it broke loose." Janie looked down at her feet. "That he has made little progress in so long a period would indicate that he is not going to get much better."

Johnny picked up the conversation again. "I have been in touch with his mother, actually. She tells me Walter lived alone and had an on-again, off-again girlfriend. When she couldn't reach him for a couple of days she went to check on him. She found him unconscious and was unable to rouse him. He regains consciousness now and then for a minute or so, but those episodes are getting more rare. His mother says the doctors have told her she will have to make a decision soon about putting him on life support."

Lucille had sat down next to me and whispered in my ear, "What is it?"

I patted her knee and told her I would tell her in a little while.

Johnny continued. "Walter has no dependents, so his mother is his *de facto* next of kin and power of attorney. She has the key to a safe deposit box and is going to check it to see if there is a box holding a 12 inch reel to reel tape. If so, she will overnight it to us and will sign any release forms she needs to sign,"

"She was always so supportive of us. Whenever we played Philly she would insist we stay with her and she cooked for us." Howard smiled.

"She was a great cook," Dog said.

"As for Mr. Blevins, I have sent a message to the management company listed on his Facebook page. Hopefully I will hear from them soon."

It got very quiet around the ring, the occasional pop of a pine knot sending sparks into the air. I felt my phone vibrate in my pocket.

I read the text, typed out a response, and put the phone back into my pocket.

"Hector's mother just passed," I informed the group. That did it for Indie, who began to sob and buried her face into Howard's chest. I'm not much good at handling these kinds of things, either, so I slowly stood and, Lucille in tow, headed for the rec room.

Lucille perched on the pool table while I sat in the rocking chair, explaining everything that had been going on. Janie came in and grabbed a beer out of my mini cooler and jumped up on the table beside her, spilling a drop of beer onto the cover. As she wiped it off with her hand, I said, "Be careful up there, I just had that cloth professionally cleaned."

The two girls looked at each other, and before I knew it we were all three laughing our heads off. I assumed that Janie had told Lucille about the non-billiard action that the table sees from time to time. The somber mood shattered, we went back out to the ring to find Howard and Tex regaling Indie and Johnny with tales from the road.

"How are any of you still alive?" Johnny asked, shaking his head. He looked over to me. "How is Hector?" I told him I would know more tomorrow.

It stormed that night. I didn't hear any frogs hitting the roof this time, thank goodness. It was cool and cloudy the next morning. I met Johnny on my morning walk around. He handed me a paper with a string of digits written on it. "Please give this to Howard, and tell him to call between 9:30 and 10:00 this morning." I looked at my phone. I had forgotten about the time change, and it was already 9:00.

"Okay. I'd better go roust him now." I found Tex at the ring, his hat off. I was surprised again at the shininess of his bald dome. He was poking at the ashes of last night's fire with a stick. He looked up at me.

"At least yours is just turning gray. Mine has turned loose."

I chuckled at that. "I'm headed to Howard's." I held up the paper.

"He's not there. I slept in his bunk last night." I pointed to the RV parked in number eight and raised my eyebrows at him. "You know it, brother. Even when we were young, Ole Zoom had a thing for them thick gals."

I knocked on Indie's door. I heard a sleepy "It's open," so I gently pushed open the door. The two were bundled up like Eskimos. Howard opened one sleepy eye.

"What's up, chief?" I held up the paper.

"It is an international telephone number. Johnny says you need to ring it in about thirty minutes." That got him moving.

"Toss me those boxers, please, if you don't mind." He was smiling, and pointing. They were on the table on top of Indie's laptop, along with a large pair of lacy panties and matching bra. I gingerly picked up Howard's boxers by the waistband, using my fingernails, and tossed them to him. I stuck the paper under the laptop and left him to it.

I discovered Janie wrapped up in a Beatles blanket, sitting in her lawn chair, cradling a steaming cup. "Make enough for two?" I asked her, as I had not had my morning cuppa.

"Go fix it." She nodded toward her door. She had a single cup maker, so I put a little container labeled 'Breakfast Blend' into the machine and got it going.

"Found any damage from the storm? Any more duffel bags or sky frogs from outer space?" she asked.

"So far, so good." We sat and sipped our coffee in silence, occasionally looking at each other and smiling. Then I was stricken with a sinister thought. *Just like an old married couple.* I shook it off, finished my coffee, and stood up. "I need to go check on Chad and Darcy's palace and open a couple of windows for a little while," I announced.

"Have fun," she said, rocking in her cocoon.

It was the first time I had seen the inside of the rock star motor palace of Chad. It had not one, not two, but three large LED TV sets, along with virtually every brand and style of gaming system ever made. There was a big pile of dirty laundry, and as I researched my memory banks, I could not remember ever seeing them utilize the washer and dryer I had for guests, which are in the same room as the shower. At least they used that fairly often.

I could reach one window fairly easily, and opened the front and back doors. "That should suffice," I thought. I would not do their laundry, though. I did a lot for my guests, but there is a line I refuse to cross. Not to mention that the thought sort of grossed me out. Maybe if I had the meth lab haz-mat gear that I always kid Eddie and Mary Beth about...

As I came around Hector's place, I noticed some scum and trash in his fish tanks. This I would clean, when it warmed up a little later in the day.

As if on cue, my phone rang. It was Hector. We talked for about fifteen minutes; he should be finished with everything in about a week. I told him about Wild Dog, and about Samuel coming. He said he was very interested to meet them, and that he had told the duffel bag story a dozen times in Mexico. I went ahead and opened his windows. I noted that his living quarters were quite spartan compared to the palace three doors down.

The three amigos, as I had come to think of Indie, Howard, and Tex, were up and dressed, gathered around the ring getting the fire going. All had coffee. I looked up and noticed the sun high in the sky already. I looked at my phone, already after noon. I wondered where the time went. "I thought we were supposed to gain an hour, not lose two," I muttered, to no one.

"I talked to Lucky." I looked at Howard, as he continued. "They won't be back in the states for another four months. The tour is going through Eastern Europe and several stops along the Mediterranean." He poked at the small, but catching, fire with a stick. "His wife has the tape at their house in Pasadena, California, locked up in a safe. She is staying at her sister's cabin in the redwoods. They live completely off the grid, and he has no way to contact her."

"When can you call him back?" I asked.

"Tomorrow, about the same time."

"Okay, when you do, ask if he has an address for the place, and get their names. I may have an idea of how to get a message to her."

I had an old friend who was in the military for a little while, and it hadn't gone very well. When he got out he had moved in with a woman he had just met, and went on a wild ride with the excesses available to a young man in California in the early 1980's. His mother had become worried when six months or so had gone by, and she had not heard from him. When the two policemen knocked on his door for a welfare visit, he was terrified that his 'business' had been discovered. Of course, the cops didn't care two cents about that, they simply told him to call his mother, so I had a notion that the local po-po's could help us out.

I began to notice a scent in the air. The smell of roasting flesh. Could it be? I walked around Janie's place, and sure enough, Eddie and Mary Beth were back. I wondered how I had missed them pulling in. It must have been while I was on the phone with Hector.

I walked over to greet them, and ask how they enjoyed NOLA.

"We had such a good time," Eddie started. "That is one wild place. We went down to Bourbon Street in our cosplay garb and no one even noticed."

Mary Beth continued. "I wasn't the only Daenerys, though. One of them got booted out because her suit wouldn't stay pinned up and she kept flashing her boobs at everyone. There were a slew of kids at that event, so that really was not cool."

Eddie was grinning. Mary Beth punched him in the arm, pretty hard.

"What was that for? I didn't say a word!"

"Yeah, but you were thinking it." Mary Beth looked at me. "Eddie didn't think she was uncool at all."

"You brought it up, doggone it," Eddie whined, rubbing his arm.

I quickly changed the subject. "What is that I smell? It smells like heaven."

"Hamburgers," they replied in unison. "Jinx!" they said, pointing at each other and laughing.

"I was expecting you back a few days ago," I said.

Eddie replied, "We found a cool spot and hung around for a few days."

I brought them up to speed of all the happenings while they were gone. "We really are one big family," I thought to myself as I related the events they had missed.

"I wondered whose Aztek that was. You don't see many of those anymore," Mary Beth said.

I couldn't resist. "Yeah, if it was olive green, it would be a perfect match for your ersatz meth lab-on-wheels."

They just looked at me, both of them stone faced.

Johnny had joined the group at the ring. He had emailed Storm's mother a release/permission form and she was including a signed copy of that as well as a copy of her court-mandated power-of-attorney, should any question arise, along with the tape. It should arrive at the park in the next two days.

"All we need now is Lucky, and we are golden," Howard said.

I suddenly remembered Chad and Darcy, and excused myself to go close up their palace. I received a start when I went inside to close the window. There, rooting around in the pile of dirty clothes, was a large dog. I had never seen him before. "Hey, get out of that stuff," I scolded him. He turned and looked at me. He came over and jumped up on me, his paws on my chest, and a pair of yellow panties on his head, his snout sticking through one of the leg holes. Again, gingerly by the waistband, I took the panties off his head and tossed them back over to the pile.

He was white, short-haired, with brown and black spots. I noticed a couple of ticks on his ears as I scratched his neck. "You're a real beauty, aren't you, huh?" He had no collar. "Where in the world did you come from?" He sat and looked up at me, his head cocked to the side as he whimpered.

"I suppose you're hungry. Follow me." I finished my duties at the palace and at Hector's with my new-found friend by my side. When we got back to the ring, the hound introduced himself to everyone there, then sniffed the air, and took off toward Eddie's, where he was flipping a grill load of burgers. He looked at the dog, who had a seat in front of the grill, tail wagging in the dirt.

"Well, hi there! I guess it's a good thing I made extras, huh." He flipped one of the burgers off the grill towards the dog, who snatched it clean out of the air and chomped it down in a microsecond. "Wow," Eddie said, standing with arms akimbo. "Wait right there." He disappeared into their house.

The dog said, "Roop, roop, roop."

Eddie returned with a plastic bag. "We have some chicken that we aren't going to get to before it's out of date." He walked up by the lake and dumped out the contents of the bag. "Come on, Rooper," he said. The dog trotted up and gobbled up the chicken. Then he walked over to the lake and slurped up some water.

"Rooper, huh? I like it. Great name," I said. Just then Rooper took off into the woods, and we didn't see him anymore that evening.

The next morning dawned bright and airish. I fixed my coffee and donned a light jacket as I went outside. I walked around the ring to find Rooper back, and getting some love from Janie, who was out in her blanket.

"You need to take him to the vet if we're going to keep him," she announced. I thought about it.

"Do you have a mouse in your pocket, or something? I didn't 'get' him, okay? He wandered up on his own. I have no idea where he came from. As far as keeping him, he looks grown enough to decide for himself whether or not he wants to stay."

"Look at his poor ears. I bet someone just threw him out. I know he needs a rabies shot and wormer and that shot for that other stuff dogs get."

"You mean Parvo," I said.

"Yes, that's right. You know there is a feed and supply store in town that has a vet there in house. It says so on their sign. Go get your keys, and let's go. We will get a chip put in him, too, in case he gets lost."

And that is how Rooper, the dog, became a semi-permanent fixture at the Tiwanawiki RV Park. Everyone fell for him immediately, he could catch and fetch anything, and only rooped occasionally. Of course, he would disappear, sometimes for a few days, and would look a little rugged sometimes when he returned.

Howard and Johnny finally made contact with Lucky's wife, and a week before the deadline they had all four tapes, and found a studio not far away that digitized the entire album, and we all got copies.

And so it was, that a week before Christmas, on the day Chad and Darcy and Hector returned, and the day after Samuel arrived from Halifax to meet everyone and collect his father's belongings, that I pulled Godzilla around to the ring, and utilizing the bluetooth feature on my phone, I found a station on the interwebs that broadcast the Christmas Special Edition of The House of Hair radio program. The incredible speaker system of Godzilla blasted into the woods around Lake Wakitani Taniki, some thirty-odd years after it was recorded, the World Premiere of the latest, unreleased single from The Penetrators, *Shakin and Bakin*.

Samuel spent about a week with us. I let him have the bedroom in the tiny house and I stayed with Janie. He had some nice stories about his Dad and Mom. He was sorry that his sister couldn't make the trip with him, but we got to meet her and her family on Skype.

We rang in the New Year with fireworks; Rooper enjoyed it as much as any of the humans, and the year's first snow. Janie had a hard time letting me go back to my house after Samuel left, but we agreed that is was best for us to keep things just the way they were, and maintain a semblance of single life, even though it seemed very much that we were committed to each other in spirit. And life carried on at the park.

After the snow, Rooper was a no-show for quite a while. We had a few sunny days, around five each sunny afternoon found us in our lawn chairs up by the lake, often wrapped in blankets. As I sat there one afternoon, watching another majestic sunset, now just touching the tree line to the south, I began to contemplate everything that had happened over the past several months, beginning with Janie and I huddled naked in a doorway as a waterspout rained frogs on the park.

The sun dropped about halfway over the horizon, igniting the splendors in the atmosphere. I pulled a stick out of my hoodie pocket and struck fire to the end of it, inhaling the smoke of wiki enhancement. I felt a tap on my left ear, as I was not wearing any shades this day.

Tradition.

We had one of the coldest winters on record that year, as a Canadian trough settled in in early January and took a month to move on. The lake iced over completely, for the first time since I had been here. Hector tried his hand at ice fishing, with little luck. It was cloudy and overcast most days, so not many sunsets to enjoy.

Wild Dog, Howard, and Indie struck out in the Aztek shortly after New Year's; The Penetrators had been offered a spot on the Monsters of Rock cruise later in the year, so they had to find a new lead singer and guitarist. Lucky's gig with Pink had been extended to South America and then Australia. Dog begged and begged Janie to join the band, but she would have none of it.

Chad and Darcy had split for warmer climates shortly after they returned. Chad said I could look for the palace to come rolling back in to spot number one when the weather warmed back up. Lucille had accompanied Eddie and Mary Beth back to New Orleans, saying she planned to spend a week or so there collecting 'stuff,' then heading to South Florida to open her winter booth at the Swap Shop.

So Johnny, Hector, the lovely Janie, and I rode out the winter in style. Hector had a frequent visitor; the manager of *Payaso's* had become quite fond of the tamale maker. Johnny stayed in touch with his new friends in Chattanooga as well as Halifax. Samuel had collected the duffel and all its contents, with the exception of one set of Lieutenant's bars, which immediately became Johnny's most prized possession.

Winter turned into spring. Hector began tilling his garden spot for his special peppers, and preparing his jugs for the inevitable return of the delicacy that had made *Payaso's* famous. One warm spring evening found us once again watching the sunset, and the inevitable tap on my RayBans. I wondered what had become of Rooper, who had been absent all winter.

Janie and I finished our sunset routine, complete with long neck Budweisers. The pleasant aroma of searing meat wafted toward my nostrils, as Eddie and Mary Beth had been back for several weeks and had begun their cooking, much to my delight. I sat on that ridge and felt like nothing could possibly go wrong, my life was pretty sweet.

I spotted movement out of the corner of my eye then, and noticed Rooper was back. He was under the picnic table, chewing on a stick. Janie turned to see what I was looking at, and all of a sudden she jumped up and exclaimed "Holy Shit!" and walked down to the table. She pulled the stick out from under the table that Rooper had been gnawing on. It was flared on each end, about two feet long with a ball on one end.

"That's not a stick," I said, stunned.

"No. It certainly is not. This is a human femur."

The End

August-October, 2021

Made in the USA
Columbia, SC
07 September 2023